I0742149

Stolen

This is a work of fiction. Names, characters, businesses, places, events, locales, and incidents are either the products of the author's imagination or used in a fictitious manner. Any resemblance to actual persons, living or dead, or actual events is purely coincidental.

Copyright © 2019 by Caroline Klug

All rights reserved. No part of this publication may be reproduced, distributed, or transmitted in any form or by any means, including photocopying, recording, or other electronic or mechanical methods, without the prior written permission of the author, except in the case of brief quotations embodied in critical reviews and certain other noncommercial uses permitted by copyright law. For permission requests, contact the author using the contact page on www.CarolineKlug.com. Please be sure to include "Permission Request" in the subject line.

All Scriptures are taken from the Holy Bible, New International Version®, NIV®. Copyright © 1973, 1978, 1984, 2011 from Biblica, Inc.® Used with permission.

Song lyrics are taken from Fielding, B./Morgan, R. (2018). Who You Say I Am [Recorded by Hillsong Worship]. On *There is more*. Capitol Christian Music Group. Used with permission.

Cover design by Tim Fitzpatrick
Author photograph by James Klug

To request Caroline Klug for a speaking event or appearance, please contact the author using the contact page on www.CarolineKlug.com. Please be sure to include "Event Request" in the subject line.

ISBN: 978-1-7339008-0-5 (eBook)
ISBN: 978-1-7339008-1-2 (paperback)

Printed in the United States of America

Although content is not graphic in nature, this book contains elements readers may find sensitive, such as physical abuse, sexual assault and drug use. Content is intended to represent the very real struggles in this present world, as well as the hope of something better.

This book is dedicated to anyone who feels lost, imprisoned, unreachable or unredeemable. May your shackles be no more, and may you be brave enough to walk out of your prison and into the Sonlight.

~ C.K.

STOLEN

Caroline Klug

A Novel

FOR HE HAS RESCUED US FROM THE DOMINION OF DARKNESS AND BROUGHT US INTO THE KINGDOM OF THE SON HE LOVES, IN WHOM WE HAVE REDEMPTION, THE FORGIVENESS OF SINS.

COLOSSIANS 1:13–14

Caroline Klug

CHAPTER 1

Star had no idea if her screams were audible or only locked away in her head. Her vision was blurred from his punch, and she fought to clear her head as she pulled herself up and onto her hands and knees.

The man grabbed her forcefully by her long, black hair, pulling a chunk out from the roots. With one hand clutching her hair and the other under her arm, he dragged her to the open side door of the van.

Star kicked her feet and screamed, working desperately to pry his fingers from her hair. When they got to the van, she grabbed the doorframe, trying to resist his push. Fighting to get past the searing pain on her scalp, she struggled to keep her grip as he shoved her inside.

The back of the van was completely empty and stripped to the metal. Star grabbed on to the front passenger seat, pulling herself up and away from him. As the man reached for her again, she kicked back with all her might, sending her 3-inch stiletto into his upper thigh.

The man shrieked. Enraged, he grabbed her ankle, pulled her back onto the floor, and delivered another swift punch to the side of her face.

Star couldn't open her eyes, but could feel the man tightening something around her wrists and ankles. When he was done securing her, he slammed the door shut, got into the van, and took off.

The fight for consciousness clouded her sense of reality and regret painted her thoughts – for which particular thing, she wasn't even sure where to start. Which was the first of her awful decisions that made all the others follow behind, forcing her down this fast-paced highway of remorse? How did this seventeen-year-old Midwest-friendly girl end up a nineteen-year-old prostitute, hooked on heroin? In her altered state, the audacity of it almost made her laugh out loud. It certainly wasn't funny. It was the kind of laughter you experience when all the other emotions fail you.

She couldn't seem to move. Couldn't seem to press past the lethargy holding her body down. Star lay on the van floor, longing to be back in that small apartment she thought she hated. Listening to Lacey would have been the better thing to do. She was right. She should have stayed home. Closing her eyes, her mind went back to earlier that evening.

★ ★ ★

Lacey burst through the door and slammed it behind her, pressing her whole backside against the door.

Star flinched, but kept her desperate focus on the syringe.

"It's Gus," said Lacey, chewing on her bottom lip. She turned to face the door and watched quietly through the peephole. "He's looking for our rent."

After a few moments, she left the door and walked into the kitchen. Seeing Star with the syringe brought her to an abrupt stop.

"What's wrong with you, Star?"

Star remained silent and focused on her task, tightening the tourniquet.

"That was supposed to go toward our rent! We don't have enough as it is. You want to end up sleeping on the street again?"

Ignoring Lacey's words, she lowered herself to the floor and sat with her back resting against the cabinet door. Star tightened the tourniquet once more, slid the needle into her arm, and took in a deep breath. She relaxed her head back and let her eyes roll backwards, feeling the drug wash over her.

Lacey stormed out of the kitchen and into her bedroom.

Star could hear her crying, but the high kept her from caring in that moment. She closed her eyes and drank in the euphoria.

Everything felt warm and safe. She could hear the birds overhead as she lay in the tall grass, feeling the tips of the blades caressing her cheeks. It was perfect, safe, and far from the reality she lived in. After a while, the blades of grass and soft ground beneath her hardened back to the familiar and cold tile floor. With her eyes still closed, she ran the palms of her hands slowly from side to side, reconnecting with reality. Jagged edges of broken tiles against her fingertips came in conflict with the now dwindling sensations of pleasure. Slowly, she pulled her elbows back and propped herself up, blinking to acclimate her eyes to the kitchen light.

She got up off the floor, staggered into the bedroom, and sat silently next to Lacey, combing her fingers through Lacey's tear-dampened hair.

"I'm sorry, Lace. I'll make this right. I promise. I'll go out tonight and make it back. I'll give whatever I make to Gus first thing in the morning."

Lacey just nodded, letting the silence condemn her.

Star went to the closet to pull out a skirt and her lucky blue heels with the silver studs. She emerged, swinging the heels around her head and stumbling onto the floor, still feeling the effects of the heroin.

"Maybe you should wait until your head is clear," Lacey said. "Stay home."

"My head is fine," Star said, as she lifted her leg into her skirt and fell sideways, catching herself with the side of the dresser. She ignored Lacey's stare and kept one hand on the dresser to steady herself as she finished pulling her skirt up. After fussing clumsily with the straps on her heels, she sprayed on perfume, lifted her t-shirt for a quick glide of deodorant, and was out the door.

Lacey sat staring at the door for a long while. She could hear men catcalling out their car windows at Star as they drove by. She loved Star like a sister, and felt responsible for the path Star had found herself on.

The abrupt sound of screaming jarred Lacey, and she ran to the window. There was a dark brown van parked on the street below, and a tall man wearing a baseball cap. It was dark, but she could see him wrestling with someone in the van. She scanned the street looking for Star but couldn't see her, and panic rose in her chest. She watched as the man slammed the van door shut, jumped into the driver's seat, and squealed off.

Lacey's face fell. The only thing left on the road was one bright blue stiletto with silver studs. She wanted to reach for her phone, but her arms felt paralyzed. She was afraid to call the police. There were so many reasons it was a bad idea, but maybe they could help. Maybe they could find her. She stood shaking, trying to push out thoughts of Star's body lying somewhere, lifeless. She knew what she had to do.

Lacey pulled out her phone, took a deep breath, and dialed 9-1-1.

* * *

Star's body jerked with every bump they drove over. She could feel the warmth of the blood from her head wound running down the side of her face and neck, and fear made it hard to breathe. Two years on the streets had taught her how to appear hard on the outside, but that never really caught up on the inside.

She had gotten in a lot of cars over the last year. Most were regulars, but when someone new showed up, she looked them over carefully, trying to decide if the situation would be safe. Well, safe *enough*. In the moment, it never seemed to matter who they were or what their names were, just as long as they had the right amount of money.

This was it. This is what she had become in such a short amount of time. Her life was the sum of Johns she had sold her soul to, and now she was about to pay the ultimate price. Grief ripped through her as she flashed back to when she had let life swallow her whole.

* * *

Star spent the better portion of the day walking the streets, trying to familiarize herself with the area. She had never been by herself in such a large city. There were a lot of strange people. To her relief, she found if she avoided eye contact, they often lent her the same consideration. By the end of the day, she was tired, and made her way back to the alley to sleep. Being on the streets was not what she had expected, and Star knew this was much bigger than she could handle alone. As she got closer to the alley, she saw lights flashing and could hear voices arguing. Out of fear, she crossed the street and continued walking past the alley, where a cop car was stopped with its lights on.

So many times, Star replayed that moment in her head. It would have been so easy to be noticed, put into the back of their squad car, and driven home. Had that happened, she never would have unknowingly walked down the track and stopped there to rest.

It was a classic case of being in the wrong place at the wrong time. Before she knew it, she found herself surrounded by men making lewd comments and trying to touch her. Some even had money in their hands, waving it in front of her face. Star grabbed the pack off her shoulders and held it tight against her chest as she pushed her way out of the circle, and right into Ronny.

"You a renegade? In my track?" Ronny hissed. "You trying to do business behind my back?"

Star had no idea what he meant. "What? No. I mean, I don't know. Please let me pass."

Ronny burst out laughing. He slapped his man, Leo, on the shoulder, and he too started laughing. The tone of Ronny's whimsical laughter lowered until it was barely audible. The look in his eyes followed suit with his laugh. In one swift movement, he grabbed Star. He spun her around and pressed her backside into the front of him, holding her tightly while she wiggled and pleaded.

"No one sells for free here, little girl. So, who you workin' for?"

"I don't know what you mean! Please let me go!"

"So now you're going to insult my intelligence too? A pretty little thing like you, down on the track, and you don't know what I'm talking about?"

Lacey, one of Ronny's girls, had been watching the whole scene. She took pity on Star and made her way closer.

"Hey, Ronny," Lacey said. "Why don't you just have her choose up?"

An intrigued look crossed Ronny's face, and he released his hold on her. He grabbed her arm and dragged her down the block. Star yelled and clawed at him while still trying to keep hold of her backpack, the only thing she had to her name. Ronny stopped at the end of the street and threw her inside a circle of pimps. As she got up off the ground, the first person she locked eyes with was Ronny. Without realizing it, she had made her selection. Now standing at a distance, Ronny took one long look up and down her body and smiled from ear to ear.

"She's a pretty one." He grinned, imagining the money she could bring to the table. "All right. She can stay. But she's your responsibility, Lace. I don't wanna hear about any problems with this one, and I want nightly check-ins."

Lacey nodded, put her arm around the young girl and ushered her around the corner and out of earshot. "Girl, you gotta be more careful than that," she said. "What's your name?"

She started to answer, but Lacey silenced her with a hand over her mouth.

"Were you about to tell me your real name?"

"Yes," she said, confused.

"That's your first mistake. Well, maybe your second, after that run-in with Ronny. Never use your real name." Lacey stopped and leaned against the building as she lifted her foot and picked something off the bottom of her shoe. "I assume you're out here running for a reason. If you don't want to be found, then don't use your real name. Also, if something goes down, the cops don't know who you are. Makes it harder for them to find you." Lacey looked her up and down and spun her around awkwardly, until it made the girl crack a smile. "Star! You look like a star. That's what we'll call you."

From then on, she introduced herself as Star.

"Where were you going, anyway?" Lacey asked, tilting her head to one side. "How'd you end up here?"

"It's a long story," Star said, her voice catching on the last word. "I don't really know where I was going. Just trying to figure out where I could sleep for the night."

Lacey looked hard at Star, then grabbed her hand and led her down the block a few more feet until they were standing in front of the doorway into an apartment building.

"You're in luck. This is where I live." Lacey led her into the building and up the stairs to her apartment. "I had a roommate but, well, she... she didn't work out."

Star squirmed at the implication.

Lacey produced a big smile. "You're in! You can stay with me."

"I can? Really?"

"Yeah. But not for free, though. You'd need to come up with half the rent."

Star drew in a deep breath and let her cheeks puff while she blew out.

"Don't worry, it's not a lot. This isn't exactly a luxury apartment." Lacey glanced around. "It's not much to look at, but it's a place to sleep, and it's warm-ish in the winter."

"How much?"

"$200 a month. That's half. The rent is $400 and includes utilities."

Star looked at the floor for a long moment, then returned eye contact. "Okay. I'll do it. I just need to find a waitressing job or something. Do you know any good places to go?"

"But, Star... don't you understand what happened back there?"

"You helped me get away from that creep."

"That *creep* is one of the more ruthless pimps in this area. When you say you're in, you're in. There's no out. He knows who you are now. If you run, it's going to be me he comes looking for. No one screws with Ronny." The pitch in Lacey's voice heightened with every word she spoke.

Star shook with nervousness. "But... I've... I'm not... I mean..."

"You're a virgin?" Lacey asked matter-of-factly.

Star's gaze hit the ground. "Yes." There was a long pause. "I don't think I can do what you do."

"And what's that, princess? Make a living? Pay for this apartment? Put food on the table?"

It was clear Lacey was offended as she tensed her whole body into a defensive posture.

"No... I mean, yes... well, that's not what I mean. It's just..."

"Stop." Lacey softened her tone. "I know what you meant. I get it. I didn't mean to snap. I know how it looks. If I tell myself enough times it's the only way to survive, eventually I start believing it."

Star drew in a deep and nervous breath at the thought of it all.

Lacey could see the look on her face. "Hey, I know you're scared, but I'm telling you it's a sure thing. When I ran away, I tried to get a normal job, but no one's gonna hire you because of your age and, well, lack of doc-u-men-ta-tion." She said documentation comically, as if it were five different words.

Star slumped her shoulders and looked off to the side. That was a problem she had not considered.

"Ronny's a jerk, but at least he lets us keep enough of the money to pay for all of this." Lacey gestured widely around her, as if she were in the middle of a grand estate.

Star took a slow look around and felt a sense of nausea creeping in as she tried to imagine what it would be like to be a prostitute. She recalled earlier in the year when she made out with Alex Draper. He was a ginger soccer player and all the girls swooned over him. She felt elated to be making out with him, but when he tried to unbutton her jeans, she bolted to her feet and screamed at him for his inappropriate behavior. She thought he wanted to have sex with her, and she had already made up her mind to wait until marriage. The poor kid was so scared, he ran out the door and all the way home, long soccer hair flapping in the wind behind him. The nausea came again, and Star felt herself reeling. She didn't know anyone and only had $22.32 in her jean pocket.

The two girls sat talking in the small apartment for a long time. Star liked Lacey, but this was all too much for her. A girl who had never crossed over to second base becoming a prostitute? It just wasn't going to happen. This place she found herself in was more foreign to her than another country, but it was just what she needed to make her realize how immature she had been about leaving home in the first place. She thought being her own boss would be exciting and fun. After what she experienced tonight, that was a load of crap. She needed to go home. She would get some sleep and go home in the morning. Maybe Lacey could come with her so *she* wouldn't have to worry anymore either. The two girls settled in and turned off the lights.

Abrupt knocking sent both girls jumping off the bed. Lacey ran to the door and looked through the peephole. Star could hear her gulp – hard – and watched her slowly move the deadbolt over and back up from the door as it was forced open from the other side.

"There's my girls!" yelled Ronny. Leo was trailing close behind him.

"Ro... Ronny? What's up?" Lacey asked, trembling.

"I just wanted to see how our new girl was settling in, and if you ladies needed anything."

"No. No, thanks. We're good," Lacey said quickly, shooting a look over to Star, who could see Lacey silently begging for her to stay quiet. Ronny moved past Lacey and stood next to Star. With every step backwards Star took, Ronny took one even closer to her.

Ronny turned around and nodded at Leo, who grabbed Lacey by both arms and dragged her out the front door. Star locked eyes with Lacey. The look of terror in Lacey's eyes confirmed what she was already fearing, and

Star screamed for help. She tried to run past Ronny, but he pushed her forcefully to the ground. She watched as Leo pulled Lacey into the hallway and closed the door, leaving her alone with Ronny.

"Shut up! Shut up!" Ronny straddled her and held her hands down.

Star could hear Lacey screaming for her from the hallway.

"You belong to me now. And when things belong to me, that means I use them first. I take what's mine before anyone else gets to."

Star burst into tears, shook her head no and pleaded with Ronny to let her go. After a few minutes, things got quiet, except for Star's crying.

After a short while, Ronny left the apartment. Lacey looked at the floor as he passed, then broke free from Leo and rushed in to get to Star. Lacey helped her up and brought her to the bedroom, easing her onto the bed.

"I'm so sorry, Star," Lacey said quietly. "I didn't know he was going to come here."

Star sat on the bed with her arms around her knees. She could hardly process what just happened.

"Are you... are you hurt?"

Star buried her face in her arms and cried. Every part of her wanted to go back home, but then she'd have to look her dad in the face and tell him what happened. It would destroy him. She couldn't put him through any more pain.

Lacey brought her a roll of toilet paper to blow her nose. Star couldn't speak. She could only cry. Lacey put her arm gently around her and sat in silence. After a short time passed, Lacey moved quietly away, and slid into her own bed.

Star followed her lead, and put her head down on her pillow. She tossed and turned, struggling with the horrible images that filled her head. When morning came, Star remained curled up in her bed, facing the wall. She was glad Lacey let her be. She wasn't ready to talk about it. She wasn't sure if she ever would be. Hours turned into days as she tried to find the courage to go home. The more she thought about it, the more she wanted to die. Every time she closed her eyes, images of Ronny on top of her would play over and over in her mind. The violation seemed as real in her mind as the night it happened. Nothing seemed to remove the ugliness. She felt like a toy that was dirty, broken, and no longer suitable for anyone. Lacey wouldn't be able to afford feeding both of them for much longer, but her guilt kept her trying.

Days turned to weeks, and Ronny approached Star with a business proposition. Star was pretty, and he could get a high royalty if he could get her to dance at the club. Ronny convinced Star if she danced, she wouldn't have to work the streets. Seeing how she took so poorly to being with him, he told her he only had her best interest in mind and would see to it she was taken care of.

Ronny had brought her to the club and showed her the way into the back room where she could get ready. Star could hardly look at herself in the mirror. She felt broken beyond repair.

"Here," said Ronny, handing her a pill. "Take this. It will help you relax."

"What is it?"

"It will help you shake your nerves. It's like what you'd take before you get on a plane if you're afraid of flying or some crap like that. No big deal."

Star looked at Ronny, uncertain. She glanced down at the pill in her hand and then looked past the curtain at the stage waiting for her. Filled with anxiety, she popped the pill in her mouth and chased it down with a bottle of water Ronny handed to her. That pill she popped was the candy Ronny hooked her with to stop her pain. It was like the treat she got for rolling over and playing dead, which is what she felt inside when she was up on that stage. If she went through the motions, she got a fix that would dull the pain for a while, and it paid the rent.

Night after night, Star popped her painkiller and danced for the faces without names. Soon the painkillers weren't enough to obliterate her feelings and she no longer wanted to dance. She sat slouched in her chair, her eyes fixed on the remnant of a person she was staring at in the mirror. She remained motionless while her name was called from the stage, and Star could see Ronny enter the room from her peripheral.

Ronny didn't say anything. He didn't have to. He cleared a spot off the vanity, poured a small amount of the chalk-like substance in front of her, and laid the casing of an empty ink pen next to it. "Take this."

Star continued looking into the mirror. "What is it?"

"Meth. You snort it with that," he said, pointing to the pen casing.

Star remained focused forward, and simply nodded. She waited for him to leave before looking down at what he laid out in front of her. Deep down, a part of her knew picking up that make-shift straw was a fast fade to a place she once thought only existed in the movies. Yet, here she was. Star glanced over at the stage once more. Her stomach dropped along with her hope, and she reached down to grab the weapon of her impending demise. She was unprepared for the euphoria that rushed through every part of her. It was the false courage she needed to get back on the stage. Soon, crystal meth turned to heroin, and dancing could no longer pay for her addictions. In desperation, she hit the streets. She was already broken, so what did it matter?

It was a fast fade all right. The stuff of movies was now her reality.

* * *

Star lay on the cold van floor trying to shake off the memories. She wasn't sure what was more painful – her present circumstances or how she got here. Despite the heroin pulsing through her veins, the pain still made her head throb. She opened her eyes long enough for the blur of the lights going by to nauseate her stomach. Maybe it was better not to fight. She closed her eyes, feeling herself fade into the blackness.

Star came to again and could no longer feel the motion under her. They had stopped. She opened her eyes to a blurred view of the ceiling, and tried to make sense of where she was. It wasn't the van. It was dark, and a strong, musty smell filled her nose. As she rolled onto her side, she was quickly reminded of her raw scalp. She lifted her hand to run her fingers tenderly over the wound. She could feel the blood, but it was dried. How long had she been lying there?

Star let out a quiet moan as she tried to sit up. Pain shot up her right leg as the sharp edge of the metal clamp around her ankle dug deep into her skin. She reached down and surveyed the cold metal with her hands, feeling chain links extending to the wall beside the bed. Star slid her hands around, feeling a tattered box spring and metal frame beneath her. There was a blanket on the bed and one small pillow. All of it smelled like a damp cellar. Her mind felt clearer, but her physical body was struggling to catch up. She tried to come out of her fog, blinking to clear her vision and see through the blackness. As she did, both terror and adrenaline brought her to attention when she realized she wasn't alone.

CHAPTER 2

Sarah was bustling through the kitchen, making her list. It was Wednesday. Wednesday was grocery day. As soon as she heard the shower turn off, she went over to the coffee machine, popped in a vanilla hazelnut coffee pod, and listened to the stream of coffee fill Jack's mug. Sarah preferred the salted caramel. It was delicious and smooth, and reminded her of pleasant thoughts she couldn't quite put pictures to. It was like feeling sentimental for a memory you couldn't recall.

She grabbed the hot mug and walked carefully down the hall, into the bedroom. She knocked gently on the door, waiting for Jack's permissive grunt before opening it and setting it on the bathroom countertop. Averting her eyes from his body, she drew her hand away from the mug, and slipped quietly out of the bathroom, closing the door behind her. Her mind quickly went to her list, and she opened the refrigerator door to inventory the essentials – eggs, milk, yogurt, broccoli, lunch meat, salad. She closed the door and moved over to the pantry. Looking inside was like looking into the soul of a serial killer, she mused. It was his way. Everything had order, and everything had its place. She always made sure the labels on the cans were facing forward, and in alignment with each other. That was the way he liked it.

"I'm ready," Sarah said, as Jack walked into the kitchen.

"Good. We need to make it quick today. I have stuff to do."

Sarah took in a quick breath and turned to hide her disappointment.

Jack swallowed down the last of his coffee and put his mug into the sink. "Come on. Let's go."

They got in the van and made a quiet drive to the local grocery store. There were a lot of big chain stores in town, but they always went to a store not far from their house, owned by a quiet but friendly Latino woman. It was small, but quaint, and Sarah loved the smell of the meat smoker that filled the entire store. Sarah smiled fondly at the owner as they rolled the cart past the service desk and into the produce section.

"I'm going to grab some stuff from the aisles while you get the produce we need," Jack said. "I'll be back here in a few."

Sarah was relieved to have a little space and walked along the wooden boxes filled with fruit. She stopped at the nectarines, surveyed them carefully and selected one looking free of bruises. She brought it to her nose, closed her eyes, and inhaled deeply. The sound of laughter brought her back to attention, and she opened her eyes.

Across the aisle was a couple by the strawberries. Sarah could hear them flirting playfully with each other.

"Well, aren't you being particular about each strawberry. Are they for royalty or something?" said the man with a grin.

The woman threw her arms around his neck and smiled. "They certainly are, and you won't be disappointed in how particular I am with them tonight, my king."

They both giggled and exchanged a sweet kiss.

Sarah flushed at the comment, suddenly feeling intrusive. She looked away but couldn't help herself from glancing back a few seconds later. As the woman continued picking through the strawberries, the man ran his fingers tenderly up and down her back.

The smile on Sarah's face turned to sadness. There was a longing in her heart that made it difficult to suppress tears. She tried not to dwell on such things. She knew how well she had it. Jack reminded her of that all the time. She knew beggars shouldn't be choosers.

She moved to the next bin to select apples. They were stacked neatly in a pyramid, like something you see in an advertisement. Despite the beautiful presentation, she was unable to take her eyes off the loving couple, fixated on their dance. She found herself leaning in toward them a little when she heard him whisper to her.

"I love you."

As soon as the man said it, he glanced up and saw Sarah looking at them. Startled, and somewhat embarrassed, Sarah swung around abruptly, hitting the side of the bin, and sending several apples rolling forward and onto the floor. It made more noise than apples should, and she stood shocked for a moment, feeling the heat come into her face. She dropped into a squat and gathered the apples on the floor.

"Please, let me help you with that," said the man, as he too bent down to pick up apples.

"Oh, gosh... thank you. I'm so embarrassed, really."

"That's nothing to be embarrassed about. You didn't see me last week when I knocked down the display of pineapples!"

They both laughed as they finished reassembling the leaning tower of apples.

"Thank you, again. I really appreciate your help."

"I'd say anytime, but I'd hate to encourage you," said the man.

Sarah giggled again, gave a brief wave and turned her cart around. Standing there in front of her was Jack, and his face was redder than hers.

"What exactly do you think you're doing? I leave you for ten minutes and I come back to find you flirting with another man?"

Sarah was gripped with fear and couldn't get the words out fast enough. "No, Jack! It wasn't like that!" Sarah clasped her hands together, as if to portray a silent plea. "I'm sorry, Jack! I'm sorry!"

Jack's fists clenched, and his jaw tightened. "Let's go."

"There are still a few more things I–"

Jack interrupted and said more firmly, gritting his teeth, "Let's go. Now."

They made their way in silence to the checkout. It wasn't the usual smiles the cashier was used to. Sarah could tell she knew something wasn't quite right, but the quieting, almost pleading look in Sarah's eyes told her not to say anything. The woman smiled politely as she punched the grocery item numbers into her outdated cash machine. Sarah used to think it was quaint but, in this moment, was wishing for a scanner. She could feel every second tick by like a grandfather clock at the top of the hour.

Jack was staring forward, avoiding any interaction with either of the women. She could tell he was upset, and she was lamenting the thought of the ride home. Or worse, what would happen once they got home.

"$102.34, please," said the cashier.

Sarah let out an audible gasp, which she quickly stifled in response to Jack's glare. She was so preoccupied with trying to read Jack that she hadn't seen all the items being scanned through. Considering she only got a small amount of the groceries she needed, she wondered what in the world Jack bought. Jack paid and ushered Sarah out into the parking lot.

"Get in the van. I'll put the groceries in the back," said Jack.

Sarah knew not to argue. She quietly complied and got into the front passenger seat. As Jack finished putting the groceries away, her heart sank. Given what just happened, she assumed they would no longer be stopping by the café for a coffee, as was their grocery outing tradition. She watched through her side mirror as Jack brought the cart back to the return. He pushed the cart in with so much fury, it smashed into the other carts, sending some out the other side. The noise was so loud, Sarah jumped in her seat. She held her breath as fear ran through her.

Jack got into the van but didn't start it right away. He just sat there. Sarah sat quietly, rubbing her fingers. After what felt like minutes, he spoke calmly but sternly.

"I do a lot for you, right?"

Sarah nodded.

"Then show me some respect."

"Yes. Yes, I'm sorry. I will."

Jack started the engine and drove out of the lot. Sarah sat, unsettled, waiting for the other shoe to drop. It wasn't like Jack to take such things in stride. It put her on edge. Maybe he was just waiting to catch her off guard.

There had been a time when she accidentally talked to the gas station attendant. She was trying to find the Pepto-Bismol. It had taken a lot of convincing to get Jack to stop on the way home for it, as she wasn't feeling well. The attendant could see she was searching, so he came over to lend some assistance. Jack caught her talking to him, which was really just a simple thank you. But Jack never saw anything as simple.

In the moment, he said nothing, other than with his eyes. In fact, he was strangely kind. After they got home, he offered to rub Sarah's feet. A minute or so into the foot rub, Jack grabbed her foot at the ankle and twisted it sharply to one side. Sarah yelled in pain while Jack sat on her legs until she apologized for what she did wrong. Today felt a little like that time. She felt like she was waiting for the foot massage.

When they got home, Sarah put the groceries away and started dinner while Jack ran out to do more errands. Again, she was glad for the space, hoping that would calm him down as well.

Jack stayed out well past the normal time of dinner, so Sarah ate and made a plate for him, which she wrapped carefully in foil and placed in the oven. She scrolled through the TV menu and stopped on a favorite reality TV show, where people live on an island and compete against each other. It was a new season and the first two episodes had already aired. She had missed them both. Jack didn't want her watching too much television, and often monitored her viewing time like a mother over her grade school child.

She heard Jack come in through the kitchen and hoped the meal he found would uplift his mood enough to allow her a little mindless TV time. She hit enter on the remote and the theme song came loudly through the speakers. Startled, she dropped the remote. Fumbling to regain it, she lowered the volume as quickly as she could. She sat upright on the couch, her body rigid with tension, waiting for that familiar bellow from the kitchen.

Silence. She eased herself more comfortably in the chair, half watching the show, and half imagining what it would be like to live like an island native. She could stomach all the fish she'd have to eat. It was the only non–plant–based protein that didn't make her squeamish. She wasn't sure about the coconuts though. She thought she remembered hearing they were a diuretic, and didn't that mean you went to the bathroom a lot?

She thought about having to squat in the brush of an unpopulated island, along with countless spiders, snakes, and other creatures she probably wouldn't recognize.

The sound of silverware hitting the floor of the kitchen snapped Sarah out of her daydream. She tensed again for a moment, listening for any sounds of disapproval coming from Jack but, again, there was silence. She relaxed a little, and let her mind wander to what it was like to leave your family and all of your worldly possessions behind like these contestants did.

Sarah found herself sitting upright again when Jack walked into the room. He sat on the other end of the couch with his dinner plate on his lap and stared ahead at the TV. Sarah avoided eye contact, so she didn't seem confrontational. After a few minutes, she was reassured, and relaxed once more, this time slumping into the arm of the sofa and resting her head against the soft throw pillow.

When Jack was finished with his meal, he put his plate on the coffee table and sat back on the couch. After a few moments, Sarah felt the warmth of his hand on her ankle, which made her flinch a little, but she dared not pull back. Hot tears blurred her vision as she stared straight ahead at the TV. She drew in a deep breath of air, breathing out even more slowly, trying to ward off the tears before they spilled out. She returned her focus to the show and wished she could trade places with one of them. Any of them.

After daydreaming for a few minutes, Sarah took a deep breath and brought her attention back to the TV as a local news broadcast cut in.

"Tonight, we interrupt this show to bring you coverage of a local teen abduction. Rachel McGinnis was reported abducted this evening from the south side of Milwaukee."

Jack took his hand off Sarah's leg and sat up.

"An eyewitness confirms Rachel was pulled against her will into a dark-colored van near the corner of 22nd and Greenfield. The witness estimated a white male. Suspect was wearing a baseball hat and dark-colored hooded sweatshirt. After talking with the witness, police suspect this young girl may be involved in a local prostitution ring. Stay tuned as we bring you more updates at 10 p.m."

Sarah sat, motionless, as she watched the video of the reporter walking around an area all too familiar to her. A rush of memories invaded her mind and tears streamed down her face. She was so lost in her mind she was unaware of Jack's hot stare.

"Why are you crying?" he barked. "You don't even know that girl."

Sarah snapped awake, gave Jack a blank stare, and began to stutter. "No! No, I don't think so. I... I just..."

"I just what?" he snapped again.

Sarah tensed. After a few moments, she spoke slowly and deliberately. "It's hard to watch that video without thinking about who I used to be."

Jack let out a condescending laugh. "Don't you mean *what* you used to be?"

Sarah's cheeks flushed with embarrassment. Her gaze hit the floor as she could still feel his judging stare.

"And let's be honest here," he said. "It's what you still are."

More tears ran down her cheeks. "Please stop," she said softly. "I'm not that person anymore, and I..." Her words were cut short as Jack jumped from the couch and loomed over her, an assailant poised to attack. The volume of his voice caused her to shut her eyes.

"I can't believe how ungrateful you are! If it wasn't for me, you'd probably be dead. I saved you and gave you a home. I've spent my hard-earned money to feed you and give you clothes to wear. And how do you thank me? By flirting with another man and talking back? You're pathetic, Sarah. You don't deserve the kindness I've shown you."

Sarah cowered under the weight of his words. "Maybe you're right. Maybe I don't deserve what you've done for me. I could leave if you want, and..."

"And what? Where would you go? Back on the street? Or how about jail?" His cruel words set her off and she found a small amount of courage.

"I could go back home!" Her volume startled even her, and silence hung between them like a thick wall. Before a dam breaks, there's a small crack that penetrates a piece of the wall. In their silence, she could hear the crackle and popping expanding around Jack. The weight of what was behind that wall would surely kill her.

It was only seconds, but it seemed like minutes to her, as she watched the imaginary lines take shape and prepare to burst. It was as if he could smell her fear. He seemed to like it, actually. Like an animal likes the sound of its prey screaming for help.

Sarah closed her eyes, trying to escape in her mind to anywhere that would protect her from the pending destruction. She was back on the island, floating on the wooden pallet used for fishing. She could feel the warmth of the sun on her back and the pleasant temperature of the water that wet the bottom of her suit. She imagined she could look over the side and see a school of zebra fish, their colorful scales throwing shimmers from the sun above. As she reached her hand into the water and toward the fish, the school of fish blurred as the weight of Jack's fist sent her onto the floor.

"Stay on the island, stay on the island," she kept telling herself, while cupping her injured face in her hands.

His words were loud and cutting. "You. Dirty. Ingrate. I saved you and protected you all this time from the world that hates you. I can't believe you'd be so stupid to think, of all of those people, your father would want you back. He hates you. He told me so. He knows what you did, and he's embarrassed by you. No. He's worse than embarrassed. He's ashamed."

Sarah felt sick, and resigned herself to the floor. A small pool of blood collected on the floor around her lip and cheek.

"So, if you think, even for a minute, that leaving here is an option, you're out of your fool mind. You are so lucky I'm the man I am, or I'd throw you out on the street right now." Jack grabbed the remote and shut off the TV.

"Now get up and clean up this mess." He pointed to his plate and the blood on the floor. "Clean yourself up and go to bed. I don't want to hear another word about it. Maybe you can spend the night thinking about how to act grateful instead of like a little brat."

Jack went into the kitchen. She could hear him rifling around but was too groggy to put together whatever he was doing. He came back into the living room, grabbed his sweatshirt and let the door slam as he left. Sarah lay on the floor, hot tears streaming down her swollen cheek and mixing with the blood. She wasn't angry. That emotion had been conditioned out of her early on. Anger only brought more physical pain. She was resigned to hurt quietly inside.

Sarah picked herself up and went to the bathroom for antiseptic and Band-Aids. She used the ones that looked like little butterflies to close the part of her cheek he had split open.

"That will definitely leave a scar," she said out loud. She ran her finger gently over the bandaged area, trying to imagine what it would look like. Sarah stared at her reflection. She used to think she was pretty. Even well above average. When she was in high school, she was never short on boys asking her out, and people were constantly calling her pretty. Especially her dad. He would always tell her how beautiful she was.

But Jack said he cared enough to tell her the truth. He said people just say that stuff to make you feel good. Jack said now that her dad knew what she had done, he would never think she was beautiful again.

Tears filled her eyes once more. She turned off the lights and crawled into bed. All she could think about was Rachel. Rachel McGinnis. She wondered where she was or if she was still alive. That poor girl. That easily could have been her. It probably would have been, if it wasn't for Jack.

She opened the window a few inches, laid down, and turned onto her side. The street light outside made the partially open nightstand drawer on the side of her bed visible. After a few minutes, Sarah sat up and opened the drawer. She pulled out a small Bible. She got it from a guy on the street handing them out, and was surprised Jack let her keep it. He said it was better than watching TV. She had read the whole thing several times. It felt like a fictional story, but she couldn't quite shake how she felt when she read it. It was the only time she didn't feel alone. Maybe that's why she read it so many times. She opened to a page that was dog eared, to a scripture she was particularly drawn to, and read it aloud. She remembered her mom reading that passage to her as a child. Her mom made her memorize it, along with many others. Even though she couldn't really connect with it as a child, now it brought her a strange comfort. Perhaps it was the familiarity of it all.

She closed her eyes, still gripping the Bible, and let herself drift off to sleep.

CHAPTER 3

Star closed her eyes tightly, then re-opened them. She was still in the dark room. She was still chained to the wall. The nightmares she had were real. The man stood silent in the darkened doorway.

"Who are you?" stammered Star. "What do you want with me?"

The man took a step backwards and swung the heavy door closed, leaving her alone. Star could hear the sound of the metal lock clicking, and instinctually tried to jump to her feet to stop it from locking.

"No!" screamed Star. The chain stopped her short as she fell onto the floor, pain screaming up her leg as the metal clamp dug deep. The pit in her stomach felt worse than her ankle.

Star reached down to feel the shackle and ran her fingers over the blood around it. She gave the chain a good tug. Hearing the chain scrape loudly along the cement floor made her realize what she was up against, and immediately resigned her to the futility of her actions. Why was she still alive? Who was this man and why did he want to hurt her? Every part of her wanted to break down. Every part of her wanted more heroin. She wanted to escape to a beautiful place. Any place but here.

Star looked around, looking for anything that could help her. Her bed frame was bolted to the cement floor, as was the chain to the wall. There was a water spicket coming out from the lower part of the wall and a small floor drain nearby. Nothing big enough to escape through. The only other thing in there was a bucket. Star's stomach turned as she realized what that bucket was for. She wasn't sure if she felt sicker about the idea of going to the bathroom in a bucket, or the idea that she'd be in this hellhole long enough to need one.

With her head still pounding, she crawled onto the bed and lay flat on her back. She ran her hands gently over her mouth and chin, surveying the damage done by the man's punches. It felt like there was a split in the lower left side of her lip, and the whole left side of her face felt swollen. She moved her jaw back and forth a little, squinting with the pain. Star closed her eyes, trying to ignore the insatiable craving for the high that sent her to a happier place. It was her constant companion. More like her constant intruder. Star allowed the images in. The ones she kept hidden away for times when the heroin wasn't an option.

★ ★ ★

"Daddddyyyy!" squealed Star, as she ran through the lawn trying to avoid the stream of water coming from the garden hose. It was almost ninety degrees outside and pretending she didn't want to be sprayed was a fun game. She had learned that her protest just made him spray her more.

Her dad was in the driveway handwashing the car. It was pearly white, and the sun sent iridescent colors shimmering off it in all directions. She watched intently as he sloshed the soft, fuzzy, blue glove around in the bucket of soapy water and slapped it onto the car window, leaving a thick trail of water between the bucket and the car. It looked fun, and she wanted to help.

"Daddy, can I help you wash the car?"

"Sure, Bean," he said with a smile. "Just grab another cloth from the garage shelf and you can work on sparkling up those tires."

Star skipped over to the shelf and selected the one that had the brightest color. She skipped back, fixated on the yellow remnant of what was once a sweatshirt she remembered her dad wearing. A mysterious and faded brown spot on the cloth brought a wry smile to her face, as the spot was not so much of a mystery to her. Her mom had donated the sweatshirt to the rag pile after being unsuccessful in getting out the ugly stains. After much inquiry, neither of Star's parents knew how it had gotten there. Had they asked her, they would have known it was grease, motor oil or a combination of the two.

Star had been bored one Saturday and wanted to play mechanic. Channeling her inner Dad, she threw on his well oversized yellow sweatshirt and went to work. She was very proud of herself for figuring out how to open the hood of the car, and even prouder to be able to crawl up onto the engine, although it involved two precariously stacked cans of paint. She lay face down on the engine, pretending to pull hoses and replace batteries – all things she had seen her dad do in his auto shop. The car fared well after her imaginary work, but the streaks of black left on the bright yellow sweatshirt were not so imaginary. Star's daydreaming smile turned into a shriek as cold water hit her from head to toe.

"DAAAAD!" she screamed, brought back into the present. "I wasn't ready for that!"

"That's when it's the most fun!" he laughed. "Come over here and help me refill this bucket."

"But you're going to spray me with the hose again!" she protested, arms folded around herself.

"No, Bean. I won't."

"You promise?"

"I promise, I won't get you with the hose, and you can't get me with the hose either," he said with a grin. Confident in their negotiations, Star continued to skip toward him to the bucket. He handed her the hose and poured more soap into the bucket. She loved watching the bubbles pile up on themselves and spill over the side and onto the driveway. They looked like shades of blue and green as the sun rays refracted the light. With each spray of the hose, a small rainbow became visible. She thought it was beautiful, mesmerized by all the colors. He finished the body of the car and she finished all four wheels with her bright yellow cloth. He let her spray all the suds off the car while he dumped out the bucket of dirty water.

"Why don't you refill this bucket, so we can rinse it out?" he said to her. Happily, she filled the bucket to the brim. He waited for her to put the hose on the ground, grabbed the bucket, smiled, and walked in her direction.

"You promised!" she yelled with nervous laughter.

"I did. I promised I wouldn't get you with the hose. I didn't say anything about the bucket!" Star took off running and her dad took off right behind her. Star's laughter slowed her down and her dad closed the gap. As soon as he got within throwing distance, her mom came outside, putting her hair up in a ponytail. She had a large grin on her face as she stood in the yard and watched the two of them play. Star finally stopped, giggling, hands out in a defensive posture, as if that would stop the water, but ready to accept her fate.

"Give it to her!" laughed her mom.

Star and her dad's attention moved to her mom, and they exchanged a conspiring look. Star's dad gave her a wink, turned quickly to the side and launched the bucket of water at her mom. Star's mom gasped in surprise, which quickly turned into a mischievous smile as she bolted for the hose. There was so much laughter.

* * *

Star opened her eyes to the darkness for just a moment. Just long enough to remind her where she was. She shut them again, trying hard to regain the memories of sun and laughter. It felt like so long ago. It was so long ago. She ached to be in her front yard again, with her only worry in the world being about a bucket of water.

Star jumped, startled by the familiar sound of the lock on the door opening. She sat up quickly and pressed her back into the wall, knees up and arms wrapped around herself. She could feel the anxiety welling up inside as the door swung open. With the sound of a snap, the room was flooded with light. Star wanted to shield her eyes, but she needed to see. She needed to see him. Struggling to adjust her eyes, she squinted as much as she could, while still maintaining vision. He was taller than she first thought. He was still wearing his baseball cap, but she could tell his hair was dark. His eyes were a piercing ice blue and his skin was more olive than white. Under any other circumstance, she might think he was attractive. But as it was, he was only a monster.

The man pulled a brown paper bag inside, closed the door and stood at a distance, looking inquisitively at her. "How are you feeling?" His words had something like compassion mixed in with them. Star's eyes dropped to the bag beside him. He reached down into the bag, pulled out a plain bagel and handed it to Star. She was starving but felt afraid to take it. After a moment, he set it down on the bed beside her. She felt a little feral as she tore off pieces with her fingers and stuffed them into her mouth, as if she was afraid he would take the rest. He watched her eat the entire bagel, and then handed her a bottle of water.

"Who are you? Why am I here?" she stammered.

The man remained silent.

Star pressed herself even more tightly into the wall as he walked toward her. She knew she was too weak to fight him, especially with the shackle around her foot, so she remained still and tense. She held her breath as he moved close and sat on the bed next to her.

"What's your name?" asked the man.

Star remained silent for a moment, then thought better of herself. She had watched a lot of movies where girls try to fight the bad guy, and it always got ugly. The same philosophy always applied with the Johns. It was one of the first things Lacey taught her about turning tricks. Pretend to be their friend and pretend to be into whatever it was they were asking you to do, even if you had no intention of doing it. It kept them calm and warded off a lot of unwanted force and violence. If they thought they could trust you, they would let their guard down and you had a better chance of being able to get out of wherever you were, unharmed or, more importantly, alive. Alive. That's what she needed to stay.

"Star. My name is Star." She paused hesitantly. "What's yours?"

The man seemed to relax a little. "Star. Is that your real name?"

Star sat silent for some time.

"Star it is," he finally said with a smile. "I'm sure you have a lot of questions about why you're here, but I want to assure you that I'm here to help you."

"Help me?" Star blurted out, as she pulled against the chain on her foot in a gesture of accusation. She immediately regretted her outburst, as he stood quickly with a displeased look on his face. Star trembled but wasn't sure how much of it was because she was scared, and how much was because of the withdrawal she was feeling. She wondered if he could see that, because he eased his voice a little. "Yes. I'm here to help you. It may not seem like it, but I'm here to save you. I know you may not understand it now, but you will in time."

Star's eyes widened. She was stuck on his words, "in time." She wondered how much time. Her anxiety returned, and she shook violently. He took a step toward her and grabbed her shoulders with his hands, as if to steady her. Star felt too weak to fight his contact.

"In order to help you, I need you to help me. Star, I need you to remain calm and trust that, if you work with me, I won't hurt you." He looked down at where she was holding her ankle with her hand and could see the blood around the shackle. "I can see the metal is cutting against your ankle. Will you let me help you with that?"

Star fought to clear her mind. If she agreed, maybe he would take it off, and she could run. She nodded her head at him.

"If I take it off, will you be a good girl and stay put?"

Again, Star nodded silently. She sucked in a deep breath as he sat down beside her. Trembling, she remained quiet as he slowly ran his hand over her knee and down her leg. She flinched abruptly when he got to where the shackle was on her ankle, and he pulled his hand back. Without breaking his eye contact with her, he put his hand back on the shackle. She winced as he slowly turned it around until the lock was facing him. With his right hand, he reached into his jean pocket, fumbled around, and produced a small iron key.

Star held her breath while he inserted the key into the lock on the shackle and turned it a quarter turn to the left. There was a clicking sound, and the shackle came apart on one side. He pulled it out from under her foot and Star let out an audible groan. As soon as she was free, she brought her leg in toward her body and tucked it away, out of reach of his hand. She continued to press herself into the wall behind her, wishing she could become one with it for just a little while.

"There," he said softly. "I'm sure that feels a bit better."

Star sat quietly, trying to control her shaking and steady her mind.

"Star, I'm going to leave now. But I need to know I can trust you not to cause any trouble if I leave the anklet off. I have a choice to offer you. Do you want to hear it?"

Star nodded.

"You were high when I picked you up, and I can see you're really struggling with the effects of the drugs leaving your system. I'm going to help you with that, and we can go one of two ways with this. It's all going to depend on you. Your first option is to cut this thing cold turkey, which means you never have another drop of that drug in your body. The withdrawals will be severe, and you'll feel very sick for several days. Your second option is that we wean you off of it. That means I give you small, periodic doses. It takes a little longer but will lessen the effects of your withdrawals. Which do you want?"

Star looked at him in a bit of disbelief. "Are you really going to give me a fix if I ask for it or is this some kinda trick question?"

He smiled. "No. No tricks. Just a choice."

Star was still trembling, trying to fight for logic. She knew if she took more of the drug, she would remain helpless to defend herself. She could feel sweat beading on her forehead. Every part of her body was screaming for the drug.

Come on, Star! Fight. Fight. She wanted nothing more than to stay strong and reject his offer, but she was too weak to do anything no matter what she chose. Before she knew it, she was releasing herself from the safety of the cold cement wall and inching her way toward him.

"I see," said the man. He had a look of disappointment on his face, but she paid no attention as her eyes kept drifting to the brown paper bag, imagining her next trip to paradise was inside. He followed her eyes down to the bag. His face twisted into something of disgust and he let out a sigh. "Okay, then. Let's get you what you want."

Star's pulse quickened as he reached down into the bag and pulled out a small bag of white powder. Star's anticipation turned slowly to anxiety and fear. She had only snorted it once before but remembered that it took a long time to feel the effects of it. She knew it was better than nothing, so she waited restlessly, while he took out a small, flat piece of hard plastic and a straw. She watched as he tapped the powder onto the plastic tray.

"Before I give this to you, you need to promise me, if I leave the anklet off, that you won't try anything, and you won't cause any trouble after I leave." She could hardly control herself. In that moment, she felt like a dog in front of her food dish, waiting for her master to say okay. She would have probably agreed to anything. "Do we have a deal?"

"Yes. Yes, we have a deal," Star said, feeling like she had just sold her soul to the devil. He carried the small plastic tray over to the bed, set it carefully onto the mattress, and handed Star the straw. As she grabbed for it, he pulled it back at the last second, with a final warning.

"If you try *anything*, this will never happen again. There'll be no more, and you'll have to quit cold turkey. Do you understand?"

At this point, Star was hardly processing anything he was saying. She mumbled a yes and looked at him like a starving child, waiting for her ration. He handed the straw over to Star. She fumbled to get it in the correct position and held it gently over the fine powder. Placing the straw at the opening of one of her nostrils, and closing the other with her finger, she breathed in deeply through her nose, vacuuming all the powder, leaving nothing behind. She wished she could feel the effects right away, but she'd need to manage through the next ten minutes or so before she could be transported from this prison.

"There. It shouldn't be too long now and that should give you what you're looking for," he said, coldly. Any hint of compassion Star heard earlier was now gone, and the man's face looked angry. His movements became more exaggerated as he gathered the items on the bed. "I'll never understand what it is you junkies want with this stuff. You say you don't have any choice but to sell yourselves out, so you can afford a place to stay and food to eat. But then you go and get twisted up with drugs and booze. It's not like the stuff is cheap either. Why would you make a trade off like that?"

He was now staring hard at Star, as if his question were not rhetorical, and he was waiting for her response. The silence hung thick between them like a fog.

"I... I don't know. It's just that..." Star spoke softly.

"It's just that what?" blurted the man. "It's just that you're a junkie and you use your situation to justify what you're doing? You make people think it's not your fault when it really is your fault. It's always their fault. She said it wasn't, but it was. I knew it all along. She gave me no choice."

At this point, he was pacing back and forth, rubbing his temples with his hands, as if he were trying to calm himself down. Although she was still fighting through her physical discomforts, the high hadn't kicked in yet, so Star was acutely aware of his babbling and erratic behavior. She felt the fear welling up in her but, almost simultaneously, felt the heroin taking over her body. She must have snorted more than she thought for it to hit so quickly. She couldn't worry about him anymore. She lay back onto the bed as she felt the familiar rush. She no longer felt her ankle throbbing. She no longer felt the presence of the monster who locked her in a room for God knows why. God. She hadn't thought about God in a while. She imagined heaven might be something like the bright lights currently invading her mind. She closed her eyes even tighter and drifted off into her memories, letting her thoughts skip around like a stone on the water.

The brilliant lights seemed to dance in the background of her memories, as she lay replaying better times in her head. When Star finally opened her eyes again, there were no more brilliant lights. Her prison was dark and quiet. The man was gone. She wondered what time it was, and if it were day or night. She no longer had the shackle on, so she could get up and turn the light on if she wanted. As funny as it sounded in her own mind, a part of her was afraid to turn the light on. She was afraid to get a good look at her prison. And her isolation.

CHAPTER 4

Sarah woke, startled by the sound of the Bible hitting the floor. She must have fallen asleep still holding it. She grabbed for it, opened the drawer of the nightstand, and tucked it tenderly back inside. She could see the bright orange sun making its way into the sky. Streams of light cascaded through her window and danced off the glass of the lamp beside her bed. She looked alongside her, expecting to see Jack, but he wasn't there. The sheets were smooth and the blanket on the edge of the bed was tucked neatly under his undisturbed pillow.

A pit formed in her stomach, and she ran her fingers across her swollen lip as she thought of what had happened the night before. Maybe he was still angry with her, and had slept on the couch. That wasn't his normal go to, but it was the only other place she imagined he might be.

A cool breeze came through the window, sending a wave of goose bumps over Sarah's skin. She pulled the covers up higher and decided to take a few extra minutes to herself, enjoying the space and stretching out across the width of the bed. She loved the feel of being wrapped up in the sheets. It was a strange comfort to her, as if arms enveloped and held her. The breeze continued to caress her cheek and, before she knew it, the sun was climbing higher into the sky.

Sarah got up out of bed, walked down the hall and into the living room. Everything seemed so quiet. She focused her eyes as she looked to the couch. It was empty.

"He must be outside," she mumbled. She picked up the TV remote, turned it on, and continued on to the kitchen. The thought of a hot cup of coffee distracted her, and she grabbed a mug from the cupboard. She favored the large mug with colorful flowers from the little café she and Jack would go to after grocery shopping. For weeks, she had been looking at that mug. Every time they went in there, she would walk over to the shelf and pick it up gingerly. She would twist it all the way around, using her fingers to trace the ceramic flowers that were slightly raised from the rest of the cup. After about the fourth week of that routine, Jack bought it for her. He had been in an especially good mood that day. Those days seemed fewer and farther between, but they were what kept her going. They were what kept her believing that things could be okay.

Sarah opened the refrigerator and grabbed the container of skim milk. She filled her mug about a quarter of the way, then set it down on the platform of the Keurig machine. Placing a new pod inside, she closed the top, and selected the 12oz setting. Sarah allowed herself a smile as she listened to the whirl of the machine and inhaled the pleasant smells of the salted caramel coffee. She opened the window, and sat quietly at the kitchen table, both hands wrapped around the mug, as she watched the sun finish its daily climb.

Mornings were the only time of the day she ever really felt like herself. Maybe it was the fact that she was alone and didn't need to be anything for anyone. Maybe it was something about the sun rising – the promise of a new day.

Her thoughts went to the couple from the grocery store. She imagined the two of them waking and having a cup of coffee together. They would hold their mugs with one hand and, with the other, intertwine their fingers with each other across the table. They would probably talk about whatever fun things they had planned for the day. He would tease her some more, and she would pretend she didn't like it. Eventually, he would pull her close for a kiss and they would watch the sunrise in each other's arms.

Sarah was snapped out of her daydream by the slam of the neighbors' screen door. Two of the neighbor kids had already gotten a start on their play day. They ran over to a group of trees by the edge of the front yard, where they knelt down and went to work digging at the base of one of the trees. They were fussing over something when the small boy stopped and pulled up a worm. The pride on his face turned to mischief as he stuck it in the girl's face, making a wild noise as he did it. The girl shrieked and jumped to her feet. The boy jumped up in pursuit, dangling the confused worm in front of him and teasing the young girl he was chasing.

The two ran in zig zags around the house, giggling all the while, and Sarah found herself smiling as she thought of Teddy. Teddy had been the neighborhood thug when they were growing up. Sarah had the unfortunate luck of living in the house next door to him. Through a series of community events and forced neighborhood cookouts, Sarah got to know Teddy, and they became close friends. She learned he wasn't really the thug everyone made him out to be. It was all a big act to cover up what life was like for him. No one knew what was really going on in his house. They only knew his dad had one too many at each of the neighborhood cookouts. What they didn't know was that after everyone went home, Teddy's dad would find a reason to get angry with his mom and hit her, usually until she was on the floor begging for him to stop.

When Teddy turned twelve, he went through a sudden growth spurt. He was already big for his age, but over the course of one summer, got four inches taller and what seemed like twenty pounds heavier. This must have given Teddy some confidence, as there was an unexpected turn of events after the Labor Day cookout. That night, Teddy's dad had three too many and made a giant scene by embarrassing his wife in front of everyone. Sarah could see the look in Teddy's eyes as he watched his dad swing his wife around, asking which of the men there thought she was attractive. She pushed him away and ran into their house, crying and ashamed.

Teddy was mortified. His face reddened and his eyes stung with tears. In a fury, he rushed his dad and bulldozed him right into the ground. Teddy threw punches, yelling and screaming at his dad the whole time. It was a string of profanities so colorful, it made most of them just stop and stare.

A few of the other dads broke them apart and tried to settle things down. They escorted Teddy's dad back to his house, not wanting him to be alone with his wife after what had just happened. Sarah's parents brought Teddy over to their house. She and Teddy sat on the couch together watching reruns of old comedies. Neither of them laughed. They didn't speak a word to each other. They didn't have to. It was the first time Sarah and Teddy had ever held hands.

Sarah gripped her coffee mug a little harder as she recalled the events that followed.

It was getting late, and her parents told Teddy it was okay to go home. The men who had escorted his dad home said he had calmed down, and things should be okay. Teddy and Sarah exchanged an anxious glance, and he reluctantly let go of Sarah's hand. He thanked her parents and left. Sarah watched him walk slowly across the lawn and in through the side door to their kitchen. She continued to watch until all the lights went out. Sarah got ready for bed and went to sleep.

Police sirens woke her. She raced out the front door, caught just in time by her dad who wouldn't allow her to get any closer. After everyone had gone to bed, another fight broke out between Teddy's parents. This time his dad pulled a knife on his mom. In an attempt to help his mom, Teddy hit his dad over the head with a lamp. It didn't knock him out, but it was enough to leave him confused enough for Teddy to wrestle the knife away from him. Once Teddy had the knife in his hand, they suspect he snapped. That's when he stabbed his dad to death. In the weeks that followed, with a lot of supporting testimony from the neighbors, they determined Teddy was only acting out of defense of his mother and was ordered to complete some kind of juvenile probation. Teddy was pretty torn up about all of it but did his probation. He never hassled another kid.

Sarah loosened her grip on the mug and sighed. She missed him. She missed his kindness. He had a way about him that always made her feel appreciated and even interesting. Whenever she was talking, he would stop what he was doing and listen intently. Sarah closed her eyes and imagined what it might be like to kiss Teddy.

"Mmm..." she said out loud. A smile formed on her face as she let their imaginary kiss play out in her mind.

Sarah suddenly felt flushed and embarrassed by her thoughts. If Jack knew she was daydreaming about that, he would go crazy on her for sure. She shook the thoughts from her head and returned to reality.

She had to think for a moment about what day it was. Thursday. It was Thursday. That meant laundry. After eating a bowl of cereal, Sarah put her dishes in the dishwasher, grabbed the basket out of the laundry room, and walked back into the bedroom. She paused for a moment as she took another long look at the half-slept-in bed. She shrugged it off and fixed her side up.

There were clothes on the floor, which brought her mentally back to the task at hand. Thursday was always laundry day. She picked up the clothes on the floor, threw them into the basket, and walked it over to the brown wicker hamper beside the dresser. The hamper was beginning to bulge a little at the bottom, as the weight of the dirty clothes pressed against the aging pieces of wicker woven loosely together. She lifted the top and grabbed the dirty clothes by the handful, transferring them into the basket. As she was grabbing a handful, something caught her eye.

She dropped what was in her hands into the basket, and turned her attention back to the hamper, staring down into it. She reached in and pulled out one of Jack's sweatshirts. Sarah tilted her head to the side as she held the sweatshirt a little closer to her face and analyzed what looked like a large stain of blood on the front of it. She racked her brain to think of some event that might have happened in the last few days to cause such a stain. She couldn't think of anything. Nothing here at home, and no stories from work.

Maybe he hurt himself and didn't tell her. Maybe this wasn't even his blood. Maybe it was someone at work.

She could probably get the stain out. She would at least try, because he would be angry if he had to throw it away. Sarah brought the sweatshirt into the laundry room and laid it out across the top of the dryer. Dousing the stain with an Oxy spray, she decided to let it sit for a few minutes while the scrubbing bubbles fulfilled all their marketing promises.

Sarah walked back into the kitchen and placed her cup of coffee into the microwave to reheat it. She would delay her chores long enough to finish her coffee. By then, she would be able to work on the stain. Just as she was sitting back down at the table, she watched Jack drive the van into the driveway and come to an abrupt stop. He hit the brakes so hard, the van skidded along the gravel another foot or so, and stopped inches from the side deck. A surge of dread ran through her, but she knew she had to act normal when he came in, or she would make the matter from last night even worse.

Sarah felt her body stiffen with tension as she watched Jack get out of the van and slam the door. He was moving quickly, as if he were in a hurry. He walked around to the back of the van, swung the doors open and climbed in. She could see him rummaging around but couldn't quite make out what he was doing inside. After a few minutes, he jumped out the back of the van and stood staring inside it. Sarah's curiosity was about to get the best of her when he slammed the heavy back doors closed and made his way to the side door of the house. Still gripping her mug with both hands, she turned her body to face the door as Jack walked in.

"Hi," she said softly, not wanting to ignore him and risk another outburst.

"What are you doing up so early?" There was a hint of accusation in his tone.

She wanted to ask him the same thing but knew better. "I thought I would start the laundry."

Jack ignored the response to his question and continued moving around the kitchen sporadically. He opened cupboards and drawers, as if he was searching for something.

Before she could think twice about her question, Sarah asked, "Are you okay? What are you looking for?"

This only increased Jack's agitation and he picked up the pace of his search. "Maybe if this place wasn't such a disaster, I could find what I'm looking for!"

Sarah looked around. Despite seeing nothing out of place, her heart started racing and she could feel the heat rising in her cheeks.

"Seriously, Sarah. It's not like you have that much to do. You don't have a job. All you have to do is take care of the house. Things should be in their place. Is that so much to ask?"

"Um . . . yes . . . I mean, no. Maybe if you tell me what you're looking for I can help."

"What are you? My mother? Get out of here!"

Sarah bolted up from her chair, fear surging through her. She wasn't sure whether she should run out of the room like he said or stay still.

"I said get out of here!"

Sarah pushed off against the chair, sending it screeching across the kitchen floor. She avoided eye contact with him while she scurried out of the room, down the hallway, and into the bedroom. Shaking, she tried to close the door quietly, afraid to alert him to the fact that she had shut herself in.

She looked down at the lock on the handle. Her breathing quickened as she thought through her choices. None of them ended well. Especially the one where he came to get her and found the door locked.

Her hand hovered just above the lock. Against her better judgement, she lowered her hand and backed slowly away from the door. She stepped backwards and tripped over the laundry basket she had set down earlier. Sarah flailed her arms, looking for anything to break her fall. Her arm circled behind her, and she slammed her wrist into the top edge of the dresser. She let out a gasp and fell onto the floor. Crying out in pain, she brought her good hand over her mouth to stifle the sound.

Sarah lay on the floor gripping her throbbing wrist and hoping desperately that Jack hadn't heard her cry out. She lay as silently as she could, straining to listen. Her heart sank along with her stomach as she heard footsteps coming down the hallway toward her room. Although fear of the impending interaction gripped her, she felt relieved she hadn't locked the door. How much worse that would have made things.

Sarah jumped as the door flung wide open and knocked hard against the wall. Using one hand, she propped herself up and tried to regain her composure.

"What the heck happened in here?" Jack scowled.

"Nothing. I mean, I just tripped and hurt my wrist. I'm fine. Really." Sarah stood to her feet, still trembling a little, partly from the shock of the fall and partly because of the look in Jack's eyes. His left eye was visibly twitching, and his right fist was clenched. Sarah watched as the look on his face went from anger to distraction, as if he remembered something else that needed his attention.

"Clean up this mess." Jack pointed to the laundry that was now strewn around the overturned basket. Sarah nodded her head, and he turned abruptly and walked out of the room.

Sarah let out the deep breath she was holding and stood motionless as she watched him walk away. Once he was out of sight, she grabbed her wrist once more and looked over the discoloration forming where she had slammed it against the dresser.

"I don't think it's broken," she mumbled to herself, once again feeling relieved. She cradled her forearm on her thigh as she squatted down and used her other hand to pick up the laundry on the floor and put it back in the basket. She sat on the side of her bed, looking down, trying to summon the energy to squat down again and pick up the basket with one arm. Sarah was brought out of her daze by the sound of the news on the TV. She rose from the bed and walked softly to the door, watching and listening for any sign of Jack. She started down the hallway, picking up the conversation from the TV.

"...with Rachel McGinnis." It sounded like an update on the recent abduction. Like a small child awake past her bedtime, she peered cautiously around the corner in both directions before entering the living room.

"An eyewitness identified a dark brown van with the rear windows painted black."

Sarah's throat tightened, along with her chest. Adrenaline raced through her, as she looked through the window at Jack's van. Jack's dark brown van with painted rear windows. She had always hated those windows and never quite knew why.

"Although this is not the actual van, police have put together a composite showing what the van make and model looks like, based on the eyewitnesses. Police are asking viewers to be alert and keep a watch out."

Sarah stopped as she rounded the corner into the living room. Terrified, she turned her body in slow motion toward the television screen. Her gaze followed second, trying to emotionally postpone what she was most afraid to see. Her eyes locked onto the composite drawing. She stood motionless for a few seconds as she took in the picture.

"This van is estimated to be relatively new, maybe two or three years old."

A surge of relief caused tears to spill down her cheeks. It couldn't possibly be Jack's van. Jack's van was at least ten years old. He already had it when she had met him, and that was more than five years ago. It didn't look anything close to new now. It had rust spots already forming all along the bottom and had a roof rack Jack had installed a few years ago.

Sarah lowered herself to the couch and sat uncomfortably on the edge, trying to settle herself. It was ridiculous to let her mind go there. Maybe Jack was right. Maybe she shouldn't be watching this stuff. She grabbed the remote and turned off the TV.

Pulling the box of tissues toward her, she grabbed one for her nose and one for her eyes. She took deep breaths in and blew out through her lips as if they were pursed around a straw. With each breath in and out, she felt a little calmer. After she felt like herself, she stood and peered out the window into the driveway again. This time the van was gone. She hadn't heard Jack leave but was grateful for his absence.

Remembering Jack's sweatshirt was still lying across the dryer with the cleaner soaking into it made Sarah jump to her feet. It was only supposed to soak for about ten minutes but by this time she wasn't really sure how much time had gone by. She hurried into the laundry room, brought the sweatshirt to the sink and rubbed out the cleaner and the stain under the faucet of cold water. Some of it came out, but not everything. Then she picked through the cleaners in the cabinet and decided against putting something else on it. Instead, she went for something her mom used to use, which was nothing more than a piece of old-fashioned bar soap. It was unusually strong, and she kept it for things like this.

For the next twenty minutes, Sarah rotated between rubbing the shirt with bar soap and the old toothbrush she kept for cleaning stains. Slowly, the sweatshirt returned to its normal color. It was slightly faded where the stain used to be, but Sarah was convinced that was better than the stain. She gave it one more good rinse with the cold water, rung it out as tightly as she could, and placed the wet garment into the washer. She was about to go get the rest of the laundry when she heard the screen door creak open in the kitchen. Jack was back.

She heard voices. He wasn't alone. She couldn't remember the last time Jack brought someone to the house with him. She remained silent, in the doorway of the laundry room, trying to identify the unknown man, or what they were talking about.

"Are you sure about this?" asked the man.

"Yes," Jack said staunchly. "She needs this to learn a lesson."

Sarah's eyes widened, her breathing quickened and her mind went to horrible places.

"I'm not here to judge," said the man. "Just pay me what you promised and let's get on with this."

Sarah panicked and searched in her mind for a place to hide. There was no way past them without being seen, and there was no place in this room she could make herself invisible. Maybe this wasn't real. After her questioning of him earlier this morning, maybe this was Jack's way of trying to scare her and teach her a lesson not to ask what he's up to. Yes. That was it. He was simply baiting her to see if she came storming out to find out what this was all about.

Feeling a combination of hope and risk, she decided to show him she'd learned her lesson. Sarah walked as calmly as she could into the kitchen. She looked at Jack for a moment, but then directed her eyes to the floor and avoided all eye contact with the other man. She continued to walk past them. She could feel the trembling overtaking her just as her back was to them. There was a solid lump in her throat as she waited to hear something from Jack.

Nothing.

She kept walking and headed back into the bedroom. She wasn't sure what to make of what just happened, but there was only silence. She told herself she had just passed his test, and felt her anxiety lessen with each passing second. Sarah closed her eyes and was about to relax when she heard footsteps coming down the hallway. The lump in her throat was back, and she found herself searching again for a way to make herself invisible. Fear turned to terror when she realized it wasn't a set of footsteps she was hearing. It was two sets of footsteps.

CHAPTER 5

Star spent most of the night tossing and turning, trying to sleep through her cravings and avoid the monsters in her head. There were no windows in the room. There were only cement walls which seemed to be closing in on her with each passing hour. The only sense of day she had was when the man opened the door. Although she could not see outside, she could see daylight streaming in, so she figured there must be two doors he came in and out through. Maybe there was one that separated her from the hallway, and one which led outside. To freedom.

Star could hardly bring herself to dwell on the word. Freedom seemed about a million miles away. Every part of her knew she had to start fighting for her life if she wanted to keep it. The physical discomfort from the withdrawals was keeping her feeling slow and unclear. Even if she could push past that, she was still in a mental prison. The walls of that prison were not made of cement, but of every bad decision she'd made over the last two years. She couldn't wrap her head around how wrong someone's life could go in a mere twenty-four months. Maybe this was just punishment for her crimes. Maybe this was God's way of putting her in hell where she belonged. After all, her actions had caused so much hurt. Not to just her own family. So many families.

* * *

"How much?" asked the man nervously as Star poked her head inside his passenger side window.

"Depends on what you want, sweetheart," replied Star playfully.

The man paused for a moment, then said more boldly, "All of it. I want all of it."

"Well, okay, then. That would be..." Star looked up as if she were calculating all the options, dragging out his anticipation. "$150. You got $150?"

"Yes."

Star flicked her head up, silently asking to see the cash before the transaction took place. He dug into his back pocket for his wallet, opened it, and leafed through the twenty-dollar bills, all facing the same way. He looked clean cut and she wondered if this was his first time picking up a prostitute.

Star opened the passenger door and jumped into the front seat. The man's eyes were fixed on her legs.

"Let's go already, or the price is going up."

He put the car in drive but hesitated, his foot still on the brake. Without making eye contact with Star, he looked down, pulled the wedding band off his finger, and placed it into the cupholder. Star felt a pang of guilt but brushed it off. After all, it was his choice, right? After another moment of silence, he lifted his foot off the brake and took off. They drove down the dark streets until the man broke the silence.

"Where do we go?"

This was definitely his first time picking up a girl.

"Keep going straight and turn left down that street," she said, pointing to the next street down. He followed her instructions and turned left without using his blinker. He hit the brake to hesitate for a moment when he saw the alley.

"We could park and do it right on the main drag if you prefer."

The man shot her a quick look and released his foot from the brake. Star knew she should probably go easier on him, being his first time and all, but her run-in with Ronny right before this ran her agitation high and her patience low. Star hadn't made her quota the last few nights, and Ronny was all over her for it. She needed money from this guy. This would be her last shot tonight. She took in a deep and slow breath to relax and change her demeanor.

It had been a little chilly out, so she was glad to at least be in a car. They crept slowly to the end of the alley and stopped. There was one, dim streetlight illuminating a large dumpster, which had garbage overflowing from it, and they faced a brick wall with an old, rusted No Parking sign. It hung by only one of the top corners, swinging down diagonally.

Star looked over and could see the man was sweating, despite the chill in the air. She felt a sense of pity for him, so she softened her tone and tried to help.

"Don't worry. No one's gonna see us here. You can relax."

The man smiled a little but seemed afraid to do anything but look ahead. He kept staring at the No Parking sign, a nervous jitter causing his right leg to bounce up and down, transferring all of his anxiety into it. Star figured she should make the first move, so she leaned in to kiss the man's neck. He put up a hand to stop her and continued looking forward.

"I'm sorry. I don't think I can do this. You're real pretty and all. It's just that..."

"It's your first time picking up a girl?"

"Yes. I've never done this before."

"Well, lucky for you, I have," Star said with a jest, trying to lighten the mood. Normally, she would take this as her cue to bail but, with Ronny all over her, she really needed the money. It was already getting late and if she didn't get this John's money, she'd be in a world of hurt. Not to mention Lacey being angry for lack of rent money. She wasn't as good at this as Lacey. Maybe it was because Lacey cared less.

"Why don't you just relax and let me do all the work?"

"Her name is Miranda," he said with a smile. "We've been married for almost twenty years. She's a good woman, but not much for sex. I guess it hurts her. She's got that endermeterosis, or whatever you call it."

Star smiled. "Endometriosis?"

"Yeah. That's it. I feel bad even trying sometimes. We got into a big fight about it tonight. I was angry. So, I came here. I wasn't thinking. I don't know what I was thinking."

"I totally get it. There are a lot of men like you." She continued to try to kiss him and he grabbed her arms and pushed her gently back into her seat.

It would have been easy to get out of the car or even ask him to drive her back. Star was sure he would. But she'd be getting out of the car without the money she needed. Star sat silent for a moment. Then, against her better judgement, she brought out all the stops. Before he knew it, the man gave in to her. When they were finished, Star returned to the passenger seat. The silence between them was awkward as she struggled to put her top on in the tight space. While straightening her clothes she heard a muffled sound that caused her to turn her head and look in the man's direction.

He was crying. She thought it sounded like the kind of crying you see at a funeral after someone dies. Quiet and painful. Star was struck with the reality of her role in this. She opened the door and stepped quietly out of the car. As she stepped out, the man sniffed and tried to regain himself for a moment.

"Your money," he said. She watched him reach back into his wallet and pull out the money he owed her. He handed Star the money and she turned to leave, consumed by both guilt and relief.

* * *

Star's stomach turned and she felt sick. She assumed it was her body screaming for a fix, but a deeper part of her knew it was the shame. She lay still on the bed, trying to figure out why she was in this place. Why she deserved to stay in this prison.

If she stayed here, he would probably end up killing her, and maybe that wouldn't be so bad after all. It would end her misery, and it would prevent her from hurting any more families. Isn't that what they called a win–win? Warm tears pooled in her eyes as she lay making peace with her sorely earned consequences. She missed Lacey. She missed home. She thought about all the people she would never get the chance to see again. Then again, loss was no stranger to her.

***

Star hid around the corner and watched as her dad threw her mom's things out onto the garage floor. She snuck down the stairs and into the basement, out of sight from her parents.

"Why are you doing this?" cried her mom.

"Because you're giving up. That's why!" yelled her dad, as he threw his hands into the air.

Reluctantly, her mom sat at the kitchen table and buried her face in her hands.

They had been arguing a lot more, but today it was unlike anything Star had seen. She just wanted to go somewhere she felt safe. She was out of sight, but she could still hear her mom sobbing.

"I just don't understand why you're doing this to me. It's my choice. You don't know what it's like. You don't know how painful it is." Eli stopped and stared sadly at Maggie, who now had her head lying on the kitchen table. He softened, and walked over to crouch beside her.

"Magpie. Listen to me. Please. I can't begin to know what you're going through, and I understand why you think this is just your choice, but can you please, please see it from my eyes too? This isn't just about you. It's about us too. We don't want to lose you. We're not ready to lose you." Eli's voice cracked under his emotions. "I'm not ready to lose you." He could no longer speak.

Maggie lifted her head, looked him in the eyes and ran the palm of her hand down the side of his face. "I'm not ready to lose you either, but, Eli, it's time. The doctors can't do anything more for me than they already have. I'm tired. I'm so tired." Maggie wrapped her arms around herself, trying to steady her shaking.

Eli moved to the chair across from her and the two sat silently for a long time.

Star could no longer hear anything, but she had heard enough. Her mom had told her she would try the experimental treatment, but now felt it was all too much for her. The cancer was spreading rapidly now, and the mom she used to know was no longer with them. She was a hollow version of herself, stifled by the set of monsters in her body.

Star couldn't handle the thought of it all. She ran up the stairs and out the front door before either of them could say anything to her.

* * *

Her dad's words echoed through Star's mind as she lay on the bed fighting for clarity. It had been so long ago, but his words seemed like yesterday. He was right. She had to fight. Her life *did* depend on it. Star forced herself into an upright position and opened her eyes. It was still dark, and she remembered the room had a light. Startled by the memory, she ran her hand quickly to her ankle and felt a glimmer of hope. The shackle was off. It wasn't just some daydream she conjured up out of self-preservation.

Star slid her body off the side of the bed and onto the cold floor. Her feet were bare, and she wondered for the first time where her blue heels were. On her hands and knees, she made her way slowly forward, feeling her way to where she recalled the light switch was. When she hit the cement brick, she moved her hands up the wall and out to the sides as she searched for the switch. Her pulse quickened when her fingers ran over the protrusion in the wall, and she snapped the light on frantically.

She looked down and squinted as light flooded the room. In some ways, she felt more afraid now than when he was in there with her. Star scanned the room. It was everything she remembered from last time, including the bucket. As soon as she saw it, she was overcome with the sensation of needing to go to the bathroom. No part of her wanted to use it, but the alternative would have done nothing for her living conditions. She was suddenly very aware of the pressure on her bladder and sighed as she pulled the bucket away from the wall and stared down for a moment. She looked around bashfully, as if there were windows to see through. Satisfied there were no eyes on her, she pulled up her skirt, pulled down her underwear and tried to balance herself over the bucket. The pressure on her bladder left, and she felt a sensation of comfort as she relieved herself. It felt so good, she closed her eyes for a moment to drink in the relief.

In the matter of a moment, Star lost her balance and fell backwards. Her foot kicked the bottom of the bucket, sending it flying against the wall and sideways onto the floor. Her urine spilled out and formed a pool on the hard, cement floor. Mortified, Star tried to regain her composure and fix her skirt. She stared at the pool of urine. It was a few feet from the floor drain, but not at the point where the floor declined.

Gravity was not going to do its job, so she had to. Star walked over and picked up the bucket, careful to avoid getting her bare foot in the puddle. The edges of the bucket were rough, and she suspected the holes in the side were from the metal handle that was probably removed. She tilted the bucket under the water spicket and went to turn the faucet handle. It wouldn't budge. She knew she was weak but thought maybe it was rusted.

Using all the force she could muster, Star let out a loud groan as she muscled the faucet open, hearing a loud creak as the handle turned counterclockwise. No water came out. Now that it was loose, Star turned the handle back and forth, praying the water would come, but none did. With a loud cry, she threw the bucket against the wall with both hands and then kicked the wall with her foot. She immediately regretted that, as that was the foot the shackle had been on, and it throbbed all over again.

Star sank to the floor and cried. The clink of the lock opening shot panic through her and she bolted to the bed like it was the safe zone in a game of freeze tag. The man stepped around the corner, closed the door behind him and set down the brown paper bag he was carrying. He was about to say something, but closed his mouth when he saw the bucket lying on its side and a puddle on the floor. He shot a questioning look at Star, and her eyes hit the floor.

"Is that what I think it is?"

Star's cheeks flushed, and she nodded.

"Seriously?"

His question went unanswered. He turned around and went back out the door. He had left the bag behind, but Star was too scared to move off the bed to look in it. She was glad she didn't move, because it was only a minute later when the door swung open and he came back inside. He was wearing gloves that looked like something a woman would wear cleaning toilets. They were bright yellow, and she fought the urge to escape to her childhood daydream. She had to stay alert if she was going to fight. He walked swiftly to the water spicket and turned the knob counterclockwise. In a moment, there was a gurgling noise, and water sputtered out of the faucet.

Star stammered, "I tried to do that. I tried to clean it. No water came out."

He ignored her and went to work rinsing out the bucket, then used the bucket to rinse the urine into the floor drain. When he was finished, he set the bucket back against the wall.

"You need to get clean," he said, matter of fact. He walked over to the paper bag and pulled out a worn looking washcloth and a little bottle of body wash – the kind you see in the travel section of a grocery store. "Take off your clothes."

Star felt her chest tighten and her heart race. She sat very still, uncertain of what she should do.

"Take. Off. Your. Clothes. I'm not going to say it again."

Fear stung her, and she removed her clothes, stripping down to her bra and underwear.

"Take it all off. You need to get clean. I have clean clothes for you."

Star gave him a pleading look, and the man turned his body to the side, just enough to comply, but still able to see her movement out of his peripheral. Shaking, Star removed the rest of her clothes and stood with one hand between her legs and the other arm tight across her chest. She had gotten naked for strangers many times, but this was different. Those other times were her choice. This time, it wasn't.

Remaining turned to the side, the man instructed her to go over to the water spicket and use the towel and soap to clean herself. Star worked as quickly as her altered body would allow her to, still continuing to conceal herself as best she could. When she was finished, she remained crouched down next to the wall. He grabbed a bath towel out of the bag, threw it to her, and then tossed a set of clean clothes onto the bed. Star wrapped herself in the towel, still dripping as she raced to put the clothes on.

The underwear looked used, and she winced at the thought of it. Clean, but used. The sports bra was a little too small, but it was better than nothing. She pulled the t-shirt over her head and pulled up the sweatpants. Those, too, were a little small and pinched her waist uncomfortably.

The man pulled the brown paper bag closer to himself, reached inside and pulled out some bandages, cotton balls, and what looked like hydrogen peroxide. He approached her slowly and sat on the bed beside her.

"May I clean the cuts on your ankle?"

Star couldn't bear the thought of him touching her anywhere, especially after what just happened, but she knew she needed to play nice if she had any hope of catching him off guard. She had been clear minded enough to listen when he was coming in and out of the room. She hadn't heard the lock clink shut like normal. It might be unlocked. This might be her chance.

Star nodded, moved her foot from underneath her and stretched her leg out on the bed. The man handled her foot with care, as he swabbed the cuts with the peroxide and placed band-aids on them. The peroxide stung, but she wasn't thinking about that. The bottle of peroxide was sitting on the bed between them. It wasn't heavy, but it might be enough to stun him long enough for her to get to the other side of the door and lock him in. She tried to slow her breathing and focus on the pain in her ankle as a means to clear her head.

★ ★ ★

"Come on, Bean! You can do this," smiled Star's dad.

She hated putting her head underwater, but his grin was convincing enough for her to feel she would *probably* be okay.

"Just like we practiced now. Deep breath in and blow it out. That's right. Again."

After a few quick breaths in and out, she plunged below the surface of the pool in a squatting position, so her head remained underwater. After a few seconds, she felt her dad tap her gently on the shoulder, and she opened her eyes. It was the first time she ever opened her eyes under water. She couldn't believe how well she could see everything, and the ray of sunshine cutting at an angle into the water and onto the floor of the pool looked magnificent.

★ ★ ★

Star opened her eyes again. He was still sitting on the bed and his hands were full. Gaining a little courage from her memory, she decided it was now or never. She grabbed the bottle of peroxide and, with every ounce of strength she had left in her, she swung the bottle and her fist into the back of his head. The man fell to the floor, grabbing his head where she had hit him.

Now! Run! Star ran for the door, leaping over and just out of reach of him. Adrenaline surged through her as she grabbed at the edges of the metal door and opened it. She could hear him getting up off the floor, but dared not take the extra second to look behind her. She was going to need every second she could get.

She could see the second door but would worry about that after she got this one closed and locked. Spinning around, she reached for the handle. To her horror, there was no handle on her side, only a key hole. Her heart sank. Her only hope was to shut it, to slow him down long enough to open the other door and make a run for it. Reaching back in, she grabbed the edge of the door to pull it shut.

The man was on his feet now, staring at her through the crack of the door opening. His face was red with fury and he thrust himself against the door. Star shrieked as her fingers pinched between the metal door and frame. She could hear her bones cracking under the weight. The man swung the door back open and grabbed Star by the hair. She couldn't defend herself with her mangled fingers, and he dragged her back inside. The man was huffing and puffing, trying to catch his breath.

"I told you! I told you not to try anything! You told me you'd be good."

Star lay curled up on the floor, moaning, with her hands pulled up toward her face.

"I brought you clean clothes, gave you water and see what you made me do? You good for nothing junkie! I'm trying to help you people, and you're all the same. If you can't see that, then I can't help you! I was going to give you a fix before I left, but now you're just going to have to suffer and do it the hard way."

He grabbed her again, this time dragging her up and onto the bed. Star pleaded with him as he grabbed the shackle. She tried to kick at it, but he sat on her. She tried beating him with her one good hand, but it wasn't enough to prevent him from getting the shackle back on her ankle. The man flipped off the light and stormed angrily out of the room. The sound of the door slamming sent waves of pain through Star, reliving the incident of a few moments ago. She cradled her hand, letting out quiet moans, looking around once more at the darkness.

CHAPTER 6

Sarah could hear the men coming down the hallway. She looked around the room for anything she could find to defend herself. There was almost nothing substantial in there. Nothing she could pick up but the lamp on the night stand. There was a chance this wouldn't be anything like what her imagination was conjuring up, and how stupid would she look if the men entered the room to find her in the corner swinging a lamp. Jack would be furious with her, and then she'd really have something to worry about. But what if they *were* coming to hurt her?

In the few seconds it took for them to reach and open her door, her mind spiraled out of control, and she stood empty handed in the middle of the room. The man standing in front of Jack was larger than he was. He was probably about 6'3" and far outweighed both of them put together. Sarah stepped backward until she reached the wall, pressing up against it as tightly as she could, as if the wall could save her.

"She looks scared. Are you sure about this?" asked the hulky man.

"Yes, I'm sure! Now get on with it," Jack snapped. "Remember, not her face."

Now the panic set in, and Sarah lunged for the lamp on the nightstand. Just as she reached out, the man grabbed her other arm and pulled her to the floor in front of him. He looked backwards at Jack just long enough for Jack to give him a nod. The man returned his focus to Sarah, who was now lying on her side. With an almost apologetic look on his face, he pulled his foot back and sent it forcefully into Sarah's stomach. She screamed in pain, horrified, not at the man, but at Jack, who stood in the doorway watching. The pain being inflicted on her was only second to the pain of knowing this was being done at Jack's bidding. She couldn't understand how he could simply stand and watch this horrific display unfold. He was leaning against the door frame, his arms folded and a slight grin on his face, as if he were catching something amusing on the TV. She lay on her back now, her eyes pleading with Jack as the man sent another blow sailing into her side. She screamed again in pain and cried.

"Please... please stop," she whispered, barely able to breathe from the swift kicks she endured. The man reached down, grabbed Sarah's arm, and forced her to her feet.

"How's that for a reminder?" Jack snarled. "Your attitude hasn't been what it should be lately. And all that talk about leaving, well, I figured you might need a reminder of what things are like out on the streets, where you came from. And, trust me, that's the only place you'd be able to return."

"No... no," Sarah cried. "I'm sorry. I wasn't going to leave. I won't leave. I'll be better. I promise."

The man turned and looked at Jack, who gave another nod. Reluctantly, the man pulled his arm back and punched her one final time in the stomach. His punch sent her stumbling backward into the nightstand and onto the floor. The nightstand slammed against the wall and sent the lamp crashing down beside her, smashing into pieces. Sarah rolled groggily over the sharp edges. She tried to open her eyes, but her vision was blurred from hitting her head. All she could make out was the towering shape over her, still looming like a dark cloud. If he was the dark cloud, then Jack was the lightning strike that followed. His tongue was sharper than any punch he could throw.

"Your money's on the kitchen table. Take it and get out," Jack said to the dark cloud. She could see the blur of a man walk out of the room, and Jack turned his attention on her. "How does it feel to be in a vulnerable position? To have a perfect stranger you don't know come in and hurt you? Huh? How does it feel?" Jack stared intensely at her, waiting for her response.

"It feels terrible," she cried.

"What do you think is going to happen if you walk out that door and go back to the streets?"

Sarah remained quiet.

"That. That is what's going to happen. Do you think you could do anything different? You're not educated to work in an office. Do you think some cute little grocery store will hire you? Or some restaurant? They do background checks. They'll find out what you did. What you are. No one is going to hire you. And you can forget going home. We already talked about that. I already told you how your dad feels. He hates you. He wants nothing to do with you."

Sarah closed her eyes. In that moment, she just wanted to die.

* * *

The argument between Sarah and her dad was even more intense than usual. Out of anger, Sarah said things she would later regret, but so did he. She ran out the door and across the lawn straight to Teddy's house, praying he was home.

"Hey!" Teddy smiled as he opened the screen door. His smile faded to a look of worry when he saw her, and he ushered her in the door. "What's the matter? What happened? Did you have another fight with your dad?"

Sarah sobbed and, without thinking, found herself in Teddy's arms, her tears soaking into his t-shirt.

"Tell me what happened."

Sarah felt better just being there with him. "Yeah, it's my dad. You wouldn't believe the things he said to me. Oh, Teddy, he hates me! I want to die. I just want to die." Again, her sobs came, and Teddy tightened his hold around her.

"I'm so sorry. I don't even know what to say." He held her for a long while until she finally stopped crying. He offered her a box of tissue as she shuffled her way back into the large arm chair in the living room, her feet dangling above the floor. Teddy used to make fun of her for that, but not today. He slid into the chair beside her. After a long while, Teddy spoke softly but deliberately. "I said before that I didn't know what to say. That's not true. I do know what to say."

Sarah looked up, surprised at his candor.

"There's something I've been wanting to tell you for a long time now. What happened with my dad a few years ago really messed me up. I mean, you know. You were there. You know it took a long time for me to feel even a little bit normal. What you don't know... what I never told you... is that I wanted to die. I almost did die." Sarah stopped crying and tilted her head at Teddy. "The weight of what I did was so heavy, and I was so tired of carrying it. No matter what he did to my mom, I knew I'd never be able to justify what I did to him. I thought I would never be able to feel happy again. I was destroyed inside, not only by what I did, but what I did to my mom too. I knew she loved me, but I didn't think she'd ever look at me the same. So, one night, when it got too bad, I decided..." She watched as Teddy paused and looked at the floor. "I decided I was going to kill myself."

Sarah bolted up and sucked in a deep breath in shock. "Teddy! No. When?"

Teddy sighed. "It was last year. After the neighborhood cookout I couldn't bring myself to go to. I know people were just trying to move on and pretend none of that ever happened, but it was nothing but a reminder of what I did. I sat in my room and tried to drown out the noise of the party outside. It seemed no matter how loud my music was, I could hear laughter, as if they were just screwing with me. I could hear my mom crying downstairs. I couldn't take it anymore. I thought it would be better for her and me if I just ended it. Then she wouldn't have to look at me anymore. I wanted it to stop. I just wanted it to stop."

Tears were forming in Sarah's eyes and she grabbed Teddy's hand.

"My mom had been taking a lot of things from her doctor, so I went into her bathroom and grabbed a bottle of the prescription sleeping pills she had. I was hoping I'd just fall asleep and not wake up."

"What happened?"

"I didn't die. That's what happened. Well, that's not all that happened."

"What else?" she asked inquisitively.

"I don't know if I can ever do a good job describing this, but all I can tell you is that I was *woken* up. I didn't wake up. I was woken up."

Sarah furrowed her eyebrows.

"I don't know who it was." Teddy looked at the floor but kept speaking. "I'm pretty sure it was an angel or something like that." Teddy lifted his eyes to see the expression on her face.

Sarah was staring intently at him, like she was riveted by a movie she was watching. He was studying her face, and she was careful not to have any sort of judgmental look, which she thought he seemed relieved about.

Teddy continued. "Don't ask me what she looked like. It wasn't like that. It was more of what I felt. I know that sounds weird, but I don't know how else to describe it. It was like an entire conversation happened in only a second or two."

"What did they say?"

Teddy took a deep breath. "I remember them saying I had to fight the lies I was being told and know the truth. That my life depended on it, and the lives of so many others."

Sarah's eyes widened. "What lives?" she asked, the tone of her voice heightening a bit.

"I don't know. I think it might be more like a metaphor or something. Anyway, I just knew I had to fight. I had to do whatever I could to put this behind me and use whatever time I have left to make a difference in this world."

Sarah nodded, as if she had just received the answer to a tough question. "So that's why you became all involved in the church last year?"

"Yes. That's why."

Sarah sat quietly for a moment, processing everything Teddy just told her. Teddy sat quietly next to her, allowing her space to take it all in.

"Has it helped you?" Sarah looked at him expectantly.

"Yes. It has. Sarah, it's helped me more than I can ever put into words." Teddy grabbed both of her hands with his. "It's what I want to do with my life now. I want to be a pastor. I want to help other people who are in pain like I was. I know your pain is different. I know it's nothing you did, and it's just something that's happening *to* you." He paused. "In some ways, that almost makes it worse. I'm not trying to dismiss what you're feeling, but I'm sure your dad doesn't hate you. He loves you and he's just worried about how you're handling things. I guess what I'm trying to say is, no matter what happens between you and your dad, no matter who's right or wrong, it's all fixable."

More tears streamed down her cheeks.

"And I know from my own experience that there's something... there's someone... out there bigger than you and I. That means there's a reason to hope. So please don't ever say you want to die. I'll do whatever you need me to, to help you through the pain you're feeling."

* * *

Sarah lay remembering that conversation like it happened yesterday. She couldn't see what Teddy saw. She wanted to, but it never happened for her like it happened for Teddy. The fights with her dad got worse and worse, until she eventually decided to leave home. She knew Teddy would only try to talk her out of it, so she did the only thing she knew to do and went out on her own. Lots of girls did that and made it. She would do the same.

Sarah was angry with Jack for allowing that man to hurt her, but she knew he was just trying to help her. He didn't want what happened to his sister to happen to her. His methods were brutal, but they certainly got the message across.

"Hey." Jack's tone softened. "I don't want to have to do stuff like this."

Sarah nodded her head, welcoming the less brutal version of him. He now sat on the floor next to her, brushing the hair from her face.

"I just want you to put all this nonsense behind you. Can you do that?"

Sarah nodded again, eyes still closed.

"Good. That's my girl." Jack let out a deep sigh and stood up. "I'm going to the shelter for a while."

For as long as she knew him, he had been volunteering at a local women's shelter not too far from their house. He said there were lots of women there who were vulnerable to going to the streets like she did, and he wanted to try to help them too. Sarah sat up, her head still spinning.

"You've been there a lot lately. Do you want me to come and try to help too?" Sarah asked nervously, hoping it sounded more like repentance than an inquisition.

"No. You stay here. That's not a good environment for you to be in, especially right now. You need to get your head straight. And clean this up," he said, pointing to the pieces of lamp now strewn across the floor.

Jack walked out of the room, and Sarah remained sitting, propped up against the side of the bed while her head cleared. She picked pieces of the lamp off the side of her shirt, and even some stuck to the bare parts of her leg. After about ten minutes, Sarah got up and walked slowly to the kitchen, pressing her hands against the walls to support herself. She gripped the handle to the freezer and pulled it open. A rush of cool air stung her face, and she stood for a minute, letting the frigid air nurse her wounds.

* * *

The cold air made her shiver as she walked to the bus stop. Her leggings were a poor barrier from the cold, as the wind rushed up her skirt and through the thin material they were made from. She picked up her pace, clutching the straps of the backpack she was wearing, wishing she had remembered a pair of mittens. It was unseasonably cold for October, and the cold weather uniform may as well have felt like shorts and a t-shirt. It practically was.

She could see the shelter of the bus stop in the distance and looked forward to a break from the cold wind. It was just before six in the morning, and still quite dark out. There was only one street light per block, and the black voids in between them made her feel alone and unsafe. She could walk the whole way to school, but it was faster and warmer to take the city bus. She had to be at school for a 6:45 a.m. practice. She'd get there early, but any later pickup and she wouldn't make it in time. Sarah trotted through the next black void and made a hopscotch-style leap into the lit circle of the street lamp just before the bus stop. She hurried around the corner of the shelter and sat on the bench. The frigid metal bench brought her back to a standing position, and she moved herself into the corner to minimize the cold air blowing through her.

Tonight was the homecoming game. It was always a big event for the students as well as parents and community. She first started on the dance squad in middle school but felt like that didn't really count. They didn't even have a real football field there. They used the green grass inside the track, and fans either stood or sat on makeshift bleachers they moved in and out for special events. Tonight, she would be in a real field with real bleachers. Even an announcers' booth and a larger than life scoreboard. Teddy would be playing. She liked watching him play and was glad to see him getting back to normal boy things. He was a junior, but his size afforded him a varsity position as a defensive lineman. She wasn't even really sure what that meant, other than he was one of the guys who stopped the other team from scoring when the other team had the ball. He was good at it too. It earned him a nickname among the high schools – Theo the Thrasher. People at school called him Theo, but she preferred Teddy. She thought he secretly liked it, because he never corrected her, not even when his friends teased him about it. He would just punch them in the shoulder, then give her a little smile as they walked away.

Whether he realized it or not, Teddy was good at flirting. He made an art out of displaying his boyish grins at just the right time. She never used to look at Teddy that way but, once they got to high school, she found herself feeling jealous of the attention he got from the other girls. It made her realize she saw something in him that was more than just a friend. She wanted to tell him, but never found the right time. That's what she told herself, anyway.

Headlights caught her attention as the large bus rounded the corner a few blocks down. Seeing the bus in sight made it feel colder, and she bounced up and down trying to warm herself. The sound of the air brakes on the bus silenced the eerie quietness of the morning, and Sarah made the four steps into the bus two, as she escaped from the cold. She looked across the empty seats as she dropped her change into the meter, then selected a seat in the middle. The rest of the stops were empty, so the bus made a straight mile and a half run to the school. She smiled politely at the bus driver and bounced down the steps and onto the pavement. The wind whipped up her skirt once more, and she tightened her grip on her backpack as she ran across the courtyard to the front doors.

Relieved to reach them, anticipating a rush of warmth, Sarah pulled on the handle only to find it locked. Pressing her forehead against the glass door, she peered inside, hoping for signs of life to open the door. Nothing. No one. Sarah sighed, and decided she would need to run around to the other side of the school and try the side doors. Those were closer to the gym and weight room where they typically practiced, so she was hopeful someone would be there. She reached the doors and gave them a tug, but they were locked too. She grimaced at the thought of having to stand out here for another thirty minutes. Resigned to her wait, she looked around for any kind of shelter.

There, along the wall of the school she saw a girl. She was sitting inside one of the window wells, so Sarah walked toward her. As she got closer, she thought better of herself, but it was too late. The girl had already seen her and was waving for her to come over. Sarah couldn't ignore her now, so she continued over. Sarah stood, looking down into the window well at the girl in a skirt and heels. She wasn't in any school uniform, so Sarah guessed her uniform was, well, professional. She had heard some teachers talking about the prostitution problem happening not far from the school, worried the teenage boys would get enticed by it.

"Hi!" the girl said with a smile. "You can come in here with me if you want."

Sarah looked at her, confused.

"It's warm in here. See the vent?" The girl pointed to the air vent by her feet. She made Sarah slightly uncomfortable, but the idea of standing in the cold for any longer made her even more uncomfortable, so she stepped inside and sat on the ground. She was right. The vent was pumping out gloriously warm air. Pleasant goosebumps ran up and down Sarah's body as she moved her hands and feet closer to the vent. The two girls sat without speaking.

Sarah tried not to stare in the girl's direction but couldn't help noticing her shiny necklace. It was a silver chain with a shiny, silver dolphin. After a few minutes, Sarah asked, "What are you doing in here?"

"Probably the same thing you're doing in here. It's warmer in here than it is out there."

Sarah smiled. "Yeah, but I mean, what are you doing *out* here?" she said, trying to clarify. "Do you go to school here?"

"I used to, but I dropped out a few years ago. I'd ask you the same thing, but I can see from your cheerleading outfit you go here."

"Dance team," Sarah clarified. "I'm part of the dance team. The cheerleaders are too stuck up." The girls exchanged a giggle and let the silence resume for a while.

"Are you a hooker?" Sarah asked, and then regretted her question.

Still staring down at the vent, the girl replied, "Yes. But we don't call it that. People call us ladies of the night. Sounds more, well, like it's something it's not."

Sarah's cheeks flushed at the girl's candor, and she immediately tried to change the subject. "I'm a freshman. It's my first year here."

The girl ignored Sarah's comment and continued. "I don't do this because I want to. It's because I have to. It's not glamorous or nothing, but it's a way to pay for food and get a place to crash at sometimes."

Sarah was now feeling increasingly uncomfortable and was elated to hear one of her teammates yelling to her from an open door. "Come on! Coach is here!"

Sarah gave the girl an apologetic look and excused herself from the warming well. She trotted quickly to the door, giving one look back at the girl who was watching her run away. Sarah wasn't sure what she thought of all of that but couldn't imagine making that kind of choice.

★ ★ ★

After all of the cold air had poured out, she grabbed a bag of frozen corn and sat at the kitchen table. She pressed it against the side of her face, wondering what ever happened to that girl she had met in the warming well. Knowing what she knew now, she wished she could go back and try to help her. She would have showed her some compassion over the choices the girl made – now that she realized how easy it was to make them.

Sarah looked out the window and saw Jack loading bags into the van. She knew he was going to the shelter but wondered what he was bringing with him. After the whole ordeal this morning, the last thing she was going to do was ask him about it. Sarah didn't want him to see her looking, so she got up from the kitchen table. She walked over to the cleaning closet where she pulled out a broom and dustpan to clean up the broken lamp.

CHAPTER 7

Time faded in and out for Star. At least three of the fingers on her right hand were broken. The swelling and discoloration extended down from her fingers, so maybe there were broken bones in her hand as well. She wasn't really sure. She guessed it had been a couple of days now since her last fix, and the withdrawals were getting harder to deal with. She hadn't eaten in a day, but she didn't much care for food anyway. Her stomach was all twisted in knots, and more parts of her body throbbed than she could count. She could feel her own heartbeat cascading through every limb. She didn't feel cold, but she couldn't stop shaking. The metal shackle cut into her already tender wounds as the sweat on her brow ran into her eyes and mixed with her tears.

Star stood up, trying to work through the haze in her head. There was a double door to who knows where, and no windows. No one would likely hear her scream. But what if they could and she didn't even try? Star took in a few quick breaths, then one long one, and then screamed at the top of her lungs. She knew the odds of someone hearing her were slim, but she had to at least try. Star drew in another long breath and screamed again. She laid on the floor as close to the door as she could get, hoping her hollers would reach through the sliver of a crack between the floor and the door frame. She even walked over to the water spicket and took a turn shouting into that.

Star yelled until her throat was horse, and then she returned to the bed, cradling her maimed hand. She felt broken. Literally and figuratively. Her spirit was broken, and she wasn't sure she had it in her to fight anymore. She hardly flinched when the lock clicked, and the door swung open. Star didn't move her eyes from the floor as the man came in and set more bags down.

"Jack," he said.

Star looked up. "What?"

"Jack. You had asked me what my name was. It's Jack."

Star looked at him a moment longer, then moved her eyes casually back to the floor as if she didn't care.

Jack pulled a plastic bag from one of the larger bags. She recognized it from one of the drug store chains. He also grabbed a small, plastic baggie with something in it, and walked over to the bed. Normally, Star would flinch at his approach, and sink backwards. She wondered if he noticed anything different. She didn't move. Not an inch. She didn't care that he was there. Star finally glanced in his direction, and could see he was studying her, probably looking at the sweat on her forehead and the tremors she was working hard to make still.

"Let me see your hand."

Star remained motionless.

"I'm guessing you've got a couple of broken fingers. I've got some stuff here to make you a splint. It should help a little with the pain and help them heal straighter."

Without looking up, Star said flatly, "How 'bout you take me to a hospital instead."

"I can't do that just yet."

Star looked up.

"Just yet?" It was the first ray of hope she'd felt all day.

Jack sat on the bed and reached for her hand. Star resisted for a moment, then let him have it. Jack pressed a little around her fingers and hand, causing her to wince and flinch with every poke and prod. He grabbed the plastic baggie and pulled out a small piece of what looked like particle board. Then he opened the drug store bag and took out a roll of medical tape.

Star sat still while he taped her three middle fingers to the little board. After he was done, he walked back over to the bag and took out a long piece of cloth, which he used to make a sling for her arm. She watched as he tied it on himself first, then he transferred it over to her and helped resize it a little. Jack put the drug store bag and plastic baggie back into one of the larger bags, then pulled out a Styrofoam container. He opened it to reveal a hamburger and French fries. Star began salivating, but she tried to hide it from Jack, so he wouldn't know how badly she wanted it. She thought he might only tease her with it, and she didn't want to give him the satisfaction. To her surprise, he walked over and set it on the bed next to her.

"Consider it a peace offering," he said with a smile. "Go ahead. Enjoy. You must be hungry."

Star only hesitated a moment before grabbing the burger with her good hand and stuffing it into her mouth.

Jack laughed. "Easy now! Make sure you taste it while you eat it."

Star slowed down only a little. She looked at the white Styrofoam carton. It wasn't the typical fast food bag she was accustomed to seeing. There was no restaurant name on it.

She wondered where it was from but realized she didn't really care all that much. It was good, and she was starving – more than she had originally thought.

Jack handed her a bottle of water. It was a generic brand. Star put the bottle between her legs and twisted off the cap with her good hand. She guzzled the water until it was almost empty. When she was finished, Jack took the food container and stuffed it back into the bag. It felt good to get rid of the hungry sensation. The food seemed to help clear her mind a little as well.

"How are you feeling? You look like hell."

Star continued with her silent treatment.

"I can see you sweating and you're still shaking. I suppose you want a fix?"

Star's heart raced, as the thought of getting a fix heightened all her senses. As quickly as the excitement came, so did reality. No. I can't do this. I can't keep doing this. If I keep doing this, I'll never be strong enough to get out.

She ran this dialogue over and over in her head for a few seconds before finally responding. "I... I don't think–"

"Come on! I'm sure you're feeling miserable and a little fix will make you feel better. I've got it right here in the bag." He pointed down.

Star could feel a single bead of sweat run from her forehead down along the side of her face. Despite drinking almost a full bottle of water, her mouth felt like it was full of cotton balls. She knew one fix could bring back daydreams of a better time. She could turn all of this horror off and forget who she was. She could remember who she used to be.

Star snapped out of her thoughts as Jack shook the bag a little, taunting her with its contents. She wanted to cry but hated the idea of being so vulnerable in front of him.

* * *

Star hustled the six long blocks back to the track, where she knew Ronny would be waiting for her. Just before she turned the corner, she stopped, looked around to ensure no one was watching her, and pulled out the cash the man had given her. She felt a little guilty about how it all went down. What he didn't know was that she already overcharged him for that evening's services. It was only a hundred dollars, but she was desperate for money, and banked on him being the kind of guy who wouldn't know any better. She had two hundred dollars in total – three fifty-dollar bills, two twenties and one ten. She took two of the fifty-dollar bills and shoved them into her pocket. Then she took the rest of it and tucked it inside her bra, toward the bottom. It was cold, and she had a small jacket on, which should prevent Ronny from seeing anything out of place.

Star resumed a casual pace and strode around the corner, avoiding a near collision with Leo, Ronny's lackey.

"Easy, baby doll!" Leo yelled.

"Yeah, yeah, sorry, sorry," Star said dismissively, as she scanned the area for Ronny. Wherever Leo was, Ronny was sure to be. He didn't go anywhere without Leo. Ronny looked at him like his bodyguard, but other people called him his pet. It was kind of a running joke amongst the family.

She saw Leo double back and pick up his pace in the direction of raised voices. That's when she spotted Ronny talking to one of the other pimps. It looked like a heated exchange, so she decided to keep her distance until it blew over. She watched Ronny poke his index finger into the chest of the other man, which she could only speculate had some threatening words attached to it. The other man puffed out his chest and pushed it forward into Ronny's finger. This was nothing unusual around the track. Pimps were always fighting over girls and territories, and whatever else happened to put someone's testosterone into question. It was still best never to get involved. After all, the last time she got involved, albeit involuntarily, it landed her in the unfortunate position she was in today, working the streets.

Star leaned back against the building and waited for the air to clear between the two men. Lacey walked up and leaned against the building alongside of her.

"How'd you do tonight?" Lacey asked expectantly.

"Don't worry, I got it."

Lacey let out a sigh of relief. "So that means we only need a little more for the rent." Lacey played with her fingers, as if she were trying to calculate.

"I have that too."

Lacey pushed off from the wall and spun herself around, so she was face to face with Star. "You do?" she said, doing a little dance in front of Star.

"Shhh!" hissed Star, as she pointed in the direction of Ronny, who was still matching wits with the other pimp. Lacey turned back around and continued leaning against the building with Star.

Now speaking more softly, Lacey asked, "So, you have what you owe Ronny, AND you have the rest of what we need to make rent?"

"Yes."

"That is so freakin' awesome." Lacey lowered the tone of her voice and looked at Star. "You don't sound very excited."

"Let's just say I don't feel great about how I got it."

Lacey gave Star a sideways look. "How'd you get it?"

"Don't worry about it. I don't really want to talk about it. I've got it and that's all that matters. But don't say anything to Ronny. Let me do all the talking at check-in. Okay?"

Star shot her a commanding look, and Lacey nodded her head. The girls watched as the pimp Ronny was talking to suddenly backed down. He and his a few of his guys raised their hands in the air.

Lacey gasped when she saw it, and she whispered, "It's a gun! Ronny's got a gun!"

The girls exchanged a worried look and stood, frozen. They watched as the pimp and his gang backed up slowly, until they eventually turned and walked in the opposite direction, a swiftness to their pace. Ronny brought the gun around to his back and tucked it in between his back and the waistline of his jeans. Ronny and Leo did a fist bump, and Ronny gave Leo a firm slap on the back. They seemed to quickly return to their world of normal. Once the other gang was completely out of site, Star and Lacey approached Ronny.

"Hey, pretty ladies!" smiled Ronny. "Is it going to be a good night or a bad night? Because, let me tell you, I'm in no mood for a bad night."

Star and Lacey chuckled nervously.

"A good night," Lacey said, looking at Star, who was trying not to glare back at her.

"I'll be the judge of that. Let's have it." Star reached into her pocket and pulled out the cash she had – from the man in the alley as well as a few other encounters prior to him.

Ronny grabbed it from her and counted it out loud. "Well, shit, Star. It's about time. Looks like you're finally getting the hang of this."

Lacey looked happier than Star did, and the two made their exit as Ronny handed the money to Leo to recount.

"Hold up!" yelled Ronny. "Why you in such a rush to leave? You wouldn't be holding out on me, would you?"

Star was thankful it was dark out, or he'd probably see the color draining from her face.

"No! No way, Ronny," blurted Lacey.

"I'm not talkin' to you Lace. I'm talkin' to brown eyes here." Ronny gave Star a hard look. Star had never been good at lying, but her life might depend on it now. She made it a point to look him directly in the eyes.

"No, Ronny. I gave you what I had. Even you said it was more than I usually do."

Without hesitation, Ronny backhanded Star across the face, sending her staggering backwards in shock.

"Never. Ever. Lip off to me again. If I question you, you just answer me. Got it?"

Star quickly nodded her head, her gaze now on the floor. Every part of her wanted to cry, but she didn't want to give Ronny that much power over her. She scrounged up every ounce of bravery she could to keep her composure. Ronny stood, giving them both a hard stare, until both girls were staring at the ground. Every part of Star wanted to throw a punch at him. Or at least tell him what a scum-sucking jerk he was. But she knew one more cross word would get her a first-class ticket to the emergency room. Or the morgue.

"Get out of here," Ronny said harshly. Without a word, the girls turned and walked home. Lacey went off on Ronny, but Star walked silently, still fuming from his backhand. She was too angry to speak. The truth was, if she spoke, she worried it would turn into tears, so it was better to just focus on the angry silence.

★ ★ ★

Star wouldn't cry. Not now. She had to be strong. She had to press past the hopelessness she felt and try again to fight. Not today, but soon. In order to do that, she had to get past this addiction. Other people went into rehab. She figured this was her rehab. It just wouldn't come with medication and a therapist. She would have to do this the hard way. It had been at least a week. Maybe longer. How much longer would she really have to feel this way? Star tried to focus on the pain in her ankle as a way to distract herself from the other physical symptoms she was feeling.

"No," Star said quietly.

At this point, Jack was already reaching into the bag for the drugs. He stopped, his hand still in the bag, and looked up.

"What did you say?" Jack looked surprised.

Star adjusted her position on the bed, fighting the pain from her ankle and hand, bringing herself to a more upright position.

"I said no," Star repeated, a little louder this time. "I don't want it anymore. I don't want to need it anymore."

Jack dropped whatever was in his hand and pulled his arm slowly from the bag, and stood to an upright position.

Star sat as tall as she could, while Jack stood looking at her. In those few moments, Star noted a shift in Jack's face. Almost a softening.

"I think you're going to make it," Jack said with a smile.

"What do you mean?"

"You're not like the other girls. You're stronger. You're going to make it. Those other girls just weren't strong enough. I tried to help them, but they didn't want to be saved."

Star's mind reeled. "Other girls?"

Jack ignored her question and returned to the bags on the floor.

"What happened to the other girls?"

"Have you ever played checkers?" Jack asked.

Star gave him a confused, yet suspicious look.

Jack pulled a travel size game of checkers from the bag and walked over to the bed. "May I?" he asked, sitting down next to her.

The game opened up like a book. The outside was the checker board, and the inside contained the small red and black circles. Each of the circles had a magnet on one side, so it stuck to the board. The idea was to be able to play in the car without all the pieces sliding around.

Star was reluctant. She wasn't sure what his angle was but thought it best to play along. "Yeah, I've played before."

Jack opened up the board and set it between the two of them. He carefully separated the black and red pieces and pushed the pile of red pieces toward Star. She winced as she picked her foot up onto the bed, so she could face the board.

Jack gave her a concerned look. "Do you want me to take that off?"

Star shot him a surprised look. "Yes."

"Are you going to be good this time? Not try something again, like last time?"

Star nodded in agreement. She watched as Jack pulled the key out of his coat pocket. She tightened her grip on the pillow beside her as he unlocked the shackle, anticipating the momentary pain of the metal releasing from her ankle. She lifted her foot up, and Jack slid the shackle off the bed. Star flinched from the loud clang as it hit the floor. She pulled her foot in toward her and cupped her good hand over her ankle.

Jack stared at it for a minute, then walked over to the bag and pulled out fresh bandages and ointment. This time, he didn't ask permission. He just looked at her. There seemed to be a silent agreement he could change her bandages. Jack finished by adding an Ace bandage wrap around it. Star tensed up a little while he applied the pressure of the wrap, but she noted that it felt better once it was secured.

"Thank you," Star said quietly, as she looked at her ankle.

Jack smiled. "You're welcome." He pulled the checker board back to the center between them and set up the pieces in the correct spots. Then he nodded his head at her, giving her the first move.

Star scanned the pieces, selected one of the front red checkers and moved it forward. Jack seemed pleased that she was playing and moved his first black checker.

"My sister, Annie, used to love playing checkers." Jack chuckled. "She wasn't very good at it, but she was determined to beat her big brother."

"How old is she?"

Jack was quiet, then took in a deep breath and sighed as he moved his next piece. "She was eighteen when she died."

Star felt oddly moved by the emotion behind his words. "Oh... I'm... I'm sorry."

Jack nodded his head in appreciation of her words and let the silence build a little as they moved a few more pieces on the board. "Annie was kind of a troubled kid in high school. Our parents were pretty strict, but Annie was stubborn. Really stubborn. If you told her to get up, she'd sleep until noon. If you told her to sleep, she'd get up at 6:30 a.m. You could pretty much count on her doing the exact opposite of whatever my parents told her to do." Jack chuckled again. "Really, I'm surprised they weren't smarter about that whole thing. They could have used that to their advantage."

Star smiled.

"Anyway, I watched her get angrier and angrier with them. I tried to talk to her about it, but she wouldn't really listen to me either. One Friday night, they caught her trying to sneak out of the house late. There was some party she wanted to go to. All I remember was waking up to all of them screaming at each other in the living room. By the time I got downstairs, Annie had run out of the house and took off with someone there waiting to give her a ride."

Star felt a small amount of nausea creeping in, but tried to keep herself steady and focused. "That sounds pretty normal for a teenager."

Jack sighed again. "I wish it were that simple or normal, but it wasn't. We didn't see her for days after that, and she wasn't in school that following Monday. I had never seen Mom so worried before, and that made me scared, so I decided to go look for her."

"Where did you go?"

"I started with some of the people I knew she hung out with at school, but they were mostly dead ends. Seems she never did go to that party, and most of her friends just thought they hadn't heard from her because she was grounded. I decided to dig a little deeper, into some of the darker social circles."

Star raised her eyebrows but kept quiet to let him continue.

"There was a group of kids that always hung out in the parking lot during lunch and after school. No one messed with these kids. They were thugs, and everyone knew they were into or dealing drugs. I had seen Annie talking to these guys a few times, but she always said she was just being friendly. I had no leads on my sister, and I was desperate. They were kind of my last resort." Jack got quiet and looked as though he were thinking through his next move on the checker board.

Star was intrigued. "Did they know where she was?"

"Yes. It's a long story, but I found out she ran away from home and was living on the streets not too far from our house. I went out looking and found her the next day. She was leaned up against the side of some guy's car, and she was dressed... well... I didn't know what to think."

"What did you do?"

"What any big brother would do. I pulled the guy out of his car and punched him until Annie got in between us and begged me to stop. I'm not proud of that, but I was upset by what I was seeing, and I didn't understand why she would want that. She agreed to let me take her to a nearby café for some food and told me this was her new life. It was the only way she could afford to be on her own. I begged her to come home. I even thought about dragging her there, but she had already turned eighteen, and it really was her choice." Jack was silent for a long while.

Star didn't say anything because he looked as though he were trying not to cry.

After another minute, he continued. "It's a night I'll regret for the rest of my life. Not the night itself, but my walking away and leaving her there. I never should have left her there. I should have made her come with me. If I had, she might still be alive today."

"How did she...?"

"The police showed up at our house two nights later. They found her body in an alley just down from the café we last saw each other at, beaten to death. They suspected it was by one of her Johns. That day, not only did I lose my sister, but my parents too. It broke them, and they were never the same."

They weren't finished with the game, but Jack collected all the pieces and started putting them back in their bags. "I know all of this seems scary, but I really am trying to help you. I couldn't... I didn't help Annie, so I'm trying to help you."

Jack got up off the bed, put his things into the bags and walked to the door. He turned to face her while he was still partway in the door frame. "I left the water bottle for you," he said, pointing to the empty plastic bottle at the foot of the bed. "You can refill it with the spicket over there. I'll leave the water turned on this time."

The heavy door shut and, once again, Star was left with only the silence. By this time, her shakes had subsided a little, but they were replaced with increasing nausea. She tried to take a few deep breaths, but it was only getting worse. She thought drinking more water might help, but the mere thought of putting anything in her stomach only turned it more. She spent one too many seconds thinking about it, and it became inevitable. She was going to throw up. She was thankful the shackle was off, allowing her to get to the bucket quicker.

Star got on her knees and wretched into the bucket until she had nothing left in her stomach. So much for the hamburger and fries. She pushed the bucket away and crawled over to the water spicket. Trickling the water into her cupped hand, she rinsed her mouth and hand, being careful to spit any unwanted water into the floor drain. She was hoping for some relief after throwing up, but the nausea was still with her. This was going to be a long night.

Caroline Klug

CHAPTER 8

Sarah stood at the kitchen sink, distracted by thoughts of the prior day. She felt an involuntary twinge run up her spine as she tried to shake off the memory of the man's fist slamming into her. She was glad it wasn't her face, as it was still pretty messed up from what Jack had done. She closed her eyes as she gently ran her hand down the side of her face and onto her chin, cradling her jaw as she slowly rotated it. It was difficult to open. Another hit there and she probably would have lost a tooth or two.

The microwave started beeping and she snapped her eyes open. Turning abruptly, her hand hit the coffee mug, sending it sliding off the counter and crashing to the floor in front of her. She cried out as the hot coffee splashed down her bare leg. She quickly brought her hand up and cupped it over her mouth, to bring silence back to the room. Sarah looked out the window and scanned the yard, letting out a sigh of relief when she saw Jack still tinkering just outside the garage.

Grabbing a hand towel, she dried the coffee off her leg and stepped awkwardly over the puddle and shards left on the floor. She could see a small amount of smoke coming out of the vents of the microwave where fresh air was supposed to go in. She pressed the button to open the door and watched the smoke and steam escape to reveal her mostly burnt turkey bacon. Finding herself standing between the burnt bacon and the pieces of her favorite coffee mug on the floor felt like too much. Tears flooded her eyes and she gave in to the sob welling in her throat.

She allowed herself only a minute to cry. She had to clean this up before Jack came back in. She tore paper towel from the roll on the counter and used that to blow her nose as she stared down at the aftermath of jagged ceramic. When she held that mug in her hands, it would remind her of hope. It was one of the only things she had that reminded her there was something caring inside of Jack. As she was bent down collecting the pieces, she couldn't help but feel like this was somehow confirmation of what life had become. What was once a symbol of hope was now only something broken.

Sarah rolled a few of the pieces around in the palm of her hand and ran her fingers gingerly over the rough edges. A part of her wondered if they would cut her. She laughed bitterly inside at her own thought. She was already cut. Tears welled once again, but she pushed them back and quickened her work to pick up all the pieces and clean up the mess.

She threw the pieces of mug into the garbage can, washed her hands and selected another mug to make a new cup of coffee. The one she chose was brown and dull. It was nothing like her colorful mug with flowers, but it seemed more fitting for what she felt inside. The Keurig machine hummed its song while she took the turkey bacon out of the refrigerator and placed a few more slices onto some paper towel and into the microwave. This time she was careful to set the time for ninety seconds, rather than hit one of the pre-programmed options.

She saw Jack walking back to the house, so she quickly grabbed his favorite mug and started another coffee for him.

Even though she was expecting it, she still jumped a little at the sound of the screen door opening, and even more so at the sound of it slamming shut. She drew in a deep, calming breath, and gripped the side of the counter to steady herself. It wasn't so much to steady her body as much as it was to steady her thoughts. Then, she turned to face him, smiling as much as her sore jaw would allow.

The microwave beeped again, and she looked down at the floor where the pieces of her mug had laid just a few minutes earlier. She could feel herself trembling a little but tried her best to act normally. Jack remained silent as he looked intently at her. Rather than looking into her eyes, he was looking around them, and she wondered if he was looking at the bruises. Maybe he was surveying the consequences of her disobedience, feeling proud of what he had accomplished. She should feel angry at that thought, but that emotion tended to get her in trouble, so she traded it in for the hurt instead.

"Is that my coffee?" he asked, looking past her to the cup sitting under the Keurig.

"Yes." Sarah took a few steps to the side as Jack pressed forward to grab his mug. He never took anything in it. Just black. "Breakfast is ready if you want to eat now."

Jack grunted in response and walked over to the kitchen table to sit down. Sarah pulled the bacon out of the microwave, split it between two plates and dished up two servings of the egg bake she had made the day before. She walked the plates to the table and sat down across from Jack. He read the paper as he ate, and she was thankful for the lack of conversation.

Normally, he would scan through each of the pages, and make it all the way through by the time his breakfast was gone. This morning, she watched him remain fixated on the front page, which spiked her curiosity. Soon, his eggs and bacon were gone, but he was still reading the front page. After a few minutes, Jack folded the paper and set it back on the table. Sarah tried to glance casually to see what the headline article was but was disappointed to see Jack had folded it the wrong way, so the headlines were inside the fold. He grabbed his mug and guzzled down the last of his coffee.

"I'm probably going to be home late tonight. Don't wait for me to eat."

Sarah wondered what he had going on but dared not ask. She simply nodded, acknowledging his comments.

"I want you to clean this place up today. Make sure you wash all the window ledges and baseboards too." Jack grabbed his things and headed out the door.

Sarah finished the last few bites on her plate while she watched him pull out of the driveway. As soon as he was out of sight, she grabbed the newspaper and opened it to a headline article about the missing girl, Rachel McGinnis. Her chest tightened and her heart skipped a beat. Taking another quick look outside, satisfied he was gone, she returned her attention to the article and continued reading. It was some kind of an exposé piece on Rachel's life – about her family and school. Sarah figured it might be a way to make the general public feel more connected with her, which might make them more willing to help if someone did see something. What she couldn't figure out was why Jack was so interested. When anything had come on the TV recently, he would always turn it off. What was different about this?

When she was done reading, she warmed her coffee in the microwave and moved to the living room. It sounded like she would have more time than usual, so she decided to take it easy this morning and relax with a little TV. She hit the power button on the remote as she shimmied herself back onto the couch as tightly as she could. She wasn't sure why, but it was comforting for her to feel all snuggled in. Sarah set the remote down and cupped both her hands around her coffee mug as she listened to the anchorwoman on the morning news program.

* * *

Jack turned up the radio in the van as he drove down 76th Street. He stopped at the red light and glanced down at the console alongside him.

"Dang it! My badge." Irritated, he let out a loud sigh, flipped his blinker on, and rounded the corner toward home.

* * *

Sarah listened as the anchorwoman concluded a segment on one of the former Vice Presidents. The next segment started with a picture of Rachel McGinnis that the police had been circulating around. She thought it might be about the exposé in the paper this morning, but as she picked up the remote to turn the channel, she stopped as the anchorwoman began,

"This morning we bring you coverage of a teen abduction quickly gaining national interest. Local teen, Rachel McGinnis, was abducted Wednesday evening from an area near downtown Milwaukee, Wisconsin. Based on information received from eyewitnesses, Milwaukee police are indicating details from the current abduction may have strong ties to several cold cases from the same area. The local police have joined forces with the FBI, as they re-open and investigate these cases. Here with us this morning, is FBI Special Agent Emmanuel Grant. Agent Grant, what can you share with us this morning?"

* * *

Jack looked nervously at the clock on the dashboard as he rounded the final corner on the way back to the house. He was skating on thin ice with his boss and couldn't be late today. Jack pressed his foot down on the gas pedal, looking ahead and down the side streets for cops. He figured it should just be a few more minutes home.

* * *

"Normally the FBI doesn't get involved with local cases. However, we were contacted by the Chief of Police, Luke Reynolds, asking for our assistance. Chief Reynolds and his team did a great job with their diligence in obtaining the eyewitness accounts and uncovering links to cases which have gone unresolved."

"So, you believe the man who took Rachel McGinnis has done this before?" the anchorwoman asked.

"Yes, we do. Descriptions received of the man and his vehicle are consistent with eyewitness accounts from prior abductions. Based on those accounts, we'd like to show you an artist rendering of both the suspect as well as the van we believe he's using to do the abductions."

The image on the screen changed to the sketches. Sarah sat up, tightening the grip on her mug, and feeling anxiety return to her chest, squeezing on her throat. She studied the sketch and couldn't ignore the resemblance to Jack. She set her coffee mug down, almost missing the end table, and buried her shaking hands in her lap. Her eyes moved over to the sketch of the van. She wondered how many vans had painted windows. Maybe a lot of them. Maybe it was more common than she thought. Maybe she was just seeing what her imagination wanted her to see.

Sarah shut her eyes, pressed them tightly together and reopened them, like a small child hoping the monster they just saw would go away if they blinked hard enough. Again, she looked at the sketches, feeling her stomach roll in discomfort.

"Unfortunately," the agent continued, "Some of the cold cases we're finding in common with our current cases involved bodies." The agent paused for a moment. "We now believe we're dealing with a serial killer." The agent's voice became more somber. "We are well aware that timing of rescue is of utmost important in all abduction cases. I'm not at liberty to share the details, due to the active investigation but, based on prior cases, if this is the same man, we have reason to believe Rachel McGinnis may still be alive. We've asked Rachel's parents to make a statement, which will be aired within the next hour or so."

The image on the screen returned to one of Rachel McGinnis, this time with her arms around her black Labrador Retriever. Sarah sat and stared at the photo on the screen, her mind whirling.

"What are you doing?" Jack bellowed.

Sarah startled so badly she almost fell off the couch. She didn't hear the van pull into the driveway. She scrambled for the remote and fumbled to turn it off.

"I... I... was just..." Her mind was reeling. How long had he been standing there? Did he only see the picture of Rachel, or did he see the sketches too?

"I'll tell you what you were NOT doing. What I asked you to do before I left. Is this what you do all day long? No wonder this place is never clean."

Sarah said nothing as Jack walked over to the TV and pulled the plug from both the wall and the back of the TV. He coiled the cord and stormed out of the living room and into the bedroom.

Sarah sat frozen, uncertain what he was going to do next. Jack rushed back through the living room. Just before he got to the door, he turned and said sternly to Sarah, "You are one lucky woman. If I wasn't in such a rush to get back to work, I'd use your face to clean one of those baseboards. If you know what's good for you, you'll stay focused on your work today, which better be done when I get home later."

Sarah nodded her head. Anything to get him to leave.

Jack turned, but then stopped once more. "And I want you to color your hair. Your roots are starting to show and that's ugly."

Once again, Sarah nodded, remaining tense and at attention. Jack gave her a final scowl and walked hurriedly out the door. Sarah held her breath until the van rounded the corner and was no longer in sight. She guessed he hadn't seen the sketches. But she had.

She sank into the couch, trying to process what she had just seen. Maybe she was losing her mind. Maybe the stress of how Jack was treating her was causing her to see things that weren't even there. The thought of that made her relax for a moment, and she realized how tight she had been squeezing all her muscles. She was just being paranoid. Wasn't she? Part of her was afraid to think such things. Another part of her was afraid not to. If he hadn't seen the sketches, it was probably in her best interest to put this behind her and get her tasks done before he got back home.

* * *

Jack sped into the work parking lot and pulled into one of the visitor spots in front of the building. This was not allowed, but it would have to be okay for today if he was going to get to his station on time. He put his hair net on as he walked through the lobby to the plant floor entrance. Delilah, the front desk receptionist, gave him a scolding look as she tapped on the surveillance screen showing where he was parked. With one hand opening the door, and the other stuffing his ear plugs in, Jack smiled and said,

"Good morning, Delilah! You look beautiful as always." He gave her a wink, which made her smile, and seemed to satisfy her initial concerns. She waved Jack through, and he disappeared through the doorway and into the plant. An enormous smile came over his face as he punched in with about thirty seconds to spare. As he made his way through the carefully taped safety walkways, he tipped his construction hat in a gesture of hello to his fellow coworkers on the machines, as they smiled and waved back.

He continued through the designated walkway and into the employee lunch room, where he stowed his lunch and soda in the refrigerator for later. He made small talk with the cleaning lady who was emptying the trash cans. His boss walked angrily into the lunch room with a look on his face that Jack knew all too well. Jack wished the cleaning lady a good day and darted for the door, in the opposite direction of his boss.

"Jack!" his boss yelled. "Get over here."

Jack stopped, turned to face his boss, and spoke with a smile. "Morning!"

"It would be a good morning if you weren't in here screwing around. You may get punched in on time, but there are expectations when you have to be at your machine and ready to run. That time has passed, and you're still in here."

"Sorry, Phil. I was just putting my lunch away. I'll get right to it."

"You do that."

Jack grabbed the door handle.

"And, Jack."

Jack stopped and turned to look at him.

"Next time... if there is a next time, you might as well come straight to my office because we're going to have to have another talk."

Jack tipped his hat again and moved quickly through the door and onto his station.

"I saw Phil yelling at you in the lunch room. Why is he such a jerk to you?" Ken asked, as he helped Jack load the large metal sheet onto the machine.

"I don't know," Jack said, as he shrugged his shoulders. The truth was, Jack knew exactly why Phil didn't like him. He worked on autopilot, as his thoughts drifted to a conversation with Phil several summers ago.

* * *

"Jack!" Phil yelled down from his upstairs office. "Turn off your machine and come up here a minute!"

Jack shut his machine down, walked up the stairs and into Phil's office. He was sitting on his big, pompous, leather chair, with documents spread out in front of him on the desk. The chair was, by far, nicer than anything else in his office. It was probably nicer than anything in the whole plant.

"Shut the door." Phil flapped his hand in the direction of the door. Phil never asked anyone to close the door. Not unless they were about to get fired. The thought made Jack break out into a sweat. He wiped his brow and sat down in the visitor chair on the other side of the desk.

"What's up, Phil?"

Phil gave Jack a hard look. "I have a problem, Jack. And I'm hoping you can help me figure it out." Phil rested the palms of his hands on the papers in front of him. "You see, I've been going over materials, and something's just not adding up."

Jack swallowed hard but kept a poker face.

"When I add up all the waste off the machines and compare that to what we're being charged to get hauled away, there's a big gap. Not like you'd think though. It's not that we're being charged too much. In fact, I suspected we were being charged too little. Now, I'm a Christian man, and it wasn't sitting good on my conscience to let that slide. So, I called the company, and had them take another look at their records to confirm we weren't short changin' them.

Turns out the gap was on our end. We were reporting more waste than we actually had. So, then I checked the inventory, and did some figuring there. But I hit a wall there too. So, best I can figure is, we've got material being reported as waste, that's finding its way out of our plant a different way. You wouldn't happen to know anything about that, would you, Jack?"

Jack adjusted his posture a little and tried to manufacture a confused look. "No, Phil. Why are you asking me?"

"Well, in doing my research, it seems the highest waste levels during those months of the gap were reported off your machines, so I started there. When I compared those months to the twelve months before that, it was obvious the spikes in waste for those months were not normal for you. I already talked to Ken, and he claims he doesn't remember the waste ever looking like what you reported. So, I'll ask you again, Jack. Do you know anything about this? Are you taking material from the shop and reporting it as waste?"

Jack looked at Phil as calmly and confidently as he could. "Maybe I screwed up when I was entering the numbers or something?"

"That still wouldn't account for the loss of material." Phil looked hard at Jack.

"I don't know what to tell you, Phil. I wish I could help explain, but I can't."

Phil watched Jack's eyes hit the floor.

"You can't, or you won't?"

Jack remained silent. He knew if he was too defensive, that would make him look just as guilty.

Phil drew in another deep breath and sighed. "Okay, then. I guess we're done here. I don't know what to think about all this, but just know I'm gonna be keeping an eye on you out there."

Jack kept his face straight and said nothing. He nodded his head and looked at the door, as if waiting for permission to leave. Phil followed his cue and gave his own nod toward the door. Jack got up and left.

* * *

It was almost 9 p.m., and Sarah was sitting on the couch reading a book when Jack walked in and set his things on the kitchen counter. She closed her book and sat tensely as he walked from room to room, observing the job she had done cleaning. When he returned to the living room, he bent down and wiped his finger along one of the baseboards. Sarah pulled her legs out from under her to the floor and sat upright. Jack stood, looking at his finger, and then smiled.

"Great job cleaning today. The place looks really nice. And so do you. Your hair looks good."

Sarah flushed. "Thank you."

"Maybe tomorrow we could go to the café and get a coffee. I know we weren't able to go after grocery shopping on Wednesday."

Sarah perked up.

"And maybe we could replace the mug you broke."

Sarah squirmed in her seat, suddenly afraid he was about to turn angry.

"I saw it in the garbage. I hope you didn't cut yourself."

She hardly knew what to think, but was relieved. The thought of going to the café lifted her spirits, and she allowed a smile to come across her face. Maybe he wasn't the monster in the news. If he was, what would she do? Where would she go? She wouldn't even be able to go to the police without getting herself in trouble. She had to hope this away. She had to let ignorance be her comfort.

CHAPTER 9

Star let out a low moan as her stomach twisted in knots. Gripping the side of the mattress with her good hand, she pulled herself up onto the bed, and curled up on her side. She kept her breathing shallow, trying to hold the nausea at bay, and pulled herself tighter into a ball as her body shook and trembled. Her head was throbbing and, although she knew this was her body going through withdrawals, she couldn't help but wonder if she might die. Hurt and anger threaded through her heart.

* * *

The room was so quiet and still, which seemed to exaggerate the sound of the machines helping her mom cling to what little life she had left. Star sat alongside the bed, holding her mom's hand while she rested her chin on the bed and leaned her head against her mom's shoulder. She found herself strangely comforted by the rhythmic beats of the machine. Maybe it was the rhythm. Maybe it was being able to close her eyes and know her mom was still with her.

Star really hadn't slept much these last few days. She was so tired, but fear kept her alert. The doctor told them it could be anytime now. If that was true, and if she closed her eyes, and drifted off to sleep, even for a moment, she might miss her last moments. Part of her thought that wouldn't be such a bad thing. Maybe if she let herself fall asleep, she could dream away this curveball life was throwing at her and wake up on the other side of the injustice. She knew that was a selfish thought, and not at all how real life goes. Star lifted her head off the bed and straightened up. Still holding her mom's hand, she took the other hand and brushed hair away from her mom's face.

"Hey, Bean," her dad called from the doorway. "Why don't you take a walk to the cafeteria with me and we'll grab something to eat."

"No thanks. I'm good."

Her dad gave her a sad look and sighed. "Honey, you haven't eaten all day. You need to eat something."

Star gave him the kind of look she would have when she was nine and wanted to have a sleepover. "Could you get me something and bring it back here to eat?"

Her dad smiled. "Sure, Bean. I'll be back in a few minutes."

Star felt relieved that he didn't make a big thing out of it. She watched him walk down the long hallway and around the corner before turning her attention back to her mom. She looked so frail laying there with a machine helping her breathe. Star couldn't imagine it away anymore. She couldn't pretend her mom wasn't sick. Wasn't dying. She couldn't look past the tubes or be deaf to the beeping of the machines. Everything around her seemed to grow larger and crowded her. Anxiety welled in her throat and she felt claustrophobic. Maybe just a quick stretch in the hallway would help.

Star stood and let go of her mom's hand, but didn't move away from the bed. She stood there for several minutes staring down at the frail woman, unsure of what emotions to allow in. She walked slowly backwards until she reached the doorway. Hesitantly, she turned around and looked out across the nurses' station. Two of the nurses were leaned against the counter, giggling and whispering at whatever they were looking at on their personal phones. A man in scrubs was talking on the desk phone and the big, bossy lady was looking over charts and making notes on the whiteboard hanging on the wall. She heard more giggling and looked to the side, where she saw two small kids peeking at her from around the door frame of the next room. She gave them a big smile and could hear them giggle as they pulled their heads back into the room and out of sight, like an easy game of hide-and-seek. For a moment, she forgot why she was there and life seemed okay.

The frenzied movements of the nurses caught her attention before the sound did. The sound of the beeps no longer beeping, but now only one, long, drawn out sound. Star could hardly process what was happening. Even though people were rushing about, it felt as though everything slowed down.

"Doctor Beck!" yelled one of the nurses. Star spun around and tried to run to her mom, but the nurse grabbed her by the shoulders and ushered her off to the side, letting the doctor through. She could hear them speaking calmly but with urgency as they moved alongside her mom.

Star watched as the doctor took the stethoscope from around her neck, placed the headset into her ears, and rested the other end on her mom's chest.

Doctor Beck shut off the monitor and all the nurses turned their heads quietly in Star's direction, with a look of pity and sorrow on their faces.

Hot tears stung Star's eyes.

"Time of death, 8:52 p.m.," said the doctor.

Star's knees gave way and she fell slowly to the floor. "Maggie?"

She could hear the sound of her dad's voice crack behind her but didn't move a muscle when the cafeteria tray hit the floor beside her. She watched as he rushed over to her mom's side. "No, no, no," he cried, burying his face in her chest. "Oh, Magpie."

The nurses quietly left the room. One of them stopped to help Star off the floor and stayed for a moment to rub her back as she cried, holding herself up at the end of the bed.

★ ★ ★

Star sobbed as the emotions of her mom's death flooded her like it had just happened. The pain of the loss. The regret of walking away from her seconds before she should have. She wanted to be holding her hand when it happened. She didn't want her to be alone when she died. Maybe this was karma. Maybe now she would die alone in this prison room. Her sobs were only upsetting her stomach more, and she knew she would throw up again. There was nothing left in her stomach, and she hung her head over the side of the bed, dry heaving until her body finally stopped convulsing. Thirst was overtaking her, and she lifted her head to see the empty water bottle lying beside her pillow. The water faucet seemed so far away, and she was exhausted. She laid her head back down for a moment.

Suddenly, as if someone had turned on a switch, she could hear music, and the sound change makes after you drop it through the slot into a vending machine. She lifted her head again and couldn't believe what she was seeing. It was a vending machine filled with Coca-Cola. She blinked twice and looked around the room wondering who had brought it in.

Star was elated and mustered all the energy she could to stand up and walk over to this gift of manna. When she got close to the vending machine, she raised her arm and placed the palm of her hand onto the front, then pressed her cheek against it. It was cool and refreshing. Just as she imagined it might taste. She opened her eyes to find her hand and cheek pressed against the cold cement wall. It wasn't real.

She had heard of people hallucinating while going through withdrawals, but she had no idea it felt so real. Her mirage was gone, and she was left with only her thirst and exhaustion. She wanted to cry, but was so dehydrated, no more tears would come out. She could feel herself soaked in sweat and needed to drink. Sliding down the wall and onto the floor, Star crawled over to the water faucet, turned it counterclockwise and drank out of the spicket like a dog. She was on her knees, lapping the water with her tongue when the metal door creaked open. Star continued guzzling the water, paying no attention as Jack walked in and closed the door behind him.

She couldn't seem to get enough of the water, and the sudden rush of fluid was too much for her stomach. She arched her back and a stream of projectile vomit painted the wall in front of her and ran down and over the water spicket. It happened so fast and so involuntarily, Star had no time to react. She sat on the floor, stunned, as vomit ran down her chin onto her shirt, and the vomit from the wall pooled on the floor around her foot. Under any normal circumstance, she would be mortified. Today, however, she felt so sick and so lethargic, she had no energy left to feel embarrassed. There she sat, motionless on the floor in her own watery bile.

"Unbelievable," Jack scowled. "Do you have any idea how disgusting this is? Just when I thought you couldn't lose any more of your dignity."

Star felt a sudden awareness of her situation and shuffled herself backwards away from the vomit creeping slowly toward her. With an apologetic look on her face, she looked at the wall in front of her, and then at Jack.

"I'll have to get the hose to clean this up. Don't move." Jack left the room and came back a few minutes later with the hose, a pair of rubber gloves, a fresh set of clothes, and another Styrofoam container. Star assumed it was a hamburger. Her stomach tightened, and the nausea heightened at the thought of it, and she tried holding back more dry heaves.

"Get up."

Star trembled unsteadily as she pulled herself to her feet. She staggered backwards and caught herself on the bed frame.

"Stop! I don't want you getting puke on the bed. Come forward so I can hose off your feet."

Star suddenly felt ashamed, and took a few steps forward, her eyes not moving from the floor in front of her. Jack put on the rubber gloves and walked carefully around the vomit to the water spicket, and turned it on. Using his gloved hands, he cupped the water and splashed it over the handle to rinse off anything on it. Once that was clean, he attached the hose and sprayed down the wall and floor around it. He turned his attention to Star and hosed down her calves and feet.

The water felt ice cold, and Star flinched at the shock of it.

"Stand still!"

Star froze and let the icy water run down her legs. After a moment, she thought it felt good. She felt herself cool down and her stomach settle a bit. She knew Jack was angry, but closed her eyes to embrace the unexpected moment of comfort while she could. Jack moved the attention of the hose from her feet to the floor. Making sweeping motions, he worked to make sure all the vomit rinsed down into the floor drain, until the floor looked clean again. He turned off the water and unscrewed the hose.

"Thank you," Star said quietly, her eyes still focused on the floor. Jack paused with the hose still in his hands. She looked up and watched his face change. Soften maybe.

"You're welcome. Are you feeling any better now?"

Star nodded her head and looked behind her at the bed, and back at Jack. He nodded, and Star backed up and sat down.

"I know this feels hard for you right now, but it will get better. You'll see. Everything is going to be all right."

For the first time since she had woken up in this prison, Star actually believed his words. Maybe this wasn't a prison. Maybe it was a second chance.

* * *

"I hate you!" screamed Star, as she slammed her bedroom door closed. She could see the door handle rotate only a fraction, and knew he'd realize the door was locked.

"Bean, come on. Open the door. I'm not the enemy here. I'm trying to help you."

"Ha! Right! If you were trying to help me, you wouldn't keep me locked away in here."

"I hate to point out the obvious, but it's you who locked the door."

Although she couldn't see his face, she could tell by his tone that he was smiling, which made her even more mad. She hated when he stayed all calm when she was so upset. It just made it harder for her to be angry. Sometimes she wished he would get upset and yell. It would help her feel justified for her own outbursts.

"What do you say, Bean? Open the door. Let's talk."

Star stood looking at the closed door for several minutes, waiting for him to walk away, but he didn't. The longer she waited, the worse she felt.

Finally, she unlocked the door and sat back down. The door handle turned, and Star watched as her dad poked his head around the door. Sitting on her bed, hands folded in her lap, and sniffling, Star gave him a look that told him it was okay to come in.

He walked over and sat on the bed next to her. "When I was your age, there were a lot of things I did that my parents didn't know about."

Star was suddenly curious but tried not to show him that. She sat still, staring into her lap.

"They were good parents. Good people. But terrible at being interested enough in what was really going on in our lives, and even less interested in doing anything about it if they did know. I guess it was probably easier that way. I know it would be easier with you, but I don't want to make the same mistakes."

"What kind of mistakes?"

Her dad smiled, sighed, and looked up at the ceiling, as if searching for words he was unprepared to speak.

"There's an awful lot I could tell you about myself when I was your age. You'll just have to trust me when I say that now may not be the right time to tell you everything. I will someday. I promise. But for now, I just want you to know that I've gone to the kind of parties you want to go to tonight. Nothing good happens at them. Nothing."

"But Dad! You don't understand–" she spoke defensively.

"Yes. Yes, I do understand. I may not be your age now, but I was at one time and, let me tell you, times haven't changed as much as you think they have. And the ways it has changed almost makes it worse than it was back then."

Star rolled her eyes and fidgeted with her hands, shooting glances at the phone on the nightstand as it buzzed with activity.

"I know you think it's social suicide not to go to this party tonight, but you're going to thank me someday."

Star rolled her eyes again, this time exaggeratingly enough to make sure he saw it.

"I get it. I know you think I'm wrong and you're right, but I love you enough to let you be mad at me, if that's what it takes to keep you safe."

"But my friends will be there with me, Dad! They'll make sure nothing bad happens."

Her dad shook his head. "It's not that simple, sweetie. I like your friends. I do. But there will be lots of boys there, and they're going to be, well, distracted."

Star's cheeks flushed, less out of embarrassment and more out of irritation.

"Besides, all it takes is one douche bag–"

"Dad!" She tried not to laugh.

"ALL it takes is one douche bag dropping a pill in the drink you say you won't have but probably will, and so many bad things can happen. I can't even count them all." He turned his body to face her and waited patiently for her to reciprocate.

Eventually, she gave in to the discomfort and turned to look at him.

"I love you. I love you so much it hurts. And even though you don't understand and you're mad at me, I just want you to know I love you."

Star felt herself softening. She was still angry, but it was hard to leave him hanging. "I love you too, Dad, but you're right. I don't understand." There was a long pause between them. "Fine. Whatever. I guess I'll be the social media laughing stock. No big deal."

"That's the spirit!" chuckled her dad, patting her twice on the leg before getting up off the bed. Star pursed her lips and gave him the most annoyed face she could without getting into more trouble.

"I'll be downstairs if you want to join me for a movie. We can even watch one of those scary flicks you like."

"Thanks, but I'm just going to go to bed," she said, folding her arms.

"Suit yourself. If you change your mind, you know where to find me. Night, Bean."

* * *

A second chance. Her own words echoed through her mind, and she couldn't help but think about that night. She was so angry at her dad. She was angry until she found out about the eighty-seven kids who got underage drinking tickets and the two alleged rapes reported weeks after the fact. It was all over the news, so her dad had to know, but never gave her the expected I told you so. It was quietly accepted between them, and never spoken of again.

Star shook off the memory and looked at Jack, suddenly wondering if she should be looking at this whole situation differently. Maybe he was trying to help her, and this was the only way. What do they call it? Tough love? He didn't know her, and certainly couldn't love her. But it sounded like he loved his sister, and maybe that was a good enough motivation to do whatever he was doing for her as a stranger. She could see he had a dark side too, which frightened her, but hope was a stronger pull for her in that moment. It was the only kind of self-preservation that might hold her together long enough for her head to clear.

"I know you're not feeling very hungry right now, but there's a salad in there for you." Jack pointed to the Styrofoam container. "I figured you might be suffering and need something you can eat later. There's no meat on it, so it should stay good for a while. I'll stop back tomorrow with something more."

Jack coiled the hose and pulled together the items he brought in. "You can change into those clothes over there after I leave, and I'll pick up the dirty ones when I'm back tomorrow." He headed for the door, stopped just short of it and turned around. "Is there something specific, like a treat of sorts, that I could bring you to cheer you up?"

Star was surprised by the question and remained silent, looking at him, uncertain how to respond. "Maybe some muffins or cookies or something?"

"Cookies?" she asked cautiously.

"What kind?" he asked, seeming surprised that she'd answered.

Star paused, her eyes searching imaginary things around her. "Chocolate chip, please?"

Jack smiled. "Chocolate chip. Okay. Sure." He turned to face the door.

Star mumbled something which made Jack turn back around.

"What?" Jack asked.

"With walnuts? Could they be chocolate chip with walnuts?" Star immediately regretted her request, worried she had now asked for too much.

Surprisingly, he smiled. "Okay. Chocolate chip cookies with walnuts."

Jack disappeared behind the door, and Star sunk into the mattress. There was really only one spot to comfortably sleep, which was right in the middle where the mattress sunk in to form to a person-like mold. She lay on her back, staring up at the ceiling, feeling grateful that her stomach was settling. It still wasn't enough to eat the salad Jack left, but it was enough to allow her what felt like one of the first moments of clarity since she'd been in there.

"Okay, Star," she said to herself. "You're going to make it through this. You're going to get out of here and then what? What's your plan? Maybe this is your second chance. So what are you going to do with it?"

She lay there thinking. I'm going to stay sober. No more drugs. Heck, maybe not even any beer or anything. I'll get a job. A real job. I'll get a place of my own too. Maybe Lacey and I could get a new place together. Away from Ronny and all that. Maybe we could even go to school.

She found herself grinning, thinking of what it would be like for her and Lace to be traipsing across some college campus with backpacks, notebooks, and iced coffees. It would be just like they see on TV. She smiled again, imagining how proud her dad would be of her. She only floated on that idea for a moment before her smile faded, and her heart hurt again. What would he think of her if he knew what she had become? Would he ever feel the same about her? She closed her eyes and tried to push away the intrusive thoughts which filled her now overly crowded mind.

Star sat up, pulled the Styrofoam container closer to her and popped open the top lid. There was a plastic fork lying on top of the salad. Several days ago, she would be plotting how she could use that to injure Jack and escape. Now, she felt oddly resigned to her prison, and the possibility that it was only a necessary evil on the way to a better place. A place she would never be able to get to on her own. She grabbed the fork and poked around the leaves of lettuce and sliced veggies on top. She hated red peppers but didn't want to seem ungrateful, so she ate them first. She was hungrier than she thought she would be. When she was finished with the salad, she set the fork back into the container and closed the lid.

Hope. It was all she had. She would either die in this prison, or she would live. A few days ago, she wanted to die. Now, she felt differently. She was starting to climb to the other side of the withdrawals and wanted her life to be different. She wanted a chance. She closed her eyes and made a silent promise to herself that she would accept wherever this prison brought her – good or bad. She had to accept the consequences – life or death. But she wanted life.

CHAPTER 10

Sarah sang along with the song on the radio as she folded the laundry. Her jaw still hurt to move, but the act of singing always lifted her mood and, right now, that outweighed any physical discomfort she was feeling. The clean clothes from yesterday remained piled in the laundry basket. She pulled each piece of clothing out of the basket and separated them into neat, organized piles on top of the bed. Socks, underwear, good shirts, work shirts. Then she focused on each individual pile, starting first with Jack's clothes and then moving on to hers.

Occasionally, she glanced out the window at the neighbor kids playing. The little girl next door was wearing a hot pink t-shirt with a yellow sun on it. It was bright and happy and reminded her of something she would have worn when she was that age. She wasn't old by any means, but she felt it in that moment. Sarah returned her focus to the piles of laundry and worked on the towels. Hearing the familiar sound of stones underneath the car tires, she looked out the window to see the van pulling in the driveway.

Jack was home early. Normally, this would make her nervous, but she was hopeful this meant Jack was going to make good on his offer to take her to the café. She allowed a small smile to grow across her face and moved more quickly to finish folding the rest of the clothes on the bed.

"Hey!" Jack yelled from the kitchen.

"Hello!" she called back. She could hear him setting bags on the kitchen table as the screen door slammed shut behind him. Sarah grabbed the stack of dish towels off the bed with her sore hand and the empty laundry basket with the other. She breezed quickly through the kitchen into the laundry room to put the basket away, then headed back into the kitchen. Fixing her eyes on the bags on the table, she placed the folded towels into the silverware drawer by mistake, closing the drawer without being aware of what she was doing. She turned to see Jack looking inquisitively between her and the silverware drawer.

Realizing what she had just done, her cheeks flushed, and she managed a small chuckle as she turned around to retrieve the towels and put them in their rightful place. She was thankful that neither her mistake nor her laugh seemed to upset him. He was busy sorting through one of the bags. Sarah hovered just near the table, pretending not to care about what he was doing.

"I needed some stuff for work, so I stopped at the store on my way home." Jack slid one of the bags off to the side against the wall and pointed to it. "Leave this one alone. I need to take that to the shop with me."

Sarah nodded.

"There's stuff in this other bag for you to make banana nut muffins."

"Sure, but I thought you didn't like bananas?" Sarah said, with her head cocked to the side.

"I don't. They're not for me. It's for..." Jack hesitated a moment, as if trying to remember. "They're for Johnny at work. And his family. They had a death in the family."

Sarah winced and then sighed. "Oh. That's too bad." Sarah reached for the bag and pulled out a box mix for banana bread and a bag of walnuts. She stopped and stared for a moment at the bag of walnuts in her hand, the hint of a memory striking her. "Wait. Did you say for Johnny?"

"Yeah," Jack said, as he rifled through the other bag.

"The really tall Asian guy?"

"Yeah," Jack replied, with more edge to his voice. Sarah could tell he was impatient with her questions, but felt what she had to say was important, so she continued.

"Um... this is a really great and thoughtful idea. I'm sure the family will really appreciate it. Do you think I should leave the walnuts out though? I remember Johnny from when he talked to us in the parking lot of the grocery store a few months back."

Jack shifted uncomfortably.

"We were coming out of the store and I was holding the bakery cookies. They were still warm, and I didn't want them to break. He's so tall. That's how I remembered him. Anyway, I remember him commenting on how good the cookies looked. We offered him one... do you remember?" Sarah asked the question but, lost in her own thoughts, didn't wait for a response. "He said he couldn't because he was *deathly* allergic to nuts." Sarah came back from her memory and looked at Jack. He still wasn't looking at her, but she could see his face reddening.

"No," Jack replied.

"No... he shouldn't have the nuts?"

"I mean, no! Don't leave the nuts out," he fired back.

"But... Jack... he said he's deathly allerg–"

"Well, you heard wrong! Leave the damn nuts in!" he interrupted, leaving her feeling uncertain what proverbial can she had just opened. Sarah swallowed hard, knowing if she said anything more there would be trouble. She stood silently, staring at the nuts, her stomach sinking. She might as well be holding a bag of bullets.

Jack paid no attention to her distress and walked out of the kitchen.

If he's deathly allergic, then he'll be smart enough to check for them first and it will be okay. Sarah took a deep breath and tried to shake off the feeling in the pit of her stomach while she put away the rest of the groceries in the bag. Reading the back of the box, she started the oven, pre-heating it to the instructed 350 degrees, and gathered her mixing bowl, eggs, oil and spoon. The silver bowl caught the sunlight coming in through the window and reflected it back into her eyes. She stood still, feeling mesmerized by it, a distant memory dancing in her mind.

★ ★ ★

Her mom handed her the bag of flour. It was heavy. Almost too heavy for her small arms, but she cradled it like a newborn and walked it over to the counter where the mixing bowl was. The bag was new, unopened, and waiting like a Christmas present. There was almost nothing she enjoyed more than baking cookies. Well, maybe eating them, but that was just the cherry on top of an already delicious sundae. Specks of flour escaped and fell to the floor as she peeled back the paper to reveal the fine powder. This next part was her favorite, but she had to wait for her mom because measurements were important in baking, and her mom always helped with that part.

"Mom, I'm ready!" Her tiny voice squeaked with expectation.

Her mom smiled and opened the drawer containing all the measuring cups, and carefully selected the ones they would need for the cookies. "Okay, sweetie. You see this one?" She pointed to the largest of the measuring cups. "We need two of these, and one of these," she said, shifting her finger to the smaller one. "Remember what I taught you about using this butter knife to make sure it's level."

Impatient, Sarah pushed up the sleeves on her pajama top and grabbed the largest measuring cup. She opened the paper flaps wide and plunged the cup deep into the flour, until even her little hand was buried in it. She liked the feel of the soft powder falling around her hand and through her fingers. She left the cup floating in the flour while she wiggled her fingers around and sifted the flour through them.

"Don't play in that flour. Just take out what we need for the cookies and then close it back up, okay?" Her mom was only half paying attention while measuring out the butter.

Sarah sighed, and pulled her hand out of the flour. She grabbed the already filled measuring cup and lifted it carefully out of the bag. Stealing a quick glance over her shoulder, she used her fingers to level off the top of the measuring cup and dumped it into the mixing bowl. She did that two more times, once again with the big cup, and lastly with the smaller one, just like her mom had instructed.

"Okay!" she called out proudly. Her mom handed her each of the ingredients, one at a time, giving instructions with each. She would tell her how much to measure out and how to add it. Sarah didn't like doing the vanilla, because it always came out of the bottle too fast, so her mom did that one. She liked packing the brown sugar, and always insisted on using the smallest measuring cup so she could do more of them. It made her feel like she was on the beach building a sand castle. They had almost everything in there now. There was just one more ingredient to add, which was her favorite.

Her mom gave her a wink. "Well, we're all done mixing the ingredients! We can spoon the dough onto the cookie sheet now!"

"Mom!" she giggled. "We can't forget the MOST important one!"

"Which one is that?" she said with a smile.

"The one that makes the cookies extra yummy."

Her mom smiled back as she pulled out a bag of walnuts from the upper cabinet. "You do love these walnuts!"

Sarah dumped walnuts into the metal bowl, scattering them as evenly as she could over the ball of dough, and watched her mom stir them in.

* * *

Sarah stood at the counter, staring into the mixing bowl, lost in her memory. The beep from the stove, signaling it was pre-heated, snapped her back into the present. The bag of walnuts caught her eye once more and she found her pleasant memory fading into unanswered questions about muffins and allergies.

There was something else bothering her. Something other than Johnny's allergy. It was like her subconscious was screaming to her, but she couldn't quite make it out. She couldn't take her eyes off the walnuts as she searched her mind for the source of her distress.

She froze as her subconscious thought broke through and her distress turned to fear. Sarah only entertained the thought for a second, and then self-preservation took center stage. No. No, it couldn't be. She found herself physically shaking her head, as if to talk herself out of her own thoughts. Pushing aside what her subconscious was desperately trying to get her to remember, she opened the bag of walnuts, poured them into the batter and gave it a good stir. Using another measuring cup, she filled each of the muffin cups and placed them into the oven.

Distracted and working on autopilot, Sarah inadvertently grabbed the grocery bag Jack had told her to leave alone and started unpacking it. She was so lost in her thoughts, she hardly noticed what she was pulling out of the bag and setting on the table. She grabbed an oblong box made of thin cardboard, and lost her grip as she was pulling it out. The box fumbled through her hands, into the side of the brown paper bag, and onto the floor. Even though it wasn't very big, it made a loud noise as the face of the box landed squarely onto the surface.

The noise brought the sound of Jack's approaching footsteps. In a matter of a moment, Sarah realized she was unpacking the bag she wasn't supposed to and worked feverishly to put the items back in before Jack got to the kitchen. Judging by the sound of his footsteps, she only had a few seconds. She squatted to the floor to grab the box that had landed at her feet. Clutching it in her hand, she raised herself back up, trying to make sense of what she was looking at.

"What are you doing?" Jack asked.

Forgetting her role in unpacking the forbidden bag, Sarah looked at Jack and showed him the box in her hand. "This hair dye," she said innocently. "Do you want me to go back to my natural color? I thought you said it wasn't safe?"

For the first time in a long time, Jack seemed left without words. In fact, he almost seemed nervous. "What? No. Ah... I must have just grabbed the wrong color by mistake."

Sarah still had questions and continued against her better judgement. "Sorry, I guess I'm confused. I just colored my hair yesterday. Why did you buy this today?"

"I don't know. It was on sale." Jack looked aware of his own nervousness and shifted his tone. "Why are you asking me all these questions? And why the hell are you even messing around with the bag I told you to leave alone? Can't you just do what you're told?"

Sarah cowered. "I know. I'm sorry. I didn't mean to. I was just busy in the kitchen making the muffins and unloaded it without thinking."

This answer seemed to appease Jack, and he grabbed the box out of her hand. "I'll exchange it at the store when I'm back."

"Seeing as I just colored my hair, I won't need it for a while. You don't have to make a special trip. We could just do that when we go to the store again next week."

For reasons unknown to Sarah, this seemed to set Jack off to a degree of seismic proportions.

"Aaaahhhh!" he yelled, frustrated. "Why are you arguing with me on this?"

"I wasn't argu–"

"I am so sick of your attitude! I'm constantly going out of my way to take care of you and give you the things you need. I do one thing wrong and suddenly you start pressuring me."

Sarah's gaze hit the floor. She knew there was no good thing to say at this point.

"You know what? You can forget about going to the café today."

Sarah felt an immediate lump in her throat, and her eyes said what her lips couldn't.

"Maybe that will teach you to know your place and know there's consequences to your actions."

She knew better than to argue with him. Instead, she stood motionless, looking at the floor, trying to hold back the tears she felt threatening her.

Jack threw the box of hair dye into the bag on the table. She felt a small amount of relief when he grabbed it and stormed out of the house. Her relief was short lived, as the screaming from her subconscious returned, this time shaking her by the shoulders. She couldn't ignore this one. Couldn't push it way. Couldn't pretend it away. It was like the pieces of a math equation all lining up, and both sides of the equal sign balanced identically. Identically and horrifically.

Her mind flashed to thoughts of Rachel McGinnis. What if buying that hair dye was no mistake? What if it was for someone else?

Sarah's already screwed up world was turning upside down again. Her mind was so paralyzed, it was difficult for her to hear the oven timer beeping behind her. After a minute or so, she realized it was going off and rushed to take the muffins out. In the midst of her frantic movements, her bare hand hit the oven grate and she let out a cry of pain. With the oven mitt in her other hand, Sarah managed to catch the pan, already halfway out, and kept the muffins from hitting the floor. Setting the pan on top of the stove, she ran to the sink to get her hand under cold water. There she stood, water running, hand throbbing, her mind still a mess. She could feel the tears welling up in her eyes.

"What happened?" Jack's voice boomed out of nowhere. "I heard you scream." His voice startled her, and she jumped back from the sink, holding her hand.

"I... I... um..." Sarah's mind was clouded by all the invading realities she was allowing in. She was unprepared to be looking at him face to face and struggled to gain her composure under her feelings of intimidation. "I burnt my hand taking the muffins out."

"You okay? Let me see it." He took a few steps toward her.

"No. I mean, yes. I'm okay. It's not that bad." Sarah countered with a few steps backward, which made Jack look at her funny. She knew it was a risky move, shutting down his help, but couldn't bear the thought of being that close to him. Not right now. Not while she was still trying to process and make sense of the connections her brain was busy making.

There was a single beep from the stove indicating it was still on. Saved by the beep. Sarah diverted her attention there and moved quickly away from Jack and over to the stove to turn it off. Although her hand felt like it was on fire, she did her best to act as though it were fine and went about her task of removing the muffins from the muffin pan, and placing them onto a towel on the counter. Never before had she felt so acutely aware of his presence. A part of her wanted to run from him. Another part of her wanted to confront him, but her fear and intimidation of him far outweighed her courage.

"What's wrong with you? You're acting weird," Jack said.

Sarah knew she had to hide her fears and accusations. She had to bury them deep and fast if she wanted to walk away from this conversation.

"Sorry. I'm okay. My hand just hurts a little, but it's okay." Sarah tried her best to act and sound as normal as possible. She avoided any lengthy eye contact with him to prevent any opportunity for him to see her real feelings.

She busied herself cleaning up the baking dishes. The warm, soapy water may as well have been a vat of acid. It made the burn on her hand flare up even more, but she winced and pressed through it, glad to keep her back to him. Without saying anything, Jack took a plastic container out of the drawer and placed the muffins inside.

"Those are still pretty warm. You might want to let them cool for a while yet before packing them up. I can do that later."

"No. I'll do it now. They can cool in the van."

Sarah wondered where he was going, torn between feelings of relief over the thought of him leaving, and the fear feeding the conspiracy theories now sprinting through her head. Sarah simply nodded and kept focused on the dishes. Jack finished packing up the muffins and disappeared into the bedroom. He emerged several minutes later with a small duffle bag, grabbed the container of muffins and headed out the door. Sarah stood at the sink, watching the van in her peripheral. She held it together until the van was out of view.

"Oh God," Sarah whispered as she lowered herself to the floor and cried. Images of the newscasts of Rachel McGinnis replayed through her already crowded mind. She knew. It was Jack. Deep down, she knew. Sitting on the floor, she pulled her knees into her chest and locked her hands together around them. It made her think she should pray, but she wasn't sure she even remembered how.

* * *

"I don't know, Teddy," Sarah said quietly. "This really isn't my thing."

"It didn't used to be my thing either, remember?" Teddy said with that charming grin that almost made her forget what they were talking about.

"But I feel scared," Sarah said, as she glanced away from Teddy's direction.

"Why?"

"Because I don't know what I'm doing," she said, embarrassed at her confession.

Teddy smiled at her. "I didn't know what I was doing at first either. Everyone is probably scared their first time. Afraid they'll screw it up."

Sarah looked up at him with a nervous look on her face, processing "screwing it up" as a possibility.

Teddy laughed at her expression, then softened his words after he could see her concern was genuine. "Look, you're not going to screw anything up. It's not like that. God's not like that. Praying is just a way of talking to him. Besides, I'll be doing it with you, so you won't be alone."

Ever since Teddy had his spiritual encounter, he had been spending a lot of time at one of the local Christian churches. Sarah had gone with him a couple of times now. Her family went to church on Christmas and Easter, with a few special events sprinkled in for good measure – baptisms, weddings, and even a first communion.

Teddy's church was something altogether new for her. She had never seen anything quite like it before. All the people at the service seemed very excited to be there, and they definitely liked to sing a lot. And raise their hands. Well, not everyone. Just some of them. When they were singing, some people would raise one or even both hands. It made her a little uncomfortable at first. She felt embarrassed for them, because it was so unusual, but Teddy really seemed to like it.

The pastor there seemed cool, but his words intimidated her a little. Not in a mean way. More that she didn't know where he learned to talk and pray like he did. It made her feel inadequate, like she did in this moment in Teddy's bedroom. He wanted her to pray with him, but she was scared she wouldn't know what to say or, worse, that she'd say something really stupid and Teddy would think less of her.

Teddy sat down next to her and offered his hands to her. She looked down at them, then nervously took them with her own. She was supposed to be entering into the presence of God, as Teddy would say, but she couldn't help feeling a little excited to be holding hands with him. Maybe she would just call that a perk. She and Teddy never formally dated, but she could feel a spark between them.

"Now, don't be afraid. You don't have to worry about saying anything wrong. God already knows what's in your heart, so just talk to him like you would me. Tell him what you feel. Tell him what you need help with." Teddy closed his eyes and bowed his head, so Sarah did the same, squinting one eye open to inconspicuously watch Teddy.

* * *

Sarah released the grip around her legs and let them fall back to the floor. She thought about that day in Teddy's bedroom, when they first prayed together. She wanted to feel that again. She wanted to feel that strange mix of fear and hope. She had the fear part down. Now she just needed hope. She remembered how Teddy closed his eyes and bowed his head, so she did that, and quietly prayed for help.

"God... it's me. Well, you know that. Sorry, I'm nervous. Anyway. I know it's been a really long time since I last talked to you. I'm sorry about that. I'm really scared right now, and I don't know what to do. I need help. I need help knowing what to do. And I think Rachel McGinnis needs your help too. Can you help her too?"

Sarah opened her eyes, then quickly shut them, as if forgetting something important. "Amen!"

She opened her eyes back up and stood to her feet. She found herself pacing back and forth in the kitchen, feeling unsettled. She found her attention returning again and again to the door. She felt like she should go, but she had no idea where. It sounded ludicrous though. Jack never permitted her to leave the house without him. Never. It was one of the foundational rules. Never leave without him. Every time she would try to go somewhere else or start doing something else, she would find herself back at the door.

Her heart raced, as she knew she had a big decision to make. Maybe this was God. Maybe he was actually answering her prayer and telling her what to do. Or maybe it was her own fear. She didn't know for sure. Then again, her fear would normally tell her to obey Jack. She stood still and silent for several minutes. She didn't move an inch, but just stared at the door. In one, unexpected and rapid moment, Sarah thrust open the door in front of her and walked down the driveway.

This is crazy. This is nuts. Jack is going to kill me if he finds out I left. She felt terrified but kept walking. To where, she had no idea. She just told herself to keep going.

Caroline Klug

CHAPTER 11

Star lay quietly for a few minutes while she took inventory of the different pains and discomforts across her body. Her arm and hand were partially falling out of the sling, and there was a dull throbbing pain working its way up her arm and into her shoulder. Her head still hurt, and her jaw was sore. She rotated both her ankles in a circular motion. The wounds where the metal had cut into her ankle were scabbing over, which made it hurt less when she brushed it across the mattress.

It took her a minute to realize her stomach had settled, and the involuntary shaking had eased a bit. Afraid the nausea would rush back and she'd be intimate with the floor drain once again, she lay there, flat on her back, not daring to move. The thought of calling that intimacy made her laugh a little on the inside, which turned into a strange rush of relief.

It occurred to her that her time in this prison was the longest she had gone in over a year without selling herself to a John. The idea of not having to do that brought a strange comfort to her, despite her terrifying circumstances. She tried to enjoy what little comfort came to her, but that was quickly overpowered by shame. She thought about all the Johns. There were so many. The more she thought of them, the more disgusted she felt with herself. How did it come to this? Starting over was a good thought but, even if she did get out of here and get a chance to start fresh, would that even be a possibility? What would people think of her if they knew what she was? What she had done? She wasn't sure she'd ever be able to escape the condemnation that would come with the names she had earned for herself. It might turn out to be a fresh start, or it might just be a different kind of prison. One where freedom was an illusion.

Star figured she couldn't feel any worse than she did in that moment, so she decided to try to sit up. Propping herself up with her good arm, she slowly guided herself to a sitting position and sat quietly while she assessed how she felt. No changes. That was good. She slid her legs over the side of the bed and onto the floor, waiting once more for anything to shift. The only change she felt was her bladder making its presence known.

Feeling more confident that her nausea had passed, Star stood to her feet, and walked slowly to the bucket. Letting out a small sigh, she worked her pants off with one hand and squatted carefully over the bucket to relieve herself. The cramping in her stomach made her realize she had to do more than pee. She hated this part, but knew she had no other options. Jack left a roll of toilet paper, which she was very grateful for. When she was finished, she walked the bucket over to the spicket and ran some of the cold water into it. It helped with the smell. Not completely, but enough to make it tolerable in the small room.

As Star set the bucket back up against the wall, she noticed a small section where the concrete was crumbling. She bent down and used her fingers to loosen one of the pieces to free it from the wall. It was smooth and flat on one side, and jagged on the other. It came to a small point, and she stood staring at it for a long while. Her eyes moved to the wall, then back to the stone, as if she were calculating an equation. Star raised the stone, pressed the sharp tip against the wall and moved it back and forth in a coloring motion. The sharp stone edge left a trail on the wall that was just visible enough to see. She cracked a faint smile at the idea of doing something other than stare at the ceiling. She wondered what she should draw. Something happy. Something that would take her emotionally away from this place, if even for the few moments it takes to look at it. There was the grassy knoll she always seemed to go to when she was high, but knew she needed a different association. She needed one that wasn't tied to her albatross. She closed her eyes and let her mind flow freely.

* * *

The sound of the waves was almost deafening, but it didn't frighten her. This was her first time being by the ocean, and she found it exhilarating. Her mom grew up in a rural farm community in the Midwest and had never been to the ocean before. She had been struggling since chemo ended, and her dad hoped a trip to the ocean would lift her mood. He hoped the salt air might provide some healing properties. It was something he heard from one of the natural healing doctors. She couldn't say much about that, but it was obvious the trip was helping lift her mom's spirits.

"Isn't this wonderful, Bean?" her mom said with a smile, as she dug her toes into the soft sand. Her dad was at the edge of the water, looking for those tiny crabs that burrow into the hard sand.

"I like it here," Star said, watching her dad run back and forth with the tide.

"Yeah? What do you like about it?" Star thought for a moment.

"I feel free here." Surprised, her mom turned her head and looked at her curiously.

"What do you mean by free?"

"I don't know. I mean, free... like there's no rules and there's just living. When I'm sitting here watching and listening to the waves, I feel like there's no such thing as good or bad. I'm just part of it. Whatever this is. Maybe that doesn't make any sense."

Her mom grabbed her hand and smiled. "I think it makes perfect sense. Bean..." She stopped, searching her own thoughts. "Sweetie, I know you think what's happening to me is bad."

Star squirmed under the discomfort of her words. She wasn't ready to acknowledge it, let alone talk about it.

"For a while, I felt like it was bad too. It was bad because it meant I might not get to be here with you and Dad. It was bad because I might not get to see you grow into a woman, get married and have kids of your own."

There were tears stinging Star's eyes, but she kept looking forward, so her mom couldn't see.

"That made me really sad. Actually, it made me angry. Really angry. I didn't think it was fair. I didn't think I deserved this and, even more, I didn't think you deserved this."

Star let out a small sob.

Her mom tightened the grip around her hand and continued. "But then I realized that was a selfish way of thinking about it."

Star turned her head slightly, as if to ask a question without using words.

"Do you remember Uncle Allen?"

Star nodded her head.

"Do you remember that he died in a car accident?"

Star nodded again.

"You were too little at the time to tell you, but he didn't just die in a car accident. He was hit by a seventeen-year-old teenager who was texting and accidentally crossed the center line."

Star's raised her eyebrows, now fully distracted by the story.

"I loved my brother. We were close. Always were. When I got to the hospital and found out he had just died, it was one of the worst moments of my life. I couldn't understand why God took him." Her mom paused and returned a wave to her husband. "I got a call last week." Her mom's voice cracked a little under the emotion that was welling up, and she took a second to collect herself. "It was the hospital calling to give me the contact information of one of the families who received some of Allen's organs. They wanted me to contact them."

Star shifted on her towel. "Did you?"

"Yes. I did." Her mom drew in a deep breath and smiled. "Turns out his heart went to a young man in Minnesota."

Star's eyebrows went up again.

"Do you remember the big story that was all over the news a few weeks ago, about that big bus explosion at a grade school in Madison?"

"Yes! We were just talking about that in school last week. About the miracle of all those kids being saved."

Her mom smiled again. "That miracle was the young man with Allen's heart. He and his family had moved to Madison a few months back. He happened to be there to pick up his son when that bus driver locked all those kids in the bus."

"Everyone at school was saying the bus driver was crazy. Like, mentally crazy, and that's why he had the bomb in there."

Her mom nodded. "That young man risked his life to save those kids, none of which were even his own son." She choked up again and took another deep breath. "Because of that man's bravery, twenty-three of the thirty-one kids were able to get off the bus before the bomb went off. Had they waited for police to show up, they all would have died in the blast. That man stayed on the bus trying to get as many off as he could. He died with the other eight." This time she couldn't hold back the tears, and it was Star now holding on to her hand. Her mom turned her body to face Star. "Twenty-three small and precious lives. Twenty-three tiny humans whose lives had hardly begun. Twenty-three future teachers and scientists and pastors and farmers and maybe even a president." Tears were spilling from her eyes, but she didn't look sad. "I know this *feels* bad. But what we see as bad and what God sees as bad are often very different things."

Star pulled away a little, wanting to hold on to her anger.

"Sweetie, please hear me. We can't see the bigger picture, but there is one. If Allen hadn't died that day, that young man who needed a heart may have and then all those kids might not have made it. Do you know what else?"

Star shook her head, still fighting her emotions.

"That girl who was texting and caused the accident... she lived. Do you know where she is now?"

Star looked up inquisitively.

"She's in a wheelchair. The accident paralyzed her from the waist down. But she writes books and speaks to kids in high school. She's dedicated her life to trying to prevent the kind of accident she caused. Because of her, who knows how many kids have made different decisions and how many lives that's saved, including their own."

"How do you know that?"

"After I talked to the other family, I looked her up. Do you see what I'm trying to say?"

Star nodded and let the sobs come.

Her mom wrapped her arms around her tightly. "I know, baby. I know. I don't know how God intends to use my cancer. We may not be able to see or understand what that means with the things we have to go through, but we have to remember that there's a reason for everything... these waves, the sun shining on us, our lives and the days we get to live them."

Star buried her face in her mom's shoulder and cried harder.

Her mom sat, rocking her and running her fingers through her long hair. "You said this place makes you feel free. Me too. I want you to know something. I'm not afraid anymore. I'm not afraid to go. I'm going to miss you and your dad, but I trust there's meaning to this that will help you or others someday. I don't have to let this rob me of peace. I don't have to be afraid and neither do you."

"Oh, Mommy!" blurted Star, as her crying now turned to uncontrollable sobs. Soon she could feel the arms of both her mom and dad around her. They sat in the sand, rocking her back and forth.

* * *

Star climbed onto the bed and knelt at the head of it, facing the wall, her mom's words ringing in her ears. Slowly and methodically, she rubbed the sharp edge of the stone back and forth, carving into the cement. She wished she could feel sun on her face or hear waves crashing onto the shore of the beach. Despite how painful it was at the time, she wished she could be back in that moment, enveloped in her mom's arms.

The familiar clink made her drop her stone, and she spun around on the bed to watch the heavy door open.

"How are you feeling?" Jack asked.

"Better," Star replied. After a few moments, his nose wrinkled a little, and Star knew he could smell the bucket. Embarrassed, her gaze hit the floor. "I'm sorry. I added water to it, so it didn't smell as bad."

"It's okay. It's not like you have a choice."

Star was surprised by his graciousness and watched him put his gloves on to remove the bucket from the room. There was another brown paper bag he left by the door, but she decided it wouldn't be smart to go rummaging through it. Jack came back a few minutes later, set the bucket back by the wall and grabbed the paper bag. He reached inside and pulled out what looked like a sub sandwich. It had a deli wrapper on it, and Star's mouth watered.

"It's turkey. I hope that's okay."

"Yes, that's great." Star paused and replied as meaningfully as she could. "Thank you."

Jack looked surprised. He smiled warmly. "If you're happy with that, I bet you'll be even more happy with this."

Reaching back into the bag, Jack pulled out a large plastic Ziplock bag filled with cookies. "Chocolate chip with walnuts!"

For the first time since she'd been in this hellhole, Star smiled. Jack handed her the bag. Like a little kid waiting for instructions on Halloween, Star sat patiently with the bag on her lap.

"Go ahead! Eat them!"

Star looked at Jack, then down at the bag. Realizing he was for real, she opened the bag and grabbed one of the cookies. She was about to put it into her mouth, but paused to offer him one.

"Nah. Go ahead. They're all yours."

Star shoved the cookie in her mouth and ate it in only a few bites. They weren't as good as her mom's cookies but, given her lack of options, they were delightful. Star ate three of the cookies before she stopped.

"Jack?"

"Yeah?"

Star opened her mouth to say something but stopped. She felt uncomfortable and adjusted her position a few times to stall her question. "I was wondering... would I be able to leave this place?" Her words were quiet, and she looked at Jack with the most submissive look she could muster, hoping her question didn't anger him.

He didn't seem upset, but simply looked at her for a minute. "I know this must all seem very, well, hard, but it's for your good. I do want to let you out of here. I just need to know the drugs are out of your system."

Star perked up. "They are! I'm feeling a lot better today. And I kept the food and cookies down!"

"I'm glad you're feeling better, but it's not that simple. It will take a little more time to make sure. It won't be safe for you to leave if you relapse."

Her shoulders dropped in disappointment, and she found herself glancing over her shoulder at the wall where she was carving.

Jack followed her eyes. "What's that?"

"Nothing. Well, just something that reminds me of my mom," Star replied, still looking at the wall. At that point, she didn't really care if he was upset or not about her carving into the wall, but he didn't react much to that. He seemed more intrigued with wanting to know about her mom.

"What is she like?" Star felt a sense of hesitation. She wasn't sure what to say. In one of the episodes of those police shows she watches, they talked about humanizing the victim. If she talked about her family, maybe that would soften him a little. Maybe he would see her as a real person and let her go.

"Was," Star said quietly.

"What?"

"Was. What *was* she like. She died."

Jack's face fell a little. "I'm sorry to hear that. What happened?"

"Cancer happened."

He didn't say anything and let the silence hang in the air until she continued.

"I miss her. I miss how things used to be with mom and dad. I wish I could go back and do it over." Star paused, surprised by her own revelation.

"What do you mean? Do what over?"

Star shrugged. "I don't know. All of it. I know going back wouldn't bring my mom back, but I could change how I handled it."

Now Jack looked fully engaged and seemed intrigued by how she felt. "What would you do differently if you could go back?"

"I used to listen to my friends talk about what things were like with their parents. The friends I was closest to, I could see for myself. In some cases, it was really awful. I mean, I knew I had it good, but I guess I never really appreciated how good. When my mom got sick, I was really scared. I didn't know what to do or say. I wanted to ask questions, but I was afraid of some of the answers, so I guess I just didn't talk much about it. Kind of buried it inside." Star paused again, looking lost in her own thoughts.

"What about your father? Were you close to him?"

The present thought of her dad stirred hope in her heart. "Yeah. Well, no. I mean, we were. Before I left home."

"Why did you leave?"

"That's one of the things I would do differently," Star said quietly, feeling the weight of her words. "When mom died, I didn't know how to handle it. I... I got really angry. At everything. Everyone. Including my dad. I know he must have been hurting, and I just kind of heaped on that with how I behaved. Even though I was a total brat, he still did his best to love me and help me. I think he was afraid too."

"What do you mean?"

"Afraid of something happening to me I think."

"Why do you say that?"

"He got a lot more protective after it was just the two of us. He asked a lot more questions and wouldn't let me go hang out with my friends. That just made me angrier. I argued with him a lot. I wanted to do what I wanted and thought I could do that if I was on my own."

"How old were you?"

Star paused. "Seventeen." Her gaze hit the floor again. She looked up just long enough to get a glimpse of Jack's face, but she couldn't read his expression. "I didn't know what I was getting myself into. By the time I did know, I didn't know how to get out." Tears formed in her eyes. "I get it now. I get what my dad was trying to do, and I didn't even appreciate it. I had it so good. Even with losing my mom, I had it good. I miss them both so much. I would give anything to see my dad. Anything." She had said more than she wanted to, but looked up at him with tear filled eyes, hoping to hear him agree.

Jack's face fell a little again, and this time she could read the expression on his face. It wasn't good. He let out a sigh.

"I was hoping to have a little more time to tell you this, but..."

Star felt her chest tighten. "What? Is my dad okay?" she said, her tone heightened.

"Yes, he's okay. It's just–"

"How do you know he's okay? Did you see him? Wait. Does he know I'm here?" She sat up straighter.

Jack put his hands up, as if to ask her to stop talking and let him finish. "Yes," Jack said somberly. "Yes, I spoke with him, and yes, he knows where you are."

Star beamed a smile larger than she had in years. "Oh my gosh! I can't believe it. Thank you! Thank you so much!" Star practically bounced on the bed. "I can't believe I'm going to see him. There are so many things I need to say to him. So many things to–"

"Star, stop!"

Star quieted, trying to understand what the urgency in his voice meant.

"Please let me finish. There's some things I need to tell you."

Star remained quiet and fidgeted with her fingers, sensing she wouldn't like what he wanted to share.

Jack sighed again. "After I got you here, I tracked down your father."

"Where was he?"

"It doesn't matter. I spoke to him and told him where you were. I told him... I told him where I found you and what you were doing."

The color drained from Star's face and she looked at Jack, partly sad and partly angry. A part of her hoped he could read the sense of invasion on her face.

Jack sighed. "I thought it was important for him to know what happened to you if he was going to help you. I thought I could help him get prepared before he saw you."

"What did he say?" she asked quietly.

Jack paused again and let his eyes linger along the bottom of the bed frame.

"I'm sorry, Star. I really am. I tried. I tried to help him understand that you could change."

Star's heart raced as she could feel her worry welling up inside. "What do you mean? Why? What did he say?"

"There's no easy way to say this, so I'm just going to say it." Jack looked hard into her eyes so there was no mistaking his words. "He's angry at you for what you've done... for what you've become. He said he doesn't want anything to do with you. He doesn't want you to contact him and he doesn't want me to anymore either. He said we should both just stay away."

Star felt sick, as the dark pit in her stomach overtook her, and tears came spilling from her eyes. "What?" she spoke rapidly, working hard to get the words out around her sobs. "I don't understand. I need to talk to him. I need to explain. He's my dad. I know he loves me. I know he would want to talk to me. I just have to try."

Jack sat on the bed next to her and put his hand on her leg. "I wish that were the case. I didn't want to have to tell you this, but I think you need to hear it, so you don't make things worse when you get out of here."

Star's head was spinning. She heard him say she was getting out of here, but her mind barely processed it through the confusion and fear of what she was hearing.

"Star, he knows what you did, and he's... well... he said he's ashamed of you. He said he can't bear to look at you and that's when he said he doesn't want either of us to contact him ever again."

Alligator tears now spilled from her eyes as she sat, unable to speak. Grief and regret crashed against her like waves, and she felt unable to breathe under the weight of them.

Jack grabbed her hand and talked softly. "There's more."

Star listened, but remained silent.

"You obviously haven't seen the news recently. The police had someone undercover in your prostitution ring and they made a major bust. Broke the whole thing up and arrested a bunch of people. They know who you are, Star, and they're looking for you."

This got her attention and she turned to look at Jack.

"They issued a warrant for your arrest."

"What?" she stammered. "But why?"

"What you were doing. You were selling sex. That's illegal. You can do a long time in jail for that. They could put you away for good."

"They can?" She was trembling.

Jack nodded.

"What am I going to do? Where am I going to go?" Star wiped the tears from her eyes.

Jack put one arm around her. "I know this all seems very confusing and scary," he said, "but I just want you to know that I'm here to help you. I'll help you through all this."

Star looked up at him, still crying.

"If I were you, I'd stop crying and try to move on. It's not worth crying over. I mean, look – your father is willing to throw you away because of what you've done. He sees you as unclean. He's willing to throw you away like trash."

Star cried harder now.

"I know this is a lot to process, but you also need to accept the consequences for your actions and decisions. You made the decisions that made you who you are. Those decisions are making your father not want to be in your life anymore, and those same decisions are what's causing the police to be looking for you, and probably will put you away for life. You think this room is bad? Think about one half this size, and for the rest of your life."

Star was now sobbing, her shoulders heaving up and down.

"Look at me."

Star kept her head down.

"Look at me, Star."

She tried to take a breath in and slowly lifted her head.

"Do you want me to help you?"

Star nodded yes between the involuntary sniffles.

"Okay then. I'll help you. But you've got to do what I say. Everything I say. Or this won't work. Or you'll end up in a jail cell. Do you understand me?"

Star nodded again, trying to regain her composure.

Jack got up from the bed and walked to the door. "Try to keep your mind off this. Just accept the consequences and be happy that you'll get to move on from this. It may not be the way you thought it would be, but you'll get to move on. There's a set of fresh clothes in the bag by the bed," he said, pointing to the bag. "Why don't you put those on? You can wash the clothes you have on now with the water spicket and hang them over the end of the bed frame to dry."

Star heard his words but sat silently, trying to stop the involuntary motions of grief unfurled.

CHAPTER 12

Over and over, Sarah repeated to herself, "This is crazy. This is nuts," as she continued to walk down the long road into town. It hadn't occurred to her until this moment how long the road was. It stretched out as far as she could see. Sarah felt vulnerable and exposed. There was no place to hide if a car came. And what if it was Jack? She found herself quickening her pace.

Her mind was reeling from all the little things she had been putting together. Jack leaving at all hours. The hair dye. The walnuts. The sketches. There were so many little things all equaling a very big thing she could no longer ignore. Not at the expense of someone who might need help.

Sarah could hardly remember the last time she had walked down a road alone. She wrapped her arms around herself, as if it were winter and she was tightening an imaginary jacket. Any arms around her seemed comforting. Even if they were her own.

* * *

Sarah threw herself onto her bed and screamed with her face in her pillow. Hot tears burned her eyes as they mixed with mascara. She sat up to grab a tissue, feeling indignant at the mess around her. Some of it she had caused, and some of it had just happened. Sarah felt like the cosmic hand of doom was looming over her.

Part of her wanted to go talk to Teddy. He always knew what to say to make her feel better, but a small part of her resented him for that. His words of hope. She knew he meant well, but hope had eluded her over this last year, and the last thing she wanted to hear was any more religious rhetoric. He would tell her that everything happens for a reason and would make her a better person.

Sarah snorted angrily and wondered what exactly a better person was, anyway. Better than who? Didn't we all have our mud? Mud can come in various shades but, at the end of the day, it's all the same.

Sarah drew in a deep breath and tried not to think about the funeral. She tried not to think about walking up to the casket. That cold, dark box containing a dead body on display. She found herself shaking her head in disgust at whoever originally thought that would be a good idea.

The counselor had assured her it was for closure. She assured him she already knew her mom was dead. He didn't think that was funny, but neither did she. Her dad wanted her to keep seeing the shrink, but she had already made up her mind after the first five minutes with him that she wouldn't be going back. She'd rather just go over to Teddy's and give him a series of obligatory mm-hm's. At least Teddy wouldn't force her to talk. Teddy was pretty good for that.

He was a great listener, but he also had a strange gift for knowing when Sarah just needed to share space. It's like he could read it on her face. He would go on and on about something meaningless, while Sarah just sat and listened. Sometimes it was about football. Sometimes it was about stuff he was doing at his new church. Sometimes it was just random things on social media. Regardless, she appreciated having a place to go where she didn't have to talk about her feelings.

Deep down, she knew her dad was trying to be there for her, even if it was awkward. That just heaped guilt on top of all the terrible things she was already feeling. There was so much she didn't know how to deal with, so avoidance became her best friend. That hurt her dad more, which just heaped on more guilt. It was a vicious cycle. Sarah could see no way out without actually sitting down with him and spilling her emotions, and that wasn't something she was willing to do. It was too hard. It would break her. And then she wouldn't know how to put herself back together.

She had to stop thinking about it. She couldn't let that level of pain in. It was too much. It was all too much. Every single thing around her reminded her of her mom. The thought that had been circling around in her mind for the last month was coming to rest hard on her now. She stared ahead, lost in thought. With a single tear running down her cheek, she got up, opened the closet door, and pulled out her backpack. She spent the next hour carefully selecting only things she thought she would really need, then sat at her desk to write her dad a note. It felt like an impossible task. What would she say? What *could* she say?

Sarah sat staring at the blank piece of paper, knowing there was nothing that would make him understand her choice. After another minute, she penned a few lines, folded the note and placed it on her pillow. She knew she needed to disconnect from the flood of emotions trying to bust down her door, or she'd never walk out. Sarah stiffened herself, mentally and emotionally, swung her backpack over her shoulder and walked out the door. She had one place to stop first.

"Hey!" Teddy said to her as she stood outside his kitchen door.

"Hi," Sarah said, running a hand over her eyes.

"What's wrong?"

"Nothing. I just wanted to see you and say..." Sarah paused, looking into Teddy's concerned eyes. "Nothing really. Just wanted to say hi. Can I come in for a few minutes?"

Teddy quickly moved to the side and gestured her in. Sarah moved past him and went right up to his bedroom. Teddy followed.

"Coach was being a real dick today," Teddy said.

Sarah threw her backpack down and sat on his bed.

Teddy was as predictable as the sunrise. He knew exactly when she just needed to share space.

"He ran us hard and when Tom laid on the ground for a second to catch his breath, Coach said if we had time for that then we'd have time for a hundred burpees."

Sarah could hear Teddy talking but wasn't paying much attention to what he was saying. She walked over to his closet and looked through his clothes on the hangers. Once in a while, she'd pull one out and hold it up against herself as if she were shopping in a department store.

"Mark fell over the side of the bench and everyone started laughing. Coach got mad again and made us do even MORE burpees. Man, I'm gonna be so sore tomorrow morning."

"Can I have this?" Sarah was holding up one of his jerseys. Teddy furrowed his brow and gave her a confused look.

"Like, have have?" Teddy asked. "Or like, borrow have?"

"I don't know. Probably borrow have."

Teddy thought for a minute, then shrugged his shoulders in a silent act of permission.

Sarah laid the jersey on top of her backpack and walked over to his window. "Do you ever wonder where you'd be right now if your dad was still alive?"

The question seemed to catch Teddy by surprise. He stood silently, trying to process the intent of her question. Even though Teddy was a good-sized kid who was often mistaken for being tough and intimidating, he was really quite sensitive when it came to people's emotions and needs. Sarah understood the sensitivity of her question, and she also knew she was one of the only people who could ask him that without him feeling attacked or offended. Sarah continued to stare out the window, not making any eye contact with him, giving him the space he needed to think.

"Um..." Teddy stalled. "I... I don't know. I guess maybe I'd still be here, playing football and stuff."

"What about the God stuff?" Sarah said, her back still to him.

"What's wrong? You seem off. Are you okay?"

"I haven't been okay for a long time now." Sarah could feel the emotion welling in her throat but pushed it down. "But that doesn't matter. I was just curious." She turned to face him. "You're in such a good place right now. All that bad stuff that happened to you... is the God stuff the reason you're doing good now, or not?"

Teddy stood searching her face, looking for anything to help him with his answer.

"I'm not sure how to answer that but, I guess so. Yeah."

Sarah smiled at him, seemingly happy with his answer, but struggling to figure out the mess going on inside of her. She wanted Teddy's answer to be her answer, but she didn't think it could be that simple.

"Seriously, are you okay? What can I do to help you?"

"I have to go. I just wanted to say hi." Sarah pushed her way past him toward the door, then stopped and turned to him again. "And Teddy, I just wanted to say how much I appreciate our friendship. You've been there for me when no one else was. With you, I could always just be myself. You're really a great guy, and I'm so glad you're happy now." Sarah moved toward him and threw her arms around his shoulders, giving him a tight hug. Then she let go and hurried out the door and down the stairs.

"Wait!" Teddy called after her. "I feel like something's wrong. What's wrong? Talk to me."

"Sorry, I have to go. I'm okay. I'm going to be okay." Sarah couldn't bring herself to look back. She hurried through the kitchen and out the side door. She made it look like she was heading back to her house, in case he was watching. She assumed he would be. Once she knew she was out of sight, she walked around the other side of her house and headed down the street toward the bus station. She still had Teddy's jersey in her hand. She pulled it up to her nose and drew in the smell. Tears ran down her cheeks and wet the jersey. The wind picked up, and she shivered as she tightened her coat around her.

* * *

The sound of the oncoming vehicle made Sarah's heart pound and the palms of her hands sweat. It was a long way down, but she could already tell it was smaller than a van. She released the breath she was holding and picked up her pace even more. The fast walk was leaving her short of breath and her legs were already getting tired.

Sarah walked about a mile and a half before making the turn towards town. It wouldn't be far now. Just a few more blocks. For as long as that road felt, being exposed and all, she realized how close she had been to what she referred to as civilization. All these years, she was only a few miles from the town she only saw once a week, if she was well behaved.

She wondered to herself how many years it had been. Four? No, five. Sarah could see where the line of houses faded into small shops and cafes. As she walked past each of the houses, she looked through the windows, wondering what life was like for each of those families. She wondered if any of them were like hers. A woman out working in her garden gave her a smile and a wave. Sarah shyly returned her wave and kept her eyes on what the woman was working on for as long as she could without it seeming weird.

She had lived so long in her current world that so much out here seemed foreign to her. It was true that she and Jack traveled down this very path almost weekly but, for some reason, there was so much she had never seen. So much she'd never paid any attention to. Maybe because she was so anxious to get where she was going, which was anywhere but the house, that she forgot to pay attention to where she was along the way.

Sarah passed another house that had a beautiful garden trestle lined with purple flowers and green leaves. There was a comfortable-looking bench and a little waterfall next to it. It was just the kind of place she would enjoy sitting down and reading. She would love to create a space like that, but Jack was uncomfortable with her being outside too long. Gardens were out of the question, let alone any kind of space she could spend any serious time in. It was for her own good. That's what Jack would say. It was for her protection.

Jack's words, which had circled around in her mind for so long, continued to play as she walked. With each old, pre-recorded thought was a new thought and, dare she say, hope, rising to take a stand. She had never felt such a myriad of emotions all crammed into such a small space. There was fear and terror. There was bravery and hope. There was confusion and speculation. There was curiosity and desire. Walking out in the open like this, all alone, was the most empowered she'd felt in a long time. It was also the most frightened she'd been in a long time.

Her mind was so occupied, she didn't realize she had reached the area where all the shops were until she found herself in the middle of a bustling Saturday crowd. Sarah was aware of the discomfort creeping up around her, feeling surrounded by so many strangers. She was about to cross the street where it looked less busy, when she came to a large opening. It looked like a large picture window, but there was no glass in it, creating an outdoor feel for the customers sitting there. Looking inside, she could see a long bar and TVs everywhere. One of them had a news channel on, and she was struck by a picture of Rachel McGinnis.

Sarah came to a jarring stop in front of the window, as the anchorwoman introduced the replay of a video conference with Rachel's parents. There she stood, in the middle of the bustling crowd, like a rock in the middle of a stream diverting water on either side. Her eyes were fixed on the television, completely unaware of the people pushing their way around her. She watched as a couple in their mid-forties walked behind the podium and adjusted the mic height. She felt her heart ache for them even before a word came out of their mouths.

"We're here today to talk to whoever took our little girl."

Rachel's dad began, but his voice broke and he was quiet for a moment while he swallowed down the emotions. Her mom's tears had already started.

"This is our daughter, Rachel McGinnis," he said, while holding up that same picture of her with her black lab. "We're asking... no, begging you... please... if you have our daughter, please let her go. She's a good person. We know she might have made some choices that put her in a bad place, and that may be why you took her, but she's a good person. She loves people and animals and has a loving personality and a big heart."

He stopped again for a moment, choked up. He took a deep breath and continued. "Please, just bring her somewhere safe. Or call and tell us where we can find her. All we care about is getting her back safely. That's all."

The mother looked overwhelmed as she pulled the microphone toward her and spoke almost frantically. "Rachel, sweetie, if you're seeing or hearing this, Mom and Dad love you so much! We're looking for you and we'll never stop looking for you!"

The woman broke down, holding her face in her hands as she cried. Her husband put his arms around her and held her there as the video faded back to the anchorwoman. This time, the FBI agent from the newscast Sarah had seen earlier was sitting next to her.

"What we just watched was a replay of an emotional plea from Mr. and Mrs. McGinnis, begging for the return of their daughter, Rachel. It's hard to watch again. So much emotion." The anchorwoman paused as if collecting herself. "Here with us is Special Agent Emmanuel Grant. Agent Grant, is there anything new you can tell us?"

Agent Grant leaned forward with his hands folded and his elbows on the news desk. "If you recall, the last time we provided an update we were looking into similarities with past cases which have gone cold. We believe we're dealing with a man, who has been abducting and killing local women for the past decade or so. Witnesses at the scene of Rachel's abduction provided details which mirror that of five cold cases we have on file. Two of the girls we're going to show you were found deceased."

Pictures of two girls were displayed on the screen.

"sixteen-year-old Amanda Kline was found deceased in a body of water just north of the Milwaukee Zoo. Seventeen-year-old Rhonda Shay was found just west of that, in Underwood Creek."

Sarah scanned their faces, feeling relieved to know neither of them.

"The next two girls we're going to show you were reported missing, but their bodies were never recovered." The screen changed to display their faces. "First is eighteen-year-old Alexa Albert, and next is sixteen-year-old Cami Roberts. The girls were from the Wauwatosa and West Allis areas, respectively."

Sarah froze as she looked at Cami Roberts. Could it be? She stared intently at Cami's face, her memory thrusting her back to that cold October Homecoming morning when she went to school early for practice. The girl in the warming well. She wondered if it was really her. They had never exchanged names that day, and now she wished she would have been kind enough to ask.

Sarah's eyes moved from Cami's face down to the necklace she was wearing in the picture. A silver chain with a silver dolphin. The sick feeling in her stomach returned, and she turned her attention to the man sitting down at the bar ordering a beer. He and the bartender were talking as if nothing else was going on. As if nothing was wrong with our world and no parents were missing their teenage kids.

Agent Grant continued. "All missing persons reports were consistently filed over summer months, which indicates a pattern. We're going to show you the artist renderings again of the suspect in question, along with the vehicle police believe him to be using during the abductions."

The anchorwoman took her cue from Agent Grant and nodded at the screen, and then the picture cut away to the drawings.

Sarah found herself face to face with a sketch of Jack and their van. She had dismissed it the first time she'd seen it, but now, all the dots she'd been connecting came pouring over her like molten lava. She felt her knees weaken and grabbed onto the brick wall beside her to steady herself.

Sarah flashed a nervous look throughout the bar, worrying people would recognize Jack from the sketch and know she was with him. It was a ridiculous thought, and she could tell most of the people in here weren't even paying attention to the screen, but her nerves still got the better of her. She expected everyone to turn around and look at her, but the man at the bar continued to drink his beer and the few tables of people carried on with conversation as though nothing interesting was on. Maybe they had seen enough. Maybe they just didn't care. Sarah wanted not to care, but she knew she had to. She had seen too much to deny it any longer. It was Jack. It had to be Jack.

The nerves and anxiety running through her caused her to begin shaking, and she thought she might be sick right there on the street. She knew that would draw too much attention, so she hurried into the bar and to the bathroom. She could hear the agent talking as she jogged past the bar.

"We have one more case to highlight of a missing girl from the West Allis area from five years ago."

Sarah ran to the first open stall, fell to her knees and wrapped her arms around the base of the toilet while she retched. She was too sick to care about what she might be touching. She was so disoriented, she didn't even realize what she was kneeling in was wet.

When she was finished, she eased herself off the floor and moved slowly over to the sink. Grabbing both sides of the sink with her hands, she stared dejectedly at the image of herself. After a minute or two, she turned on the cold water, washed her hands and rinsed out her mouth.

She had to get out of there, but she still didn't know what to do. She thought about finding the police station but worried it would only land her in a cell, like Jack had warned. She knew there was a warrant out for her arrest and she didn't want to end up back in a prison.

With her thoughts spiraling, she walked out of the bathroom and headed for the door. On her way out, she glanced one more time at the television, just as the image was changing back to the anchorwoman. Her pulse quickened, and she rushed back into the bar, standing frozen in front of the TV as her brain tried to catch up with the image she had only caught a momentary glimpse of. It looked like her dad.

"Not possible," she said out loud. She felt like she was losing it. It couldn't have been him.

Agent Grant spoke again. "The connections between this case from five years ago and Rachel's prompted us to reach out to the father. He's agreed to join forces and reintroduce his daughter's case, in the hopes of solving both."

Sarah watched as they rolled the same clip she'd seen a day or so earlier about the van in the abduction she'd thought was too new to be theirs. The clip started right at the point when Jack had ripped the cord out, but now she was seeing the rest of it roll.

"What you're seeing is what the van would have looked like at the time of the abduction five years earlier. The artist's rendering we've been showing you is what we believe the van looks like today, taking into account natural aging along with eyewitness testimony from Rachel's abduction. In a few hours, Mr. Gregor will be joining us. We will be re-broadcasting his original plea and then he'll be here with us live in the studio."

Sarah could feel the color fading from her face. She felt as though every bit of warmth was draining from her body and out through her feet.

"Thank you, Agent Grant. We appreciate your time and updates." The anchorwoman turned back to the camera, addressing the audience. "We'll be back here at 6 p.m. This is WIML, your source for the local news and live alerts."

Sarah could hardly process what she had just heard. Was it possible they were talking about the same person? Could it really be her dad? Sarah scanned the walls for a clock. She had to know what time it was. She walked over to a couple at one of the tables and tried to act as normal as possible while she asked for the time.

"3:05 p.m.," said a woman in a bright green top. The woman scanned Sarah from top to bottom. "Hey, are you okay?"

Sarah nodded and rushed out of the bar. She stood looking in each direction, reeling in disbelief.

CHAPTER 13

Star lay on her back, staring up at the ceiling. She had counted each of the visible imperfections so many times she could almost do it without looking. It felt like weeks had passed. Maybe more. She wasn't sure anymore. She closed her eyes to try to do just that, but it was an ineffective distraction from the thoughts of all the things Jack had told her about her dad.

Star sighed involuntarily, and tears welled in her eyes once more. The pit in her stomach pressed her into the bed like an anvil. Her mouth was dry, and she could see the empty water bottle on the floor beside the spicket. She sighed again, trying to will herself to sit up, but the heaviness she felt held her down. She suddenly found herself craving the heroin. It could help with the pain and the empty feeling gnawing at her from the inside out. It could make all of it go away for a little while.

Star let out a deep moan and beat her fist on the mattress. How could she entertain such thoughts? Why would she run to something that made her dad hate her? Her stomach started to roll again. She rolled onto her side and curled up in a ball like a small child.

Time went by slowly.

With each passing minute, Star came closer to acceptance of her new normal. It wasn't hope that got her there. It was hopelessness. Without her dad, she had no one. If her dad wouldn't accept her back, surely no one else in her life would. Star remained curled up facing the wall as the heavy, metal door unlocked and swung open.

Jack walked in carrying a couple of brown paper bags in one hand, and a coiled-up hose with the other. After shutting the door behind him, he set the bags down, and let the hose slide onto the floor.

She startled when the metal end of it hit the concrete floor and flipped over so she could face him. She followed the noise down to the floor, and the color ran out of her face when she saw the hose, thinking about the first time Jack used it on her.

"It's not for bathing," Jack said, as if reading the question in her eyes.

"What?" Star said, looking back and forth between Jack and the hose.

"It's for your hair." Jack reached down into one of the bags and pulled out a box of hair dye — the kind you get from the local supermarket that only carries the cheap brand.

Star could see the picture on the box of a woman with long, platinum blonde hair. She swallowed hard as she grabbed her own long, black hair into two ponytails, pulling the locks over her shoulders and holding them tight with both hands, as if somehow protecting it.

Jack bent over and pulled a pair of scissors from the bag and placed them, sharp side down, into his front pocket. Star's eyes grew large as her mind raced with frantic thoughts. No. No, I don't want to cut my hair. I *can't* cut my hair. It's what makes me pretty. Cutting it would just disappoint him more. Star lowered her head and cried, shaking her head back and forth, still gripping the mass of her black locks with both hands.

* * *

"What, Dad?" Star slapped her pen dramatically onto the table.

"Oh, nothing," he said with a smile. "You're just so beautiful. That's all."

Star smiled, keeping her eyes on her homework. She wasn't mad, exactly, but she wasn't ready for eye contact yet, either.

"Seriously, Bean. Have you seen yourself? Those beautiful, brown eyes and all that long, gorgeous, black hair? I'm going to have to sit on the porch out front with a shotgun to keep all the boys away."

"Dad!" Star said, trying not to laugh.

"You look more and more like your mother every day. You should thank her for your looks. You definitely got them from her!"

This time, she couldn't help but smile, and the tension that was hanging between them finally broke.

He pulled out the chair across from her and sat down. "You know, Bean, in all seriousness, I want you to remember something."

Star stopped playing with her pen and looked up at him.

"It's true. You are beautiful. And I'm not just saying that because I'm your dad and I have to."

Star smiled.

"You really are gorgeous. It's going to be easy for you to get things because of your looks. It will be easy for you to manipulate people and get them…" He paused. "Get men, to do things for you because of how you look. Don't rely on your looks to lead you through life. Looks fade. But you know what doesn't?"

Star waited for him to continue.

"Character and personality. It's okay for people to recognize your outward beauty, but let people see how smart you are, how caring and how funny. Let them see how you do the right thing no matter what, and especially when no one is looking. Let them see how kind you are to others and how you look to help others before yourself. If you can do those things, I guarantee you will be successful in life."

Star grinned at her dad. "Does that mean I can't blow off my math test in favor of a scary movie with you?"

Her dad laughed.

"Yes! That's exactly what it means! But I'll make you a deal. If you promise not to rush through it, and all your answers are correct when I check it, I'll let you stay up long enough to watch a short one. It has to be ninety minutes or less. Deal?"

"Deal!"

* * *

Jack sighed. "I'm sorry for this, Star, but with how you are right now, I feel it would be best to, well, secure you, while I do this."

She knew exactly what he meant and cried a little harder as she watched him walk over and grab the metal shackle hanging off the wall. The sound of the chain across the floor was like nails on a chalkboard as he walked toward her. She didn't like it but had nothing left in her.

"He wouldn't like it." Star mumbled.

"What? Who wouldn't like it?"

"My dad." Star's eyes remained on the floor.

Jack sighed loudly and worked the shackle around her ankle until it clicked in place. Star winced, more at the thought of it.

"I thought we talked about this. I don't want to seem uncaring by bringing it back up, but your father was clear. He doesn't want to see you or have a relationship with you anymore, so what does it matter what he would think anyway?"

Star's lower lip quivered, and she hid her face from him.

"I get it. It stinks, but this is all for your good. I'm trying to help you. Your father won't help you, but I will. Can you see that?"

Star studied his face intently.

"I'm the only person right now that seems to care. Do you believe that?"

Star slowly nodded. In this moment, she realized she actually did believe him. He was right. Her dad was clear about how he felt. In his eyes, she was already ugly, so what did it matter?

Star sniffled and wiped her nose against the sleeve of her shirt. She sat up a little straighter and let go of any defensive posture she might have had.

Jack smiled approvingly. He grabbed the bucket from the room and went outside to empty it. When he came back in, he used the hose to rinse it a few times and send the runoff down the floor drain.

"Come over here." Jack pointed to the bucket. He guided her down into a kneeling position and pulled her forward, so her hair was flipped over the bucket. One arm was still in a sling, so it took her a moment to balance herself right.

Star tightened her one-handed grip on the bucket as the cold water hit her scalp and neck. It was freezing, but probably what she needed to shake her from this lethargy.

"I used to help Annie dye her hair when we were in high school," Jack said, switching the hose to his other hand. "She liked experimenting with the color. It would make our parents mad sometimes, when she did something they thought was embarrassing. But I kind of liked it. I liked that she didn't care, but I think I mostly liked it because she let me help. She liked feeling like she was at a salon. Sometimes we would play that up and I would offer her drinks and pillows and dumb stuff like that."

Jack wrapped a towel around her hair to soak up the extra water. He grabbed her by her armpits, and pulled her up to a standing position. He emptied the remaining water from the bucket and flipped it upside down, so she could sit on it while he worked. Star sat motionless and accepting while Jack brushed her wet hair straight. Out of the corner of her eye, she could see him grab the silver scissors from his pocket. Her wet hair made her shirt damp all the way down her back. In seconds, Jack had taken a large lock of her hair and cut it just below her ear.

Star could feel the dull side of the scissors against her neck and could see the length of the lock hit the floor, but she was dead to the emotion of it now. In her mind, she knew how she was supposed to feel about it, but complacency took the place of her anxiety, and she sat, unflinching, as he worked his way around until it was all cut evenly under her ears.

"I'm sorry about your father."

Star stayed quiet for a moment, before responding. "Thanks."

Jack opened the hair dye box and took out its contents. "After my parents found out what Annie was doing, it was like they were torn between grieving and anger. Honestly, I think they were embarrassed more than anything. It wasn't how they raised us, and they thought others would judge them. I think that's why they stopped talking about it altogether." Jack took a clean bath towel out of one of the bags and draped it over Star's shoulders. "Maybe that's part of what your father is feeling." He grabbed the plastic gloves that came in the box and stretched them over his hands. "I was always kind of mad at them for that. It was like they forgot about me and what I needed when I was trying to get through it all."

Jack combined the two tubes of liquid, secured the top and vigorously shook the tube. Then he broke off the tip of the tube and squirted the dye in lines across Star's scalp.

Star spoke abruptly. "Are they still alive?"

He didn't answer but continued to work the thick liquid through her hair, giving special care to her side burns and hair line.

"No," he said after a few minutes. "They got into a car accident about a year after Annie died."

For the first time, Star found herself feeling pity for Jack, and saw him as an imperfect and hurting human. "I'm sorry. That must have been really hard for you."

When Jack was done working all of the dye in, he peeled off his gloves, so they ended up inside out, and tossed them into the hair dye box with the empty tubes.

"I can see you're listening and trying to work with me. That's good. It won't be long now."

"Until what?"

"Until you can leave this place."

A bolt of adrenaline ran through her at the thought of leaving and she sat up straighter.

"Really?" Her tone was lighter than it had been in the last few days.

"Yes. If you continue to trust me, I promise things will get better. I know you don't like what I've done to your hair, but it's to protect you. I think you're serious about turning your life around and I don't want to see you go to jail for the rest of your life."

Star let her mouth hang open while she took in a quick breath.

"The rest of my life?" she said, with a small crack in her voice.

"Yes, probably. With as much as they busted that ring for, and you being so directly involved and all, it could really go bad for you. I guess there were even some gang murders and stuff that they were saying the whole ring was involved in."

Star stammered a little. "Murders? I was never involved in any murders!"

"I believe you. But I don't think they will. I don't think it matters because if they can prove you're a part of the group, which they already did based on the news, then they can charge you like the rest of them."

Star sat quietly, digesting his words. She didn't know much about the law and, although some of her common sense told her what he was saying wouldn't be that simple, she still didn't know for sure. Regardless, the thought scared her, and she kept quiet.

Neither of them said anything over the next ten minutes while the hair dye cured, although Jack checked his watch occasionally.

"Okay. Time's up. I'll need you to get back on your knees and bend forward, so I can rinse it out."

Star did as he asked and gripped the side of the bucket in anticipation of the arctic water about to pour over her. The cold water sent shivers up her spine, and she arched her back in response to it.

Jack's chest brushed against her back as he leaned in to rinse her hair. She could feel his breath on her now bare neck and shivered uncontrollably. Star lost her grip on the bucket and fell forward, causing Jack to fall with her. As he threw out a hand to stop his fall, the scissors slipped from his pocket. Star's shackle clattered across the floor, and Jack looked over at her as the scissors hit the floor and skittered under the bed.

"Whoa!" yelled Jack.

"Sorry." Star responded, as she eased herself back onto her hands and knees.

"It's okay." Jack tipped the bucket back up and allowed Star to get back on her knees in front of the bucket, with her head tipped forward.

Star hardly noticed the cold water this time, as her eyes were fixed on the point where the scissors had slid under the bed. She waited for Jack to stop what he was doing to go get them, but he didn't. She wondered if he hadn't realized what happened.

When Jack was finished, he grabbed both ends of the towel draped around her shoulders and pulled them up and around her hair. He pulled her shoulders back, then guided her into a sitting position on the floor. Star sat with her legs folded as he used the towel to rub her hair like someone might towel dry their dog. Jack took the brush out again and ran it through her hair several times, until it was all straightened out.

"There!" he exclaimed proudly. "This looks good. You look good. It's going to be okay."

In the absence of any mirrors, Star grabbed the sides of her hair and pulled her hair as far up to her eyes as the length would allow. She could see the bottom few inches of it, and it was definitely blonde. She wasn't prepared for how different it would look. Her black beauty was gone and she fought the urge to cry. If she wanted to get out of here, it was best to just accept it. She needed to keep reinforcing that she trusted him and would go along with what he told her.

"Thank you," Star said.

Jack turned toward her, a little surprised. "You're welcome."

He pointed, and Star moved off the floor and onto the bed while he cleaned up. After everything was packed up, he rinsed the floor a few more times and then placed the bucket back against the wall by the spicket. Right before he left, he reached into one of the bags, pulled out a soft-sided lunch cooler, and unzipped it. He took out a wrapped sandwich, a pear, a bag of chips, and a new bottle of water, and handed it all to her as she sat on the bed.

As if no longer expecting a thank you, Jack grabbed the bags and headed out the door. She could hear him as the door was closing behind him.

"Get some sleep. You'll feel better tomorrow."

Star waited until the second door closed and then ripped the bag of chips open, being careful not to spill any of them out. She could see the flashes of platinum blonde dangle forward as she shoved a chip in her mouth.

* * *

It was Saturday afternoon, and the girls were walking downtown, window shopping through the "fancy district." Lacey stopped abruptly in front of one of the display cases, and looked through the window with both hands up, like a little kid looking in a candy store.

"Look at that, Star! Look at that beautiful wig! I bet I would look like Marilyn Monroe in it!"

"I don't think we should be in here, Lace. It's not exactly our kind of place, if you know what I mean." Star glanced both ways down the street, hoping to get Lacey to keep walking.

"And what exactly is our kind of place, Star?"

"I don't know. I mean, well, not really here. It's expensive. We don't have the money to shop here."

Lacey made a disapproving noise. "I'm going in. With or without you."

She shook Star's hand off her shoulder, grabbed the door handle and opened it with a grand gesture. Star rolled her eyes and reluctantly followed behind her. As soon as the two girls entered into the store, one of the ladies behind the counter leaned over to the other and said something under her breath.

In true Lacey fashion, she didn't let that bother her one bit.

"Hi there! How are you today?" Lacey called, wiggling her fingers at the ladies. Lacey was always larger than life. Sometimes Star envied her confidence, but was typically happy to be her side kick.

Star stood awkwardly alongside her as she slid hangers and flipped through the clothing on the racks. It seemed the more racks she went through, the more uncomfortable the women at the counter got.

"Come on, Lace. We should go," Star said nervously as she watched the women move from behind the counter out onto the floor, probably so they could keep a closer eye on them.

"Are you serious? That would just give them what they want. We have as much right to be in here as anyone else. Who do they think they are anyway?" Lacey complained.

"Yeah, I know. I get that. But it's not like we even have the money to buy anything in here." Star flipped the tag over on one of the simpler looking tops. "$65!" she exclaimed. "That's like a t-shirt! Seriously, let's go."

Lacey looked at Star with a mischievous look which made Star very uncomfortable.

"Who said we need money?" Lacey whispered, as she looked over her shoulder at the two women hovering in close company.

"No, no, no." Star whispered back. "I don't want to get in trouble. Can we please just go?"

"Girl, I can't believe you. Are you seriously going to let these over-privileged snobs decide what we will and won't do? Look at them. They've been oozing with self-righteous judgement since we walked through the door." Lacey's words caught Star off guard, and she found herself connecting with an unexpected indignance. She looked over at the women, and one of them gave her a spiteful scan up and down.

"Maybe you're right," Star said, with a confidence that surprised her.

"That's the spirit!"

One of the women scoffed at their playfulness, and Lacey and Star ducked behind a display to hide their giggles.

"Okay," Lacey stated matter-of-factly. "I'll cover you. Take something. Anything. Anything your little heart desires. You deserve it."

Star could feel her heart racing, and she tried to keep her hands from shaking as she looked through the rack. She tried to discreetly move to the back side of the rack as Lacey stayed put. As interested as the women were in keeping an eye on them, they also seemed to want to keep their distance, like a person who crosses the street when a dog starts barking at them. Star slid one of the hangers over to reveal a sequined pink camisole. It was one of the most beautiful things she had ever seen, and lights from the store ceiling danced off the jewels on the front. Her pulse quickened again, and she looked up to see the women leaning into each other and whispering.

Star gave Lacey a nod.

In a skipping motion, Lacey jumped over a display of shoe boxes, intentionally catching her foot on it, and bringing the whole thing down.

Star knew now was the time. It was now or never. While both women were fixated on Lacey's dramatics, Star grabbed the sequined camisole off the hanger and stuffed it into her purse.

Just then, one of the women yelled at Lacey. "That's enough young lady! This is a fine establishment and we won't have the likes of you chasing paying customers away!"

Lacey's mouth hung open. "You bitch!" she yelled.

Star could see one of the women scurry back behind the counter and pick up the phone.

"Come on Lace. Time to go!" Star grabbed Lacey by the sleeve and pulled her toward the front door.

Lacey looked like one side of a bar fight as she resisted against Star's pull, arms flailing as she launched her verbal assault at the women.

"You think you're better than us. You think you're better than everyone else, don't you? You and your pretentious..."

Star managed to get her out the front door but, just as they crossed the threshold, a loud siren went off. The girls looked at each other in panic.

"Run!" Lacey yelled. Both girls took off in terror and could hear the two women yelling at them from the sidewalk. By the time they rounded the corner, they were both laughing as they tried to catch their breath. They walked down the street as Lacey proudly held up the camisole, proclaiming their stand of solidarity against the pretentious housewives of Milwaukee. Although Star laughed, deep down, she was feeling guilty. She had never stolen anything before.

* * *

Star left the pear for last. She hadn't had one in years, and it tasted even more lovely than it smelled. Juice ran down over her hand with each bite she took, and she was careful to catch all the juice that ran down with her tongue. When she was finished, she wrapped up the core of the pear in the plastic wrap from the sandwich and placed it next to the base of the bucket. She grabbed the stone from under her pillow, stood on the bed and continued working on her etching on the wall.

She could see more of the platinum strands bouncing back and forth with the movement of her hand and wondered what the whole of her head looked like. Maybe she would look like Marilyn Monroe. Star stood atop the bed, looking over the carving on the wall. It was finished. She opened her fingers and let the stone roll off of them and onto the floor.

Caroline Klug

CHAPTER 14

Sarah stopped for a moment on the street, her stomach turning while the brief image of her father's picture burned in her brain. She braced herself with one hand against the building to steady herself through the wave of nausea. A cool breeze swept past her face, which momentarily eased her stomach. She let go of the wall and leaned in to let the whole side of her body lay against the brick. It felt cool against her skin.

People were passing her, but she wasn't aware, her mind assaulted with images and memories, all vying for center stage. She was trying to make sense of everything, and her thoughts pressed into each other in rapid succession, like a crowd in Times Square. Sarah drew in a deep breath, hoping to further quell the nausea, but it was all too much. She darted around the corner of the building, thankful it was a private alley.

Pressing the palms of her hands against the building, she bent forward and vomited until there was nothing but dry heaves. She straightened herself, wiped her mouth and took in several deep breaths. Clearing her stomach out was enough relief to allow her to continue moving. She felt at a loss of what to do, but the adrenaline inside her kept her going. She rounded the corner back onto the main street and pushed forward down the sidewalk, scanning the windowfronts as she went. About a block up, she saw the sign for Emma's café. The comfort of a familiar place was a welcome feeling, but not enough to outweigh the rush of anxiety which was now her constant companion.

They have internet there. She picked up her pace as she crossed the street. I need to know what's–

A blaring car horn paralyzed her as she stopped in the middle of the road. She had been so focused that she didn't see she was walking right into traffic. She waved apologetically and ran to the other side.

When she reached the door of the café, she paused to collect herself, opening the door as calmly as she could. She scanned the long row of laptops by the window, praying one of them would be open. There, at the end of the table was one open spot. Relieved, she made her way toward it. Etiquette would say to go to the counter first to make a purchase, but she didn't have any money and couldn't afford drawing that kind of attention in explaining, so she continued toward the table.

"Well, hello there!" the café owner said cheerfully, blocking Sarah's path to the laptop. "I almost didn't recognize you."

The woman stopped as she got closer. Sarah could feel her eyes examining the side of her face that still held the evidence of Jack's discipline. She gave Sarah a questioning look and her tone became more inquisitive. "I don't think I've ever seen you in here without Jack. What's he up to?"

Sarah stared at her, suddenly feeling exposed and nervous. "Um. He's working second shift this week," she replied.

"Sure. Hey, are you okay?" the woman asked, still examining her face.

"Oh." Sarah held a hand up to her face. "Yes, it's nothing. Really. I, um, I really like your skirt." Sarah looked past the owner, over her shoulder at the empty seat.

Through the corner of her eye, she could see a young man grab his coffee from the front counter and turn in the direction of the laptops. Sarah lost all congeniality and mumbled an apology as she pushed past the women in order to get to the empty seat before he did. Once seated, she exchanged a brief look with the man who was clearly irritated, but she couldn't worry about that now. Instead, she turned to the screen, feeling lost intellectually.

It had been years since she had used a computer or surfed the internet. She glanced sheepishly at the woman next to her and then returned her focus to her own screen, which appeared to be a recipe site, probably from the previous user. Sarah moved her mouse into the URL box and typed in the name of a search engine she could recall. Several of her fingers were crooked from not healing properly after a past break, so typing was more difficult for her. She had to use the backspace to fix the letters she inadvertently typed.

Once she was on the search page, she sat staring for a moment. She realized she wasn't even sure what to look for. Where would she even start? Sarah closed her eyes and took in a deep breath. She breathed it out slowly and did it again. She opened her eyes, pulled the keyboard closer to her and started typing her name. Her real name.

* * *

"Rehabilitation," Jack said. "It's the steps you take to help someone get healthy again after things like addictions or injuries. Think of it like therapy or training."

She nodded her head but her eyes scanned the air above her as if searching for understanding.

"If we're going to get you healthy again, there's some steps we're going to have to take to protect you and allow you to live a normal life. Do you understand?"

She hesitated. "I think so, but what do you mean by steps?"

"Well." Jack paused. "For starters, we're going to have to change your name."

The two sat quietly. She was uncertain what to say or how to act. Deep down, a part of her knew what was happening was somehow wrong, but her fear of what she thought was beyond those walls kept her still.

He gave her another hard look up and down. "How about Sarah? Yeah, I like Sarah. And you look like a Sarah. Let's go with that."

She took a deep breath in and tried to process her new name. "Sarah," she repeated to herself. "Sarah," she said again, committing it to memory.

* * *

Tears spilled out as she tried to process the litany of links and pictures displayed in the search results. It was so strange to see her real name – Galia Gregor – over and over again. It was even stranger to see pictures of herself from years past. She had almost forgotten what that version of herself looked like. She had forgotten how beautiful her long, black hair used to be.

Galia clicked on the first link, which said, "Gregor assisting local police in search of missing McGinnis girl." Her thoughts raced to the poor girl she suspected Jack had taken. Galia wanted to believe Jack was helping Rachel, like he had helped her, but a much darker story was becoming clear to her. She continued skimming through the articles, hardly able to process all the questions in her mind. Just like the news said, the articles pointed to other missing girls they thought were connected. Some of them were even dead. Galia's stomach dropped again and she had to fight once more through the nausea.

"Dead," she whispered. She took a deep breath and continued reading.

Her mind was spinning from all the information but came to a screeching halt when her eyes landed on a picture of her dad. It wasn't the same one on the TV. It was from much earlier. It was from around the time when she left home. There was a link to a video of her dad. Her pulse quickened and light beads of sweat formed on her face. She had to see it. She nervously hovered the mouse over the video, looked quickly on both sides of her to confirm that she had at least a little privacy, and then clicked the play icon.

Sound blasted from the speakers, and she jumped out of her seat. Her face flushed as she tried to find the volume to turn it down. People shot her agitated looks until she finally stopped the video. She desperately wanted to watch it but didn't want to draw any more attention to herself, so she continued reading through the articles instead. One after the other, she read about accounts of her own abduction and of the other girls they thought were linked.

The color ran out of her face as she stared somberly at the words in front of her. Tears formed, and anxiety turned to a dark pit in the bottom of her stomach. She stared face to face with the ugly words. Prostitution ring. Galia averted her eyes from the screen and stared into her lap as shame overtook her. He knew. Her dad knew. They all knew.

★ ★ ★

"Hey there," said the John, pulling up along the side of the curb. He was driving an Audi, the kind you didn't normally see in these parts. She thought maybe he was lost but wasn't going to waste time figuring it out. That car meant money. If she played her cards right, that could be money in her pocket.

She put on her most flirtatious smile, pulled her already short skirt up a little higher and strolled seductively to his passenger window. She leaned over so her forearms were resting on the top of the door and winked at the man.

"Hey, baby. Nice car." She scanned the man's face. He was a bit older than she was, but that never stopped her. "You looking for someone to have a little fun with in it?"

"Sure." The man smiled. "You happen to know someone?"

She smiled back at him, playing his game.

"I just might. Depends. You like blondes?"

The man looked at her for a second. "No?" he said, more like a question than an answer.

She smiled again. "Good answer. Looks like you're in luck then. I'm your gal." She opened the passenger door, pausing only long enough to catch a glimpse of him, to see if there was any protest. There was none, so she got in the car and closed the door.

"What's your name?" he asked.

"Nope. No names. Too personal."

The man raised his eyebrows but seemed satisfied to proceed. He put the car in drive and signaled to merge into the empty street.

"So, what do you do that affords you such a fancy car?"

"Nope." He winked at her. "No occupations. Too personal."

She accepted that she had been beaten at her own game. When she first started on the streets, she used to answer their questions. She used to tell them her name. Well, not her real name. Never Galia. She would tell them her street name, and nothing more. Outside of that, she never held back when the Johns wanted to talk.

She learned early on that, besides sex, the other thing they usually wanted was someone to talk to. Someone who wasn't going to judge them or hold them accountable to their words. She got good at listening. She got equally good at talking. She would spin tales and tell them whatever she thought it was they wanted to hear. There were usually hints of what they were looking for in their own words, and she just got good at playing along.

"Turn here," she instructed, pointing to the road which lead to the alley she typically brought her Johns to. The man did as he was instructed. He came to the end of the alley, turned the car off and looked at her expectantly.

"So, have you ever done this before?"

"Paid for sex?" he asked. "A few times."

She gave him an understanding nod but pushed his hand away when he tried to advance.

"Money first," she said, businesslike. The man sighed, but silently complied with her request.

"How much?"

"How much you got?"

The man squinted at her as if displeased, but pulled out his wallet, nonetheless. He directed his open wallet away from her, looking carefully through what was inside.

"$100," he said flatly. Although he tried to hide it, she could easily see the thickness of the wallet. He was lying.

"That's too bad, because it will cost you at least $200 for all the things I want to do to you." She moved her hand over to him and grabbed the inside of his thigh.

That was enough for the man, because he took another look in his wallet and agreed with her. He pulled the money out and set it on the dashboard.

"You better make this worth it," he said. For $200, she would give him whatever he asked for, which is exactly what she did.

When he was finished, he reclined his seat and rambled. "Life is all about choices. People make choices every day. Heck, every minute. And life is short. A man should be able to just do what he wants before life takes it away from him."

She thought that was a strange thing for him to say but continued to listen to him as she tucked her shirt back in.

"I mean, there's so much bad stuff going on out there. One of the other VPs I work with lost her husband in some kind of freak accident this week. Just like that. You're going along, having a fine day and BAM!"

The volume of his voice startled her.

"That really set off this other guy who works for me. Bad memories probably. Man, he's had a bad run these last few years. He lost his wife a few years back. Then, not long after, his teenage daughter goes missing. I mean, when was the last time you saw things like that happen in a town like West Allis?"

She froze, then tried to sound nonchalant. "How did his wife die?"

The man darted a look at her, but answered. "Cancer or some crap like that. Why?"

She sat up straight. "I'm sorry. I need to go back."

The man put his hand on her leg as if to slow her impatience.

"I need to go back now," she said, as she pushed his hand off her leg.

The man snorted but put his chair back up and started the engine.

★ ★ ★

Galia felt sick over the memory. She headed out the door and stumbled through the streets, trying to focus on anything other than the images from her old life. Jack was right. As much as she hated to admit it, he was right. She would never be able to look her dad in the face again.

Not after all she had done. Not after she'd slept with so many men, including his boss. Not after who she had become.

The streets were busy and despite the number of people she kept bumping into, Galia felt more alone than ever. She found herself walking back in the direction of her house. *Jack's* house. She argued with herself, trying to convince herself that he really was there to help her. Maybe he was there to help all those girls. Maybe even Rachel McGinnis. Maybe the police had it all wrong and he was some kind of prostitute rescuer, and he helped the ones who wanted help.

What about the ones who don't want help? She knew what he was capable of. Her present physical injuries would testify to that.

Fear ran through her again, and she felt more confused than before. A small, crumpled up piece of paper caught her attention, and she bent down to pick it up. She uncrumpled it and flattened it between the palms of her hands. It was a dollar bill. She looked up and around, but there was no one close by.

Galia couldn't remember the last time she'd held money of any kind. She folded it in half and tucked it carefully in her pocket. No one seemed to be looking for it. But someone was looking for Rachel McGinnis.

Conviction overtook her, and she stopped cold in the middle of the sidewalk when she saw a payphone. She stood still, just looking at it. She reached her hand in her pocket to feel for the dollar bill, and cradled it in her hand, still inside her pocket, as if it were a precious diamond. She thought people were looking at her and tightened her grip on the dollar bill. Did they recognize her? Did they know she was with Jack? Galia let out the breath she was holding as she realized people were only looking because she was standing in the middle of the sidewalk, forcing everyone to go around her again. Her paranoia got the best of her and she ducked into a nearby store.

"Hello!" said the woman behind the counter. Galia was surprised to find herself in an ice cream shop. Her eyes widened as she looked across the expanse of ice cream buckets, all encased neatly behind the glass. There was a coolness to the air inside, and the collision of smells from the ice cream and the hand-dipped chocolates pleasantly filled her nose. The bell on the door jingled as it closed shut behind her, awakening distant memories.

* * *

"Mom, are you sure you're up for this?"

"Of course, Galia. Don't be silly. I'm fine. Besides, there will never be a time when I'm not okay enough for ice cream!" She smiled until she looked at Galia's face and realized the obviousness of her contradiction.

"Hello you two! It's good to see you both in here!"

Galia, still trying to recover from her mom's faux pas, looked at the floor. The woman looked back and forth between the two, trying to figure out the source of awkwardness keeping them silent.

"Hi there. Sorry." Galia's mom smiled apologetically and put her hands on Galia's shoulders. "We're here for our birthday treat tradition! What would you like, sweetie?"

The woman smiled. "Well, happy birthday, Galia!"

Galia smiled politely and tried to act like things were normal. She tried to forget that she was getting ice cream with her dying mother who probably wouldn't live to see another one of her birthdays.

"Um..." She pointed through the glass. "Blue Moon, please. One scoop."

"But honey, you always get two scoops!"

"Thanks, but I'm just not that hungry," Galia said, still trying to get herself back to normal. Her mom tried to change the subject while the woman scooped her ice cream.

"So, I noticed you've been spending a lot more time with Teddy." She smiled, nudging Galia's elbow.

"Mom," Galia said, rolling her eyes.

"What?" her mom laughed. "I'm not dumb, you know."

"I know," Galia said quickly. "I didn't mean... I just."

Her mom put her hand on her arm. "It's okay, honey. I was just teasing. You know," her mom paused. "you don't have to walk on eggshells around me. You don't have to worry about what you say to me. I always want to know what you're thinking."

* * *

"What can I get for you today?" The woman's voice broke Galia out of her daydream. For a moment, she had forgotten about the darkness inside. But now the darkness was back.

"Um... no, I'm sorry I..." Galia stood and looked at the confused woman for a moment. She realized she was still gripping the dollar bill in her pocket and pulled it out slowly.

"Do you, uh, happen to have change for a dollar? I'm sorry I won't be buying anything, but I really need to make a phone call."

"You don't have a phone?"

"Um... no, I... I left it at home by accident."

"Oh. I would hate if I did that. It would be like leaving my brain at home." The woman laughed. "You can use the phone in the back if you want."

Galia looked over her shoulder at the crowd of people on the sidewalk. She shoved the dollar bill back in her pocket and let the woman lead her to the back room. The woman pointed at the phone, then stood there looking at Galia. Galia waited a few moments, then shot her a silent request for privacy.

"Oh! Right. I should get back to the counter in case another customer comes in." The woman turned toward the store front but ended up doing a complete circle back to Galia. "Um... try not to be too long please. I probably shouldn't have anyone back here."

Galia nodded her head and waited for the woman to walk back up front. She knew she didn't have a lot of time, so she couldn't afford to stall. Couldn't afford to think. She lifted the receiver off the desk phone and nervously dialed 9-1-1.

"9-1-1. What's your emergency?" A woman's voice came through the receiver.

Galia pulled the phone away from her face and held it just above the base, as if about to hang it up. She could hear a distant voice over the line.

"This is 9-1-1. What's your emergency, please?"

Galia took a deep breath and put the phone back to her face. "Yes... I'm here..."

"What's your emergency, ma'am?"

"I... uh... the man that's been on the news."

"What man?" the operator asked.

"The one they think took that girl... Rachel McGinnis."

"Yes, go ahead."

Galia paused and rubbed her forehead, wondering if she was doing the right thing.

"Ma'am?"

"Yes, I'm here."

"Who am I speaking with? What is your name?"

"The man... I think the man you're looking for is Jack. His name is Jack." Galia rubbed her forehead again. "He lives in Greendale and works for a mill."

"What is his last name, please?" the operator pressed.

Galia hesitated, then slammed the receiver back onto the base. She hurried out of the back room, past the woman at the counter and to the front door.

"Okay then! Have a good day!" called the woman from the counter.

Galia waved her hand without turning around. Instead, she grabbed the door handle and flung it open, the bells clashing loudly against it.

Once on the sidewalk, she felt as though every eye were on her. They knew. They all knew who she was. And soon they would know who Jack was too. She hurried down the street and turned onto the long road back to the house.

I have no idea what to do. I have no plan. No plan. So, I go back home, and the police show up looking for Jack. Then what? Then they arrest me too. Sarah, what were you thinking?

She paused for a moment, then said out loud. "Galia. My name is Galia."

Galia fought to hold back tears. If she was going to figure this out, she needed to be level headed.

"I need to grab some things and get out. I don't know where. Anywhere. I've lived on the streets before. I can do it again." Galia fell silent again. She knew opening herself up to that old world meant having to find a means to survive, and she knew she could never go back to doing what she did. Getting a regular job would be next to impossible if the police were still looking for her.

She continued on, hoping she would figure it out as she went. The long road felt like forever, and she was relieved to see the house and the driveway empty. Jack should still be at work. She would have enough time to grab some things and go.

Caroline Klug

CHAPTER 15

Star no longer had any concept of night and day. When Jack told her to get some sleep before he left, that at least told her it was evening, or close to it. She tossed and turned for a good portion of the night. After what felt like several hours, she got up and walked around to the extent her shackle would allow. It still cut into her skin, but she was becoming numb to pretty much all kinds of pain.

She sat on the floor with her legs crossed and used her fingers to trace the imperfections on the floor. Her fingers and hand were finally starting to feel a little better. The fingers looked bent in an unattractive kind of way, and she still couldn't fully rotate her wrist, but at least most of the pain had subsided.

She stared down at the brace holding her arm and thought it best to take it off. It really wasn't doing much anymore other than making her life more difficult. Getting it off her shoulder was easy, but there was a knot tied in it where it connected around her wrist. She struggled to get it untied with her one hand and looked around for anything she could use to cut through the material.

Her heart skipped a beat as she remembered what was under the bed. She could hardly believe she'd forgotten about it. In all the trauma of the hair-cutting yesterday, she had completely spaced out. Star flipped over onto her knees and peered under the bed. There it was. The shiny silver handle peeked out from behind the back leg of the frame. She crawled to the end of the bed, careful to use her forearms instead of her hands, and fished out the scissors, sliding them in front of her. Then, she sat and stared at them for a long time. She didn't think they were big enough to do any substantial damage to Jack, but it might be enough to catch him off guard and give her a fighting chance to get away.

Star sat, contemplating her choices, thinking about the first time she had tried to run and the unforeseen consequences of her failed attempt. If she tried and failed again, the consequences could be even worse. Maybe even her life. But if she succeeded… If. That was a big word.

Star felt the anxiety welling up inside of her at the thought of trying to escape. She stuck a finger in the middle of one of the small handles and twirled it in a circle on the concrete, stalling her difficult decision. Star jumped when she heard the latch moving on the metal door.

She moved quickly to tuck the scissors back behind the leg of the bed frame, so it was out of sight. Turning so her back was up against the bed, she tried to breathe deeply to bring herself back to a calmer state.

Jack came in and closed the door behind him. He flashed a lingering look at the wall where Star had been etching, then shifted his eyes to her, as if uninterested in it.

"Good morning," he said. "How did you sleep?"

Star tried hard to keep her nervousness at bay, and made sure her tone was calm when responding. "Fine. It's hard sometimes to know when night is in here, or how long I'm sleeping. I keep the light on a lot."

Jack studied her face and walked over by the bed, motioning to the space beside her as though asking to sit.

Star nodded, but kept her eyes on the floor. She pulled her legs up to her chest and wrapped her arms around them. The knotted cloth was still hanging from one of her wrists.

"Do you want me to take that off for you?"

Star followed his eyes down to the cloth around her wrist and felt grateful she hadn't cut it already. That would have certainly given away that she had the scissors. Again, Star nodded, and offered him her wrist.

Jack leaned down to work the knot with his fingers until he could pull it apart. "There. That better?"

"Yes," Star said, rubbing her wrist. "Thank you."

"Sure. No problem. Star, can you come sit here for a minute? I want to take the shackle off, and there's something I want to talk to you about."

Star looked up at him curiously. She only hesitated a moment before easing herself up off the floor with her good hand and sitting back onto the bed.

Jack produced the key from his pocket and unlocked the shackle. He caught both sides in his hand and eased it to the floor. Star tried to caress her ankle. Her wounds burned and sharp pains were shooting sporadically up her leg, so she pulled her hand back, trying not to show the discomfort she was feeling. After a minute, she dropped her foot back to the floor and turned her body in his direction.

She always felt uncomfortable looking him in the eyes but tried to give him her full attention.

"Do you know how long you've been in here?"

Star played with her hands while she thought for a second.

"I don't know. Maybe five or six weeks?"

Jack shook his head. "It's been about two months."

Star lifted her eyebrows but continued to sit silently. "Do you remember what I told you about leaving here?"

Star perked up and her heart raced. "You said I needed to be clean."

Jack smiled. "That's right. You need to be able to be free of the drugs, so you don't relapse."

Star nodded, trying not to seem too excited. "Yes. I am. I'm clean. And I feel good. And I'm eating everything you bring me and..."

Jack stopped her. "I know. That's good. I'm glad. You've done a good job lately, and I think it's time to take the next step of your rehabilitation."

Star nodded her head, but still had a look of uncertainty. "The next step of my what?"

"Rehabilitation. It's the steps you take to help someone get healthy again after things like addictions or sicknesses. Think of it like therapy or training."

Star nodded but was still feeling a little confused.

"If we're going to get you healthy again, there's some steps we're going to have to take to protect you and allow you to live a normal life. Do you understand?"

Star hesitated. "I think so, but what do you mean by steps?"

"Well." Jack paused. "For starters, we're going to have to change your name."

Star smiled. "Oh, that's okay. Star was never my real name. It was just my street name. I changed it on the street because my roommate, Lacey, told me I should never use my real name."

"Well, your roommate was real smart. And that will help you going forward. You still won't be able to use your real name, because that's how the police will find you. And you shouldn't use your street name anymore either. You don't want people to recognize it, and... well, you don't want to be *that* person anymore." Jack paused again. "Do you?" He studied her.

Star felt strangely alarmed. It was hard enough the first time to give up her real name. Now she had to give up another. If it meant her freedom, then she could do whatever he was asking.

"Okay," Star said reluctantly.

"So, what kind of name do you look like?" Jack's tone changed, and Star could only assume he was trying to lighten the moment. He backed up and looked at her up and down while smiling, making a dramatic play of things. She could tell he was trying to get her to feel a part of the game. Star sat quietly thinking, then spoke softly.

"What about Maggie?"

"Why Maggie?"

"It was my mom's name." Star looked at him, hoping he would agree, but Jack shook his head.

"I don't think so. You really shouldn't use anything that's already associated with you." He gave her another hard look up and down. "How about Sarah? Yeah, I like Sarah. And you look like a Sarah. Let's go with that."

Star took a deep breath in and tried to process her new name.

"Sarah," she repeated to herself. "Sarah," she repeated again, as if committing it to memory. "What about my last name?"

"You won't have to worry about that." Jack smiled and slapped the palms of his hands on his thighs. "Which brings us to some of the other steps."

Sarah cocked her head to the side, still listening.

"Sarah." Jack paused for dramatic effect. "You're going to leave here today. We're going to leave here today."

Sarah felt emotion welling up in her. Was this real or just some cruel trick?

"Really?" she squeaked. She cleared her throat. "Really? Today?"

Jack smiled, nodding, and she couldn't keep the tears from wetting her eyes and spilling down her cheeks.

"Now, Sarah." He smiled at her. "In order for you to stay hidden from the police and protected, there's going to be a lot of rules for you to follow. Think of it as a next step to show how you can get better. Do you think you can do that?"

Jack could have asked her if he thought she could pound nails into her own leg and she would have said yes.

"Yes. Yes, I can do whatever you ask me to."

Jack nodded in approval. "Good. Good girl. That's what I was hoping. I have a house not too far from here. I'm going to let you stay with me there, okay?"

Sarah nodded.

"Like I said, there's going to be rules."

"Like what?"

"Well, one of the most important rules there is, is never, and I mean never, go anywhere without me. We will go places, but for the first few weeks, I think it's best for you to stay inside and not be seen. You know, just get used to the place and learn the rules."

Sarah winced as she felt the proverbial nail being driven into her thigh. She tried to cover up her wince with an accepting nod.

"I know it sounds... well... limiting, but it's for your own protection. Do you believe that? It's important you believe that."

Sarah nodded her head and tried to push past the fear of the decision still looming in her head of whether or not to run. "Yes. Thank you."

"There's something else."

Sarah grimaced, reacting more to the tone of his voice than his words.

"I have a buddy at the police station. That's how I knew about them looking for you. He told me something really troubling and I feel I need to share it with you. I'm not trying to scare you. I just want you to be educated on what's going on, so you believe me when I say all of this is for your own good."

Sarah swallowed hard. "What is it?"

"Remember how I told you the police busted up that prostitution ring you were in?"

Sarah nodded.

"Well, apparently, they didn't get your ring leader."

"Ronny?" Sarah blurted out.

"Yeah!" Jack said. "That was his name. So, they didn't get Ronny, and my police buddy told me that they were finding bodies."

"What do you mean?"

"I mean, I guess this Ronny guy doesn't want to get caught, so he's going around and cleaning up business, if you know what I mean."

Sarah still had a confused look on her face, which seemed to slightly irritate Jack.

"He's killing any prostitutes that are still around and could I.D. him. He's looking for you too and he'll kill you if he finds you."

Sarah's mouth dropped open and she began to stutter. "I... I don't... Oh my God. He's a monster. I need to get out of here!"

"Shhh." Jack grabbed her shoulders and tried to calm her. She settled down a little, but looked at him, scared.

"That's why I'm doing everything I can to keep you safe."

Sarah sat, shaking from the news. Ronny was the last person she would ever want to see. She knew Jack was right. Ronny wouldn't hesitate to kill someone.

★ ★ ★

Ronny burst out laughing, and his stocky right hand, Leo, was quick to follow. "You gotta be kidding me right now. Kid, go home."

The boy stood his ground, looking Ronny in the face and sizing him up with the confidence of being twice the size he really was. Star watched from a distance, feeling afraid for the young boy.

"I'm not leaving here without my sister. She's worked for you long enough and we need her at home."

By now, others were gathering around them and observing the conversation.

"Mama's sick, and she doesn't have much time. I promised her I'd bring my sister back, and that's what I'm gonna do."

Ronny and Leo exchanged a look and laughed again. Then Ronny looked at the crowd of his people observing, cut his laughter abruptly and took a few steps toward the boy. "Listen, you little shit-face. No one's gonna tell me what I'm gonna do. Especially not someone your age. Only I'm gonna say what I'm gonna do. Didn't your sick mommy ever teach you to have respect for your elders?"

Leo laughed in support of him.

"Get the hell out of here before I make you sorry."

The girl grabbed her brother's hand and pleaded with him to leave, but he shook her hand off and took another step toward Ronny, trying to appear man to man. Ronny took a step back and then began walking around him in a circle as though sizing him up. To Star's surprise, the boy pulled a switch blade from his jean pocket and pointed it at Ronny.

"I ain't leaving without my sister. You hear me?"

Ronny smiled and took another step back, both hands in the air as if to calm the boy.

"Yeah, little man, I hear you. Okay, okay." Ronny nodded his head.

Leo took the signal and came up from behind, grabbed the boy's knife and put him in a headlock.

Ronny spoke as Leo held the boy. "This is all really too bad. I consider myself a fair man. I was going to let you go home to your mommy, and let bygones be bygones. But then you go threatening me with that knife. Not cool, little man. Not cool."

Ronny nodded again, and Leo threw the boy roughly to the ground. The boy tried to get up, but Ronny, Leo and two more of Ronny's guys took turns kicking him in the head and stomach until he was no longer conscious. His sister screamed and cried, held back by some of the other girls, pleading for them to stop.

They did, but it was only long enough to throw her to the ground and do the same thing to her. They were both lying still on the ground, and the others began walking away. Star stood off in the shadows with Lacey, waiting for all of them to leave so they could go help the boy and his sister. Ronny had taken a few steps away from the boy, then stopped and turned back around. He grabbed the boy's knife out of Leo's hand, walked swiftly over to the boy and slit his throat.

Star gasped. Lacey threw her hand over Star's mouth to quiet her and walked them both backward into the shadows. Ronny wasn't done. He walked over to the boy's sister, who lay still beside him, and did the same thing to her.

"Can't have no one comin' after me with knives." Ronny spun around in a circle, waving the knife around at anyone still watching. "That goes for the rest of you too. Don't ever try to cross me."

* * *

"Sarah, do you believe I'm trying to help you?"

Sarah was so shaken she didn't know which end was up anymore. The thought of running scared her more than ever, and she accepted the fact that she now needed Jack. She knew what Ronny was capable of and she needed Jack's protection, even if it came with his rules.

"Yes, I believe you. Please. Please help me."

Jack pulled her to him and gave her a hug. "Of course I will," he replied softly, stroking her platinum hair. "I don't want you to worry. I'm going to take all that bad stuff you did and make it go away."

Something in Sarah flipped like a light switch. Jack *was* trying to help her. He was her means of salvation. Sarah tightened her grip around him in response to his words.

Jack released his embrace and took her by the hand to bring her to her feet.

"It's time," he said, this time more somberly, as if cementing the seriousness of the moment.

Sarah reached for her water bottle, but he pulled at her hand to stop her.

"Don't worry about that. There's more at home."

Home. The word burned through her. It was such a mix of emotions to hear that word. Jack led her by the hand through the metal door. It was the first time she was able to clearly look around since she had been there. She watched as Jack closed the door and locked it with his key. Sarah shuddered a little, looking down at her hand, remembering the incident when she tried to escape. He turned to the second door.

This was the door she had always heard but never seen. It wasn't nearly as formidable in stature as the metal door. This one was made of wood, and much thinner than the other. It was an odd color green, almost seafoam, and had a regular door handle and lock on it, like the kind you'd see on a service door going into a garage. Jack opened the door, and Sarah's eyes immediately stung from the sunlight that poured in. She hadn't seen the sun in two months. Her eyes were forced shut by the brightness, but she could hear birds singing.

Jack, still holding her hand, led her to the van slowly. As her eyes adjusted, she could see the woods around her and hear the familiar sounds. Jack opened the passenger door of his van and helped her into the seat. As they drove out of the woods and onto the road, Sarah looked around, trying to take everything in. It had only been two months, yet the world around her felt almost surreal.

Sarah glanced over her shoulder and was surprised to see nothing was in the back of the van. There were no seats or carpeting. It felt strange to her, like looking at someone you know you should recognize, but you just don't.

Trees rushing past her peripheral soon turned to houses. As they drove further into the city, she realized that Jack was watching her out of the corner of his eye. She sat calmly, taking in everything around her. She would occasionally look in Jack's direction but would always turn away once he looked back.

"It's going to be okay. I promise," Jack said, still looking at the road.

Sarah let out a deep sigh and gave him an uncertain look.

"It will be. Really." Jack smiled.

Sarah could feel the speed of the car slow as they entered a quaint downtown area. The streets were lined with cute little shops and novelty stores. There was a water fountain spurting out water to the beat of a song playing nearby. Sarah used to hear about that kind of stuff happening in Las Vegas, but not, well, wherever they were.

The thought suddenly dawned on her that she had no idea where they were. She didn't have much of a recollection of how she got to that prison room, so she had no idea if she was miles or thousands of miles from her home. Her home. Where was her real home?

Sarah glanced over at the door handle, and then to the lock. The lock was down, which meant she would need to pull it up before she would be able to open the door and make her escape. Very slowly, she moved her hand off her lap and onto the seat beside her leg.

"Listen, Sarah."

Frightened, Sarah stilled her hand.

"I don't want you to worry about Ronny. I know you said this guy's a monster, but I'm going to keep you safe. I can see you really want to change your life around, so I'm going to do everything I can to help you."

Ronny. The mere mention of his name made her stomach drop. Sarah felt stupid for forgetting about him, if only for a moment. She pulled her hand back into her lap and stared forward.

The car stopped at a red light, and Sarah watched as a mom grabbed the hand of her small daughter and walked her across the street. Seeing other people and little kids seemed like a strange phenomenon after being alone for so long. The little girl was wearing leggings and a t-shirt and had one of those princess costume dresses pulled over the top. The girl looked into the van as they passed in front of it and waved her little hand at Sarah. Sarah smiled and waved back.

Jack shifted in his seat. "So, are you starting to feel better, being back in the fresh air?"

Sarah looked away from the little girl and turned her gaze to Jack. "Yes, I guess so."

The mother and daughter continued through the crosswalk and into one of the little stores on the other side as the light turned green and Jack proceeded through the intersection. As they crossed, Sarah saw a small coffee café on the corner. She turned her whole body toward it and placed a hand on her window.

"That's Emma's Café. I go there a lot for coffee. It's good. I'll take you there sometime."

"Really?"

"Yeah, sure."

Sarah's mood lifted a little as they drove through town. Jack turned onto one of the side streets, which changed the feel from the downtown area to more of a residential feel. It was a long road, but Sarah thought the houses were pretty. She liked the flower gardens and the little garden art some of them had.

She took a reassuring breath. Maybe this wouldn't be so bad after all. It seemed like a nice area, and she'd be safe and away from Ronny.

"Jack?"

"Yeah?"

"Where are we? I mean, what town are we in?"

"All in good time, Sarah. All in good time."

Sarah sighed. "How much time?"

"I don't want to do or share anything that might get you hurt."

"Hurt?"

"Yes, you know, Ronny and the cops and all."

It troubled Sarah that he wouldn't tell her, but the alternative wasn't exactly attractive. She didn't argue with him and remained quiet the rest of the ride. Jack slowed the van and pulled into a long driveway. She could hear the gravel popping underneath the tires. The house wasn't big, but it seemed well kept. Jack brought the van to a stop and slapped the top of his legs. "Well, here we are!"

"Is this where you live?"

"Yes. This is where you live now too. We're home."

Home. There was that word again.

"Wait here. I'll come get the door for you." Jack popped the locks open and opened his door.

Sarah felt fidgety. The lock was up. All she had to do was open it and run. Her mind was turning thoughts around and around like a carnival ride. All she had to do was run faster than Jack. She quickly scanned the surroundings. There was no one within shouting distance. She could do this. She could run.

Her mind flashed to Ronny beating and killing that poor boy and his sister, and fear demolished any courage that had built in those few moments. She sat quietly and waited for Jack to come around to her side and open the door.

Caroline Klug

CHAPTER 16

Galia opened the door into the kitchen. It was unlocked. She must have left it that way when she rushed out earlier. She stood in the middle of the kitchen, suddenly feeling like a stranger in a home she had lived in for five years. She couldn't help but think about how she had called herself Sarah the last time she stood here.

Her mind spiraled through the events of the past few years. Her life as Sarah. Her life before that as Star. Now, she had to find her original self again: Galia Gregor. Daughter of Eli and Maggie Gregor from West Allis. A girl on the dance team, infatuated with football star, Teddy Fenton. She had to remember who she really was. Galia Gregor.

It had been almost seven years since she had called herself by that name. Could she really do this? Could she go back to who she used to be those long seven years ago? Emotionally, it felt more like seventeen years ago. Galia hated herself for being afraid.

She had to make a decision. Should she leave and try to find herself as Galia, or stay and continue being Sarah? She thought she had made the decision on her walk back, but was now feeling gripped with fear. Jack's words from earlier penetrated her thoughts. She could hear him asking her where she would go if she left, and reminding her that her dad didn't want her anymore.

Galia's eyes fell on the half bag of walnut pieces folded shut on the counter. She thought about her conversation with Jack about Johnny's allergies, and scoffed at herself for not knowing better. For not remembering how Jack manipulated her the same way.

* * *

"Chocolate chip, please?" Star suggested.

Jack smiled. "Chocolate chip. Okay. Sure." Star was about to say more when he turned to face the door. She had almost forgotten the most important part, but worried it was too late. She wondered if asking for anything more at this point would be seen as ungrateful or greedy.

Jack took a step toward the door, and she knew she only had a moment to decide. She also knew the cookies wouldn't mean anything without them so she decided to be bold.

"With walnuts," she blurted.

Jack turned back around. "What?"

"With walnuts? Could they be chocolate chip cookies with walnuts?" Star immediately regretted her request, worried that the mean version of Jack would respond in anger. The walnuts could be her undoing but, to her surprise, he smiled.

"Okay. Chocolate chip cookies with walnuts."

* * *

Galia couldn't escape her tears any longer. Anger tore at her heart and filled the cracks with indignance. She was mad at

Jack. At herself. At the stupid walnuts on the counter that only reminded her of her own ignorance. She felt gullible and angry for not putting two and two together sooner when Jack asked for those muffins.

Rachel McGinnis. That must have been the special treat *she* requested. It made her the idiot for so many reasons. Her mind spiraled with questions. She had been so busy trying to figure out who she was in all of this, that she never stopped to ask the more obvious questions. She probably didn't want to know the answers to them anyway.

Who baked the chocolate chip walnut cookies for her when she was in that prison? Is it possible someone was here before her? She knew it wasn't Jack. He couldn't even boil an egg.

Galia felt numb from the thoughts in her head, and all of them arguing with each other. She lowered herself to the floor and gave in to the emotion crushing her from the inside out. How ironic, that the one thing she wanted most in the world, her dad, was the source of the pain from which she needed comfort. Those things were in conflict like two battering rams.

Galia lay on the floor and wept. As she turned over on her back, she could feel the coolness of the floor, and let the memories of that small apartment in Milwaukee flood back to her. Lacey. She hadn't thought about Lacey in a long time. Was she still in that little apartment? Was she still with Ronny doing, well, what she had to? There was so much pain.

For the first time in years, Galia thought about the heroin. Like an old friend, it offered itself as a helping hand. To forget. To forget all of it, if even for a short time. Just thinking about that made her feel disgusted with herself. She wondered if this is what it all came to. This moment taking her right back to everything about herself that she tried to escape. Maybe that was who she was and who she'd always be. Unworthy.

Her emotions subsided briefly while she tried to remember back to that night when she asked for the cookies. She scrolled through her memories. What was it she had said to herself? It was about all the things she was going to do when she got out of that prison. It was about a second chance.

Galia squinted at the ceiling, not really looking at it but more through it. She recalled making a promise to stay sober. She had certainly done that. Since being in that little room, she hadn't even had a beer. She was proud of that, but continued scanning her memory of that night.

She thought about getting a job and going to school and helping Lacey. All of these things seemed almost impossible now as she lay on the floor. Who was she kidding? Maybe this, this living here with Jack, *was* her second chance. Maybe all the things Jack had been saying up to this point had more truth attached than lies. Perhaps he was misguided in how he went about things, but maybe his intention was aboveboard.

Galia sat up and wiped her eyes with the bottom of her t-shirt. She was doing it again. She was making excuses, telling herself all the reasons Jack wasn't really a monster, so she didn't have to do anything hard or complicated. Her dad always used to get on her for that. He would call it taking the path of least resistance. He tried to encourage her to stand up for herself, and make her voice be heard. Galia wasn't really a fan of confrontation. She found it about as pleasurable as pulling out a nose hair and tended to avoid it at all costs.

That was one of the reasons she liked hanging out with Teddy. He was about as easygoing as it got. She couldn't think of one time when they got into a fight, or he did anything that required her to get into a fight with him. Even the day she left, when she took one of his favorite jerseys, he didn't argue. She knew he had a soft spot for her. But what would he think of her now? She assumed he felt the same way as her dad. She lay on the kitchen floor, letting her mind move away from this disaster to something less painful. She couldn't bear to taint the memory of Teddy on top of what she was already feeling about her dad. It was too much to handle.

She would give anything in this moment to have him sitting there with her, talking to her like he always did. Maybe he would understand her situation. Then again, her kind of complicated seemed so much messier than his, and not doing complicated wasn't really an option for her anymore. Not after she called the police.

Galia took in a deep breath, snapping out of her daydreams. The police. It would only be a matter of time before they used the information to connect the dots and came to the front door. If she didn't get moving, it would be a two for the price of one sale at the precinct.

She looked around the room, feeling a strong resignation to her circumstances. Galia picked herself up and made her way into the bedroom, where she grabbed one of Jack's duffle bags from the top shelf and threw it on the bed. She had no idea where she would go, or what she would have to do to survive, but she knew leaving was the only option. If Jack showed up, there would be no way to hide what she knew, and maybe she'd end up like some of those missing girls they found dead. If the police showed up first, then she'd go to jail. A part of her wondered if her slowness was because that option was beginning to sound better than the streets.

Galia filled the duffle with only the things she thought were most important. She was conservative with clothes, but enough layers to handle if it got a little colder. Galia was about to leave the bedroom when she thought about her Bible. She figured that was important too, so she turned around. She knew it was in a drawer and, in her preoccupied state, opened the top drawer of the dresser by accident. That was Jack's drawer.

She was in the process of closing it when something caught her eye. She opened it back up, moved the shirt over and saw the television cord. Galia dashed over to the night stand to turn the alarm clock around.

6:02 p.m. She wondered how long she had been lying on the floor. The newscast. Her dad. She ran back to the dresser, grabbed the cord and sprinted to the living room. Her hands were shaking as she tried to attach the cord and plug in the television. Frantically scanning the living room, she saw the remote control sticking up between two cushions of the couch. She grabbed it and flipped to the news channel, then sat perched on the edge of the sofa, leaning in toward the TV.

* * *

Jack turned out of the parking lot and headed toward home. Phil had been passing out chocolate covered coffee beans earlier, which gave Jack a taste for a good coffee. He decided to stop at the café to grab one on his way home. He pulled up to the curb and rifled through the middle compartment for some change. After dropping a few quarters into the meter, he walked inside.

"Hey!" he said to the woman as he approached the front counter. "Can I get a medium-sized mocha? Better make it decaf."

"Hi, Jack. Sure thing. I'm surprised to see you in here."

Jack squinted and tilted his head a little.

"Sarah told me today you were working second shift this week."

Jack's eyes widened. "Today?"

The woman nodded. "Yes. She stopped in earlier." She looked off to the side, as if remembering. "Come to think of it, she didn't seem herself. She seemed quite flustered. I hope everything is okay."

"What do you mean? What did she say?" Jack tried to sound more concerned than suspicious.

"It wasn't so much what she said, and more what she did."

Jack leaned in intently, motioning for the woman to continue.

"We talked for a minute or so. It was nothing significant, but there was something about her that just didn't seem right. She was very distracted. Kept looking past me and around the café. Then, while I was telling her about the new coffee mugs we just got in..." The woman smiled and pointed over to the display. "...she didn't even look at them. She just walked past me, in the middle of my sentence, and went to the computer table over there."

She pointed to the seat where Galia had been sitting. "Now I don't know exactly what she was looking at but, from over here, it seemed like a lot of articles and pictures."

"How long was she here?"

"Oh, I'd say about an hour. She looked very upset when she left. I tried calling her name before she walked out the door. I was going to see if she was okay, but I don't think she heard me. She ran out the door pretty fast and headed down the street."

The woman looked like she had more to say but hesitated a moment before continuing. "I didn't mean to pry, but..." She looked toward the laptops again. "I was worried about her, so I walked over to that laptop over there to see what she was looking at. It was just a picture of that Rachel McGinnis. Poor girl. I'm sure you've heard of her. Such a shame, what that poor family has to go through. They seem like such nice people..."

She turned back around to face Jack, but he was halfway out the café door.

* * *

"Hi, Bean. It's Dad."

Galia was frozen in place as the sound of his voice pierced through her. His hair was grayer, but he mostly looked like she remembered him.

"I know it's been a while, and I pray to God you're alive and okay."

Galia involuntarily sucked in her breath. Tears fell from her eyes and rolled down her cheeks.

"My sweet, Galia. If you're still out there – if, by God's grace, you're watching this – I want you to know I've never stopped looking for you. I know you were angry with me when you left."

Galia felt a twinge of guilt.

"I'm sorry I made you feel that way. We were both going through a lot, after losing your mom and all. I should have tried harder to be there for you. I wish I knew where you were so I could hug you and be there for you. I've heard so many things about where people have seen you. I don't know if it's true but, if it is, I don't care. I don't care about any of it. I don't care what you've done or what you think you've done. None of that matters. The only thing that matters is finding you and bringing you home to me. I'll never stop looking for you, Bean."

Her dad lowered his head, trying to recover from the emotions. "I love you. Please..." He was almost whimpering now. "Please... come home."

Tears streamed down Galia's cheeks in grand succession. She was torn between exhilaration and guilt. Her choices were what had brought them to this moment they were indirectly sharing.

After a few moments, her dad drew in a long breath and lifted his head again. "And if you are not gone by your own choice... if the man they think is behind Rachel's abduction has you, then I have another message for him."

Galia was as frozen as a statue.

★ ★ ★

Jack was visibly sweating as he jumped in the van and slammed the door shut behind him. His mind was busy with worry, wondering what she knew and what she might do with that information. What should he do when he got home? He wondered if she would even be there. He pressed harder on the gas pedal and accelerated above the speed limit.

* * *

Galia couldn't believe what she was seeing. What she was hearing. She listened as her dad continued.

"I don't know who you are. I don't know why you did what you did. I don't know the reason you took my baby girl. What I do know is that you are a human being. That means you have feelings. You are capable of understanding what I'm going through… this nightmare I'm living. The nightmare Rachel's parents are living."

He signaled off to the side, suggesting Rachel's parents were there with him. "I'm guessing you're probably not a dad. If you were, I don't think you would've done what you did. Please. I'm begging you. Please don't hurt our children. Please don't hurt my baby girl. My Bean." Eli broke down and gave in to his tears.

Watching him cry broke her, and she cried too. After a moment, he regained his composure and continued. "I've never met you, and I don't know what kind of man you are."

Surprise and hope surged through Galia.

"But I'm asking you to dig deep and do the right thing. Send our children home."

Galia fought to process all she had just heard and seen. Her mind kept returning to the words, "I've never met you."

* * *

"There's no easy way to say this, so I'm just going to say it."

Jack looked hard into her eyes so there was no mistaking his words.

"He's angry at you for what you've done... for what you've become. He said he doesn't want anything to do with you. He doesn't want you to contact him and he doesn't want me to anymore either. He said we should both just stay away."

* * *

The memory of Jack's words stung, but was immediately replaced with a feeling so foreign to her. Hope. Jack's words were a lie. Her dad said he had never met him. That meant Jack had never talked to him. That meant her dad had never said he didn't want anything to do with her.

Her tears stopped and she felt a newfound energy. Maybe if she could get to him first, he could help her with the police. That hope was enough to finally channel the missing component to her freedom. Courage.

Galia looked at her watch and panicked. It was 6:09 p.m. Jack would be home any second. She jumped from the couch and started for the door and stopped. Her things. She had to get her things. Galia ran into the back bedroom and grabbed the duffle off the bed. The clock and her sense of urgency told her there was no time to grab anything else. She needed to leave. Now.

She ran to the kitchen, stopping just short of the window. A looming sense of dread hung over her as she tried to peer discreetly through the window to see if the van was sitting there. She didn't see anything. Elation washed over her, and she thought she might cry again out of pure hope, but there was no time for that. Galia reached for the door handle and stopped, thinking better of it. This was the way Jack always came in. If he was almost home, he would surely see her if she came out this door.

She would go to the front and run around the other side of the house. Hope fueled her steps and she double-timed it to the front door. Even if he did pull up right now, she could cut through some of the backyards without being in his view from the driveway. Galia threw the straps of the duffel around her shoulder, pulled the door open and peered around the outside. She could feel herself shaking and tried to steady herself with her hands on the door frame. Sweat formed on her brow and anxiety lodged itself in her throat. Jack's van was in the driveway. He was probably going to walk into the kitchen any second now.

She closed her eyes for just a moment to summon courage, then took off running, leaving the door open behind her. She kept watch over her shoulder as she ran to the opposite side of the house. She almost felt a sensation of laughter welling up inside, caused by a strange mix of hope and adrenaline. She turned her full focus forward as she rounded the corner of the house, surveying the yards in front of her. If she sprinted, it would only be a few minutes until she was far enough away and could stop and ask for help.

She had never been much for physical endurance but felt confident her anxiety would carry the burden.

For the first time in years, she felt free. She took in a deep breath and broke past the last corner of her house, ready to sprint. Hope quickly gave way to terror as Jack came from behind and tackled her, sending her tumbling painfully to the ground. Galia screamed, first in pain as her knee twisted, then in fear, as Jack held her down.

Caroline Klug

CHAPTER 17

Jack grabbed her and pulled her tight against himself, holding one of his hands over her mouth. Leaving her duffle in the yard, he dragged her around the back of the house and into the kitchen, throwing her onto the floor.

"Why did you do that, Sarah? Why did you have to go and do that?"

Still reeling from the surprise, she eased herself up into a sitting position. "It's not Sarah."

"What?" Jack said harshly.

"It's not Sarah. It's Galia. My name is Galia." She cried and whimpered. "My name is Galia."

Jack grabbed one of the kitchen chairs and threw it against the wall.

Galia cowered as it smashed into pieces and fell on the floor.

"Sarah! Galia! Does it even matter anymore?" Jack yelled angrily. He continued pacing and rubbing his temples with his fingers. "I thought we were past all this. I thought you were better."

"I *am* better!"

Jack pounded his fist on the wall next to him. "You ungrateful little..." Jack snorted. "I pulled you out of that hellhole and gave you a better life."

"The same way you pulled Rachel McGinnis out?" Galia said boldly. Seeing his face made her feel more afraid.

Jack stared, his left eye visibly twitching. He said nothing and walked over to the counter, opening drawers and rooting around through them.

"So, you don't deny it? You have her, right? You have Rachel? Jack?"

"Shut up!" he screamed, and Galia flinched.

Jack rifled through the drawers looking for something unknown to her. She thought about getting up to run, but was still a bit groggy from the tackle.

"Here!" Jack said, sounding relieved. He spun around, holding a bag of zip ties.

Galia shook her head and tried to use her legs to push away from Jack as he grabbed her by one arm and dragged her into the back bedroom.

★ ★ ★

Star grabbed her small handbag and staggered out the door, into the hallway. She held the rail tightly as she made her way down the steps, paying extra attention to how she was stepping down on her bright blue stilettos. She could see the light of the foyer from the first floor as she made her way through the dark. The lights in the stairwell had gone out weeks ago, but they didn't dare ask Gus to fix them. They owed him rent and requesting lights would be an invitation to a conversation they were not prepared to have. Star got to the bottom step, thinking there was one more, and took a hard step onto the foyer floor.

"Ugh!" she exclaimed.

Star heard the faint sound of something drop, and looked down to see a small, shiny object. She bent down to pick it up.

"Crap!" One of the silver studs on her heel had fallen out. "These better not be all falling out now. These are the only sexy shoes I have."

Star grabbed the handle of the entryway door and pulled it open. She and Lacey lived in a run-down apartment complex right on the track. Their apartment windows faced it, so they could always see when things were quiet or when they were picking up. Tonight, it was especially slow, but she promised Lace she would make up the rent money she had wasted on heroin. She knew she had a problem but couldn't seem to kick it.

Star walked along the side of the building and turned the corner. Three main streetlights lined the track. The middle one was Star's. There were several girls that worked the area, but they all had their designated space. That's how the regulars found them.

Star walked over to the middle streetlight. She pulled her skirt up a little and leaned against the post. There weren't many cars coming past, but the few that were sent out shrill catcalls when she pulled up her skirt. Star watched as they did their slow drive by. She waved, acknowledging their comments like she had just won a prize. Looking good out there usually meant a good night.

Unfortunately for her, they were regulars, but none of them hers. They all went to another spot on the track and pulled over long enough for their evening companions to jump in. Within a minute or so, the street was quiet again. Star examined her red handbag. It was worn and there was a dark stain across one side of it, but she needed something to keep condoms in. This was a necessity in her mind, and some of the Johns didn't always have one.

Star looked up at the night sky, wishing there were stars to see. She wasn't sure if it was cloudy or if it was the city pollution creating an unwanted cover. Her attention gave way to the headlights approaching, and she pushed herself off the post to stand up straight. She double-checked her skirt and smoothed her t-shirt down. The car was coming up slowly. She had to squint past the headlights but could eventually see it was a van.

"Ahhh," she said disappointedly. "Family guy." She never really did make peace with that part of the job, but money was money, and beggars couldn't be choosers. If she didn't come home with something, Lacey would never forgive her. Star walked out closer to the curb in anticipation of the van. When it got close enough for her to see the man inside, she put up her hand, smiled a brilliant smile, and waved at him.

The van pulled up and stopped just ahead of her. Star sighed at the blatant inconvenience and walked up to where the van was. The passenger window was still up, so she tapped on it with her nails and motioned for him to put it down. Rather than respond, he just sat there, looking ahead. She hadn't seen him down here before, and figured it was his first time. He probably had cold feet and was a little nervous about what to do. Star tapped on the window again, this time accompanying her tap with some verbal encouragement. "Hey, honey! Why don't you put your window down, so we can properly meet?"

The man turned his head and looked at her. He looked down at the handbag she had and stared at it for a long time. Even though she wasn't clearheaded, she found the look in his eyes strange. Normally, she'd walk away from a guy like this, but the heroin still in her system and her urgent need for cash kept her where she was. She would have to roll the dice on this one.

"Heeeey!" She tried to make it sound like she was being playful, but she was slurring her words. After a few more seconds of awkward staring, the man put his finger on the button to bring the window halfway down. Without it down the whole way, Star couldn't lean on the top of the door and stick her head inside, like she usually did. She knew she was pretty and figured giving him the up close and personal look might help to seal the deal. She leaned her hips into the door and got as close to the window as she could.

"Well aren't you handsome. Whatcha in the mood for tonight?" She tried hard not to slur her words.

The man continued to stare at her in a way that made Star second-guess her choice. In a brief moment of clarity, she pushed off with her hands, and turned to walk back to the streetlight.

* * *

Jack threw her onto the bed, holding her down as he zip tied her wrists to the bed frame.

"Please, Jack. Please don't do this." Galia pleaded.

"*Me* don't do this? *You* did this. You brought this on. I thought you were different, but you're just like the others."

Galia struggled in the tie wraps. "What others?"

Jack didn't answer. He opened the closet door and moved things on the floor out of the way.

Galia tried to watch what he was doing but couldn't see well enough past him to see inside. Her wrists hurt from the zip ties, and her knee looked like it was swelling. She watched as Jack threw things out of the closet, clearing his way to something. She looked out the window next to the bed and her stomach flipped when she saw the neighbor kids playing outside. Her hope fell as quickly as it rose. They were pretty far away, and it was doubtful she could scream loud enough for them to hear her. With the window closed, the odds were against her. It would only anger Jack more, and who knew what he would do then.

Jack emerged from the closet holding a box. It looked like the kind of box you'd see with paper in it, or maybe files. He set it on the floor of the bedroom, sat down next to it and took the top off. From on the bed, Galia could see it contained a myriad of colorful items. Jack pulled out a yellow scarf. He held it up to his face, closing his eyes as he smelled it.

Galia scrunched her face in disapproval. He set the scarf down and reached into the box, pulling out a small, red handbag. Galia looked at the bag and felt her chest tighten.

"Is that my bag?" she said, as more of an accusation than a question. Jack looked up at her and simply nodded. He set the bag on top of the yellow scarf, got up and walked out of the room.

Galia sat there, looking at the red handbag, stunned. She thought about that night, standing under the streetlight, examining the stain across it, and all the horrible things that happened after that. She could hear Jack doing something in the kitchen. She yanked her arms, hoping to break the ties, but Jack had used more than one, and she was having no luck. The ties were cutting into her skin now, and blood was coming out from around the hard plastic.

Galia looked over at her wrist, watching the blood slowly pool under the zip tie. She looked down at her ankle, studying the scars from the shackle, and cried. She thought about how close she was to getting away. Maybe even seeing her dad again.

She only allowed herself a minute. Come on, Galia. Snap out of it. You got those scars around your ankle because you didn't fight. You've taken the easy way out your whole life. It's time to fight. It's time to fight for your freedom. For your very life. She was about to tug again when Jack rounded the corner into the bedroom.

Galia kept still hoping not to aggravate him. Jack had a mixed drink in his hand. He sat back down on the floor next to the box and reached back inside. Pushing things to the side and moving past the items on top, he reached deep to the bottom and pulled out another small handbag, which looked very similar to the one Galia had that night Jack took her.

"Annie," Jack said, still staring down at the handbag.

"What?"

"Annie. This belonged to Annie."

"Your sister, Annie?"

"Yes. She had it on her the night..." Jack paused, running his hands across the handbag. "The night she died."

"That was terrible... how she died. But, Jack, look what you're doing to me. You're hurting me. Do you really think Annie would want you to do to someone what they did to her?"

Jack slammed both his forearms into the box and rolled it over, its contents spilling out. "Don't you ever talk about Annie! Don't you talk about what you think she would or wouldn't want."

"Okay. Okay. I'm sorry," Galia said quickly. Her eyes were drawn to the contents that spilled out, and she could see a hodge-podge of newspaper clippings, articles of clothing and even some jewelry. With wide eyes, she looked slowly from the items on the floor to Jack. Jack ignored her stare and pulled the box away. She watched as he put things into piles, matching newspaper clippings with the different personal items. He grouped several clippings together, and then carefully laid a silver chain across that pile of articles. Galia could see it had a charm of sorts attached to it. She felt sick.

"Is that a dolphin?"

Jack traced the charm with his finger, but said nothing. He cocked his head strangely to the side, like a dog listening for something in the distance.

"That's Cami Roberts' necklace, isn't it?"

Jack looked up with a surprised look on his face. "Did you know her?"

Galia recoiled at his reference to her in past tense. "Yes. I mean, not well, but once. We met once."

"Was it on the street?"

"No. Well, she was but, I wasn't. I saw her at my school. I recognized her necklace when I saw her picture on the news today."

Jack look surprised again, but quickly changed his expression.

"She was a problem. Right from the start. She would never cooperate. No matter what I did or said, she just kept fighting me. I knew she wouldn't change. She didn't want to change."

"Did you keep her in that same room you kept me?"

"Yes. I kept them all there. Well, not the first two."

Galia's face dropped. "How many were there?" She held her breath, waiting for him to answer.

Jack looked to the side, as if lost in thought. He took a long, slow drink from his glass and set it back on the floor. "Eight. I think." He looked to the side again. "No, nine. Yes, nine."

Fear cascaded across Galia, standing every one of her hairs on end. "Does... does all that stuff belong to all those girls? Are they all..."

Galia stopped, afraid to say the word. "Am I going to be... ten?" she stuttered.

"No."

Galia felt herself untense a little.

"You will make twelve."

"What?" Galia's voice cracked and she struggled to regain her composure. "I thought you said there were nine girls."

Jack nodded his head. "Yes, there were. But then there were two more that weren't girls."

Jack swept items off to the side until he uncovered a photograph. He picked it up and turned it around so Galia could see it. It was a picture of a man and woman outside in a park.

"My parents met Emily. They didn't understand what I was doing. How I was trying to help her. She was Annie's friend, and I had such high hopes for her." Jack smiled, remembering. "She didn't want to end up like Annie. She wanted the help. She was the one who gave me the vision for helping you girls off the street. I brought her back here, to our house to live with us."

Galia looked around, surprised. She hadn't realized this was the house Jack had grown up in.

"At first, I tried to hide her, but that got too difficult. Then, I decided I would just tell my parents. I thought, after what happened to Annie, they would understand. They didn't. They didn't agree and told me she had to leave. Maybe it was too soon after Annie but, regardless, I couldn't send her back to the streets. Not when she wanted help. I couldn't let them get in the way of her rehabilitation."

Galia's mouth was open. "I thought you said your parents died in a car accident?"

Jack swirled the ice around in his glass. "They did."

Galia hardly knew how to process what she was hearing. "What did you do?"

Jack looked up at her again and smiled. "I got rid of the problem. That's what I did."

Galia shuddered inside, but outwardly tried not to react. "So, then what? What happened to Emily?"

Jack wrinkled up his face, as if recalling something painful. "She became... difficult." He shot Galia an accusing look, then looked out the window. Galia followed his eyes to the woods in back of their house.

"I told her it was for her. What I did was for her. So I could keep helping her. But she didn't understand either. She thought what I did was bad and wanted to call the police. I couldn't let her do that." Jack fell silent for a moment. "It turns out she wasn't better either."

Galia swallowed hard at his reference to her.

"So, I thought I would start over. I knew eventually I would find the ones who wanted to be better." Jack broke his gaze outside and scanned the items on the floor. He picked Galia's red handbag back up. "This is why I picked you up."

"My handbag?" Galia asked, confused.

"Yes. It was just like the one Annie used to carry around. I felt like it was a sign. You were a little harder in the beginning, because of the drugs, but I was prepared by then to help you. The one after Emily had a similar problem. When I picked her up, I didn't realize she was strung out on cocaine. It was hard to keep her here without constant monitoring. Things went bad with that one quickly, and I knew I needed a better plan. That's when I constructed the holding room."

"The holding room?" Galia repeated. "The place you first took me to?"

"Yes. It's worked out well, for the most part. Like I said, you were hard in the beginning, with trying to escape and all."

Galia glanced at her hand with the slightly crooked fingers.

"But I knew there was something special about you. I just knew you were going to be different." Jack became more agitated as he downed the rest of his drink. "But then you had to go and screw it all up." He stood up and advanced on Galia, as if he were going to hit her.

Galia tried to twist herself away from him, but the restraints kept her in place. He stopped just short of her, his hand in the air. Like a light switch, his whole demeanor shifted. He brought his hand down gently on her head and caressed the side of her face.

Galia tried not to recoil from his touch.

"I really thought things were going to turn out different. You were my favorite. You really were. Not just because you were here for so long, but because you really seemed like you wanted to change. I never thought I'd see you want to go back to the streets. I'm sorry, Sarah. I'm sorry for these choices you keep making. I can see now you won't get better. No matter what I do for you, you won't get better." Jack continued to caress the side of her face. "I'm going to miss you, Sarah."

Galia started to shake and her breathing became rapid. She knew she'd be taking a long nap in that woods if she didn't do something quick. Galia felt herself snap.

"Galia! My name is Galia Gregor!"

She screamed at the top of her lungs, and the bed shook as she pulled at her arms as hard as she could, paying no attention to the blood running down them as the hard plastic cut further into her skin.

"Stop!" Jack straddled her, grabbing her arms and pushing them backward into the headboard. Galia continued to scream and Jack slapped her.

Galia stopped yelling and lay slumped against the headboard, trying to clear the haze around her. Jack got off the bed and paced back and forth across the floor. She could hear him rambling to himself but couldn't make out anything recognizable.

"How..." Galia was trying to talk, but having difficulty moving her jaw. "How many girls... have you taken since I've been here with you?"

Jack ignored her and kept pacing.

"How... many..."

"A few," Jack snapped.

"Are they... Are they all... dead?" Galia was exhausted.

Jack yelled out something unintelligible as he kicked his feet through the articles and items on the floor.

"You were supposed to work! It was supposed to work with you!" Jack grabbed the alarm clock off the side table and threw it against the wall. He stood still, as if gaining a moment of clarity, and walked out of the room. He came back a minute later.

Galia's heart skipped a beat when she saw he had a knife. Jack walked over to the bed and grabbed one of her wrists.

"No, no, no..." Galia squirmed as Jack slide the tip of the blade under one set of the zip ties and pulled hard. The knife cut through the wraps and her arm fell to the bed beside her. To her surprise, he cut the other side and she found herself free from the restraints. She laid there, trembling. She was exhausted physically and emotionally.

"We're going for a little ride," Jack said. He turned around to gather the items on the floor and put them back into the box.

Galia's eyes darted back and forth between him and the door. She slowly shifted her legs onto the floor, as not to make any noise. Her heart raced, and she knew this might be her last opportunity. With as much might as she could muster, she pushed off on her legs, hoping for enough momentum to get up and out the door before he could turn around. The push caused a searing pain through her knee and she let out a whimper. Jack spun around. She had no choice. She had to keep going now. She channeled every ounce of courage she had and pushed past the fiery pain in her leg.

She made it out of the bedroom and through the living room before Jack got to his feet and came after her. She ran into the kitchen, screaming, reaching for the handle, when her knee gave way, sending her head first into the door. She yelled in pain as she hit the floor again, gripping her knee and rocking from side to side on her back.

Jack stood over her, his face red with anger. She could see the rage in his eyes and curled up on her side, bringing her hands in front of her face in a defensive posture. He grabbed her by her arms and shirt with both hands and swung her into the adjacent wall. Her left side hit the wall and she cried out in pain when she fell to the floor on top of the pieces of the chair Jack had thrown against the wall earlier.

"Please Jack! Please!" She lay there, helpless as he lifted his boot above her head. Galia, still whimpering, shook her head back and forth, terrified of the impending blow.

CHAPTER 18

Galia's head throbbed with pain as she tried to make sense of her blurred vision. She was on her side and her hands were secured with zip ties again. She realized she had no vision out of her left eye, and terror seized her as the memory of Jack's boot coming down on her head came alive in her mind. She cried out in pain as her body was sent upward from a bump in the road, and back down onto the cold metal floor.

She was in the van. She was in the back of the van. Panic fueled her awareness, and she knew she needed to get her hands free. The blood from her wrists running down her forearms felt warm against her skin. The sun had gone down, and the street lights were now creating a strobe effect through the tiny side windows as they drove. Lying there on the floor and squinting from the lights made her remember. How many times had she sat in the front seat, glancing behind her and feeling the stir of a memory too repressed to recall? She remembered it all now. The first time.

Galia's heart raced with fear, reliving her worst nightmare. Again.

★ ★ ★

Star watched the man get out of the van, open the sliding side door, and then turn toward her. The swiftness and purpose of his steps made her realize she was in trouble. She let out a scream, turning to run, but her heel caught in a crack on the sidewalk, and she fell. The man stood over her and delivered a swift punch to her face. Before she could recover, he grabbed her by the hair and lifted her, then threw her into the van.

Star grabbed for the front passenger seat and began pulling herself up, but the man grabbed her ankle and pulled her back onto the van floor. She lay on her side, fighting to clear her head as the man stood just outside the sliding door. Star pulled her knee up to her chest and drove the heel of her shoe as hard as she could into the man's leg. He cried out in pain, pulled his arm back and delivered yet another swift punch.

Star faded out into the blackness.

★ ★ ★

Galia's wrists had swollen around the new set of zip ties and the pain radiating throughout her head made it difficult to think straight. She was grateful not to have the heroin in her system this time. If only she'd been this clearheaded the first time. If only there hadn't been a first time.

Galia looked around for anything she could use to get free. The back of the van was completely stripped down, but there were large metal runners which jutted up from the floor about an inch. She suspected that was where the back seats were supposed to slide in. One of the runners was broken, exposing a sharp edge to the metal. Galia quietly shuffled over a few inches, so her hands were next to the runners. Her back was to Jack, and she tried to keep her hands low to the floor in case Jack looked back at her.

She startled when music started playing through the van speakers but kept her body still. Jack looked over his shoulder, then resumed his focus on the road. She couldn't believe it. It was like an early Christmas present beyond anything she could have asked for.

Excitedly, she kept one eye on him while she worked the tie wraps back and forth over the edge of the metal runner, the music covering over the sound of her hope. She winced in pain as the pressure of the wraps cut more deeply into her already split and swollen wrists. Silent tears fell, and she bit her already split lip, pressing as hard as she could tolerate without crying out.

Galia sucked in the air around her as the wraps snapped open. She tucked her hands back together, as if still bound, and lay as still as she could. Jack turned off the road and onto a bumpy path. Galia fought to stay clear enough to count the seconds from where he turned off.

"One one thousand, two one thousand, three one thousand..." She counted fifty-two seconds before Jack came to a stop.

Galia kept still, trying to appear unconscious. It might give her another shot at running if he thought he could leave her unattended for a minute. She slowed her breathing to calm herself as she listened to Jack get out of the van and shut his door. She could hear the ground crunching under his feet and wondered if they were in the woods beyond their house. That sounded like the place Jack took those who were being *difficult* for him. After the day's events, she would certainly fit into that category.

She flashed back to the bedroom, Jack stroking her hair and telling her he was going to miss her. If she couldn't think of something quickly, this might be where she died. Galia's mind was spinning with how to get past Jack. She couldn't die like this. She couldn't let her dad get news of a body in the woods. She tried not to jump when Jack slid the van door open. The metal on metal made a loud, screeching noise, and jarred the van and everything in it when it came to an abrupt stop.

Galia lay as still as she could. She could hear him breathing hard as he loomed over her. Watching her. Jack pressed his hand into the side of her head and Galia let out a scream. The pain radiated deeply through her head and down into her shoulders, and she was no longer able to fake oblivion.

Galia used her hands and feet to push herself backward, away from Jack, but he climbed inside and pulled her forcefully out the door and onto the ground. Pain radiated through her. She pulled her head up from the ground and opened the one eye that would work to survey her surroundings. As she scanned, she saw nothing but woods. As she moved past the other side of Jack, her eye widened in fear.

"No! No! No!" She scrambled backwards again.

Jack grabbed her by the arm and dragged her through the dirt. She looked forward and saw the door. That old, wooden, green door. She could already picture the metal one she knew was behind it.

Galia kicked and screamed as he pulled her toward the door, clawing her fingers through the dirt.

"Please! No! Not again," she cried. After a few more steps, Jack grabbed her by the wrist. She let out a painful cry and submitted to him, allowing him to lead her forward.

"Jack, please. Listen to me. You don't need to do this. You don't need to put me back in there. I'll be good. I swear."

Jack opened the wooden door and led her into the middle room.

Galia stared at the large metal door, her shoulders slumping in defeat. Jack held her with one hand while he unlocked the door with the other. Galia had enough wits about her to look around and tried to commit everything she saw to memory while he worked to open the door.

Jack swung the door open and, without saying a word, pushed Galia in and down onto the floor. He gave her a good shove to make sure she was in far enough before closing the door. Galia tumbled awkwardly, trying to catch herself, and rolled to her side as she listened to the lock click into place. She crawled over toward the door and put her hands up on it, as if begging to an unknown god. Any amount of hope she had for freeing herself dwindled like a wick snuffed out, and she bent forward on her knees and cried. She may not be lying on the floor with broken fingers this time, but the rest of her body was broken, and her spirit was in too many pieces to count.

* * *

"Time of death, 8:52 p.m." The doctor spoke quietly, looking at the clock.

Galia watched as her dad rushed over to her mom's side.

"No, no, no," he cried, burying his face in her chest. "Oh, Magpie."

She watched her dad, hardly able to process her own pain, but feeling oddly responsible for his. She went to his side and rested her arms around his shoulder. Eli lay over Maggie's body, his face in her chest, sobbing. With one hand, he reached up and tried to put his arm around Galia.

"Oh, Bean, I'm so sorry. I'm so, so sorry."

Galia broke, and the weight of the pain brought her down to the floor once more. It was too much. Too much to bear. She couldn't bring herself to look up at her mom's lifeless body. The nurses had turned the machines off, and the silence was deafening. She would give anything to hear the sound of those annoying beeps again. Anything.

Eli pushed himself back into the chair beside her bed, and sat holding Maggie's hand, tears running down his cheeks. He kept his other hand on Galia, still on the floor beside him.

"We're going to get through this, Galia. We'll get through it together."

Instead of comforting her, her dad's words made her burn with anger. Galia stood to her feet, letting her dad's hand fall off of her. Defeat hung thick in the air around her. She didn't understand why this had to happen, and she certainly didn't think things would ever be okay again.

★ ★ ★

"He... hello?" came a nervous voice from behind her.

Stunned, Galia spun around on her knees and gasped, as she looked wide-eyed at the young girl standing in front of her. Her hair was blonde and tattered, and she was wearing a t-shirt that looked familiar to Galia. She was wearing the shackle, but it was around her wrist instead of her ankle. The chain looked a little longer than she remembered.

"Oh my God! Rachel?"

Rachel whimpered in response to hearing her name. "You know me?"

Galia stood and stared at her for a long minute, then took a few steps closer to her.

Rachel countered her with a few steps backward, wrapping her arms around herself. The metal chain attached to her shackle slid across the floor as she moved, and Galia shuddered at the sound of it.

Galia took a step back to give Rachel more space, looking at her again in disbelief.

"Who are you?" Rachel asked.

Galia's face softened. She looked around the room she had all but forgotten. There were several new things since she had been in here. A small table next to the bed, a bean bag chair, and the old bathroom rug she thought Jack brought to the dump.

"I was you," Galia said somberly. "My name is Galia. Galia Gregor. Jack brought me here years ago... like you... I was a prisoner here."

"Jack?" That's his name?"

Galia nodded.

"But I don't understand. You got out? And now he brought you back?"

"It's a long story."

"How do you know who I am?" asked Rachel.

"The news. Your picture has been all over the news."

Rachel burst into tears. "They're looking for me? They're really looking for me?" she cried.

"Yes. I'm so sorry, Rachel. I didn't know. Maybe I did know, but I just didn't want to admit it."

Rachel looked at her confused. "What do you mean? Why did he... why did Jack bring you here? Why did he bring me here? What's he going to do with us?"

Galia drew in a long, slow breath and looked to the side, avoiding eye contact with Rachel. "We need to figure out how to get out of here."

Rachel shook her head. "How? I've been trying to think of something for days, and even if I could figure out how to get past him when he opens the door, I think there's another door after that."

"There is."

"So how? How do we get out?"

Galia winced in pain as she twisted her body to look around the room.

Rachel stood silent.

Galia looked at the shackle on Rachel's wrist. She could see there was some type of padding in between the shackle and her wrist, a modification she would have appreciated during her time here.

"I'm sorry. I'm not sure how to get that off your wrist, but we'll think of something." Galia's eyes moved over to the bed and emotion enveloped her face when she looked at the wall above the pillow. She walked over to the bed, leaned around it and ran her hand over the carvings.

"That was there when I got here," said Rachel.

"I know." Galia traced the lines with her fingers. "I did it."

Rachel was silent for a moment, and then spoke softly.

"It kind of comforted me when I first saw it. Gave me a weird kind of hope. In a strange way, it also made me feel not so alone because I knew someone else had been here. To be honest, it kind of scared me too. It made me wonder what happened to whoever did that."

Galia nodded, still letting her eyes wander over the words.

"Maybe this is a good thing. You're still alive, so maybe there's hope."

Galia moved down and sat on the bed. "No, Rachel. I don't think so."

Galia looked down at her wrists and touched the mixture of fresh and dried blood mixing with the dirt around her wrists. "I think we're both in a lot of trouble, and that's mostly my fault." She stared at the floor, remembering that day she made such a fateful choice to go with Jack. "I believed him," Galia said softly. "I believed every word he said to me that day. I believed he was my freedom. But he was just another prison."

"What happened to you?"

Galia sighed. "So much. I hardly know where to start. I was living on the streets. This was about five years ago. I was... well... I was... I had to make a living so I..."

Rachel sat on the bed next to her and put a hand on her leg. "Lady of the night?" Rachel said, almost sarcastically, as if she didn't approve of the title.

"Yes." Galia looked down.

"Me too."

Galia looked over at Rachel, thankful that she understood.

"I know. It was on the news."

Rachel's face dropped.

Galia knew that feeling all too well. She looked past Rachel to the small side table by the bed. Wrapped in plastic were two of the banana nut muffins, which turned her stomach.

Galia continued. "Jack came to the track and I thought he was just another John. I knew something about him wasn't right, but I was coming down off heroin, and in a desperate way for some money. But the more I got a look at his eyes, the more my gut told me to let this one pass. I tried to walk away, but he got out of his van and attacked me. He threw me in the van and brought me here."

"That's awful," Rachel said. "I know what you mean about him though. He was weird and awkward, but I needed the money, and he was offering to pay me a lot more if I agreed to go to a special spot with him. Said he'd drive me back to the track when we were done. So, I got into the van with him."

Galia shifted her eyebrows at Rachel, as if asking her to continue.

"He drove pretty far, and ended up bringing me here. Said he had a quiet place we wouldn't be disturbed and would pay me three times my normal. I followed him through the first door but, when I saw that metal one, I freaked out and turned around to leave. He grabbed me and threw me inside. Just like that. I practically did it for him. I can't believe how stupid I was."

Galia gripped Rachel's hand reassuringly.

"I don't have any memory of coming here. Well, the first time. I passed out in the van and woke up here, on the bed, with that shackle around my ankle."

"How long were you in here?" Rachel asked.

"About two months."

Rachel's face dropped again.

"I tried to escape once, but it ended badly." Galia lifted her hand and showed Rachel the broken fingers. "I was almost out, just beyond the metal door when Jack slammed my hand in it. Broke these three fingers and did something to my hand. It's never been quite right since that happened."

Galia winced again at the reminder. She put her hand back in her lap, tucking her crooked fingers in between her thighs, out of view. "After that, I kind of lost hope. I was going through withdrawals too, and that messed with me a lot. But then Jack seemed nice sometimes and kept telling me he was trying to help me. That I was in here for my own good to help me kick the addition and to protect me from the cops."

"He said the same thing to me about the cops!" Rachel blurted out.

Galia looked at her and shook her head. "I honestly don't know how much of that is true or not. He told me he found my dad and that my dad didn't want anything to do with me... because of the prostitution and all."

Rachel teared up as she listened.

"He told me all of that about my dad, and about the cops wanting to put me in prison. I started believing him. But I know that part isn't true now. The part about my dad."

"How do you know?"

"I got out of the house and saw a news broadcast about the abductions, and my dad looking for me after all this time. The police thought it was all connected, so they were opening cold cases like mine."

"What house?"

"Jack's house," Galia responded. "He brought me to his house to live."

"So, he tied you up there too, for all this time?"

Galia's face fell. Her cheeks flushed, and tears came to her eyes.

"What is it?" Rachel asked.

"I... I..." Galia sputtered. "I wasn't restrained. I just lived there." Galia wasn't sure what she felt more of. Shock or anger with herself at the obvious revelation. "I thought he was protecting me, so I followed the rules. All this time. All these years, I could have left whenever I wanted and none of this would have happened." Galia sobbed. "I'm so sorry, Rachel. None of this would have happened to you if I left. I thought I couldn't. I believed I couldn't. I'm so sorry."

Rachel grabbed Galia's hands and made Galia look her in the face. "Listen to me. That man is a monster. He fooled you. He was trying to fool me too. I don't know what I would have done. Maybe I would have done the same thing. But we're here now. We're here and we need to figure out how to get home."

Home. There was that word again. Galia let it spin in her head like a merry-go-round, flashing to the images of her grey-haired dad crying at a podium. More tears spilled down her face.

"I remember sitting right here." Galia paused. "I was sitting right here when he told me my dad knew what I did and didn't want me anymore. It destroyed me, and I let go of every hope I had on the inside of me. I let it go like a helium balloon and watched it float away in front of my face. I didn't have the energy to try to reach for it. All I felt was shame. What I had done. What I had become."

Rachel tightened her grip on Galia's hands.

"He made me feel dirty. Unforgivable. He made me believe I could never be anything more than the sum of my poor choices. I was a whore addicted to heroin. Nothing more. That's what my dad saw. That's what the news stations were saying. That's what the police said and why they wanted me off the streets and in prison."

Galia let go of Rachel's hands and wiped the tears sideways across her cheeks.

"I was scared, but I should have known better. I should have trusted what I know about my dad. About the kind of person I know he is. I don't know why I didn't. I let Jack free me from this room only to let him chain me up in a different kind of prison. I could have walked out of it, but I didn't. I got so used to trying to be what he told me I should be. I just accepted it. I feel so stupid." Galia lowered her head.

Rachel comforted her. "But you said it isn't true, right? You said you know what he said about your dad isn't true?"

Galia lifted her head.

"You're right." Galia took a deep breath and wiped her nose with her sleeve. "I'm doing it again," she said angrily. "I'm believing the lies that this is what I deserve, and this is who I am." Galia's eyes lit up. She could see the balloon she had let go of so many years ago. Her mood shifted from grief to determination. "We need to get out of here. As soon as we can. Before Jack gets back or we're both..." Galia let her words end abruptly, and the two girls exchanged a worried look. "We can figure this out."

"But you just said you tried once and look what he did to you!"

Galia looked down at her hand and sighed. She thought for a moment.

"Yes, that's true. But it was only me. There's two of us now. Together we can overpower him."

Rachel's face lifted a little. "Do you really think so?"

Galia sighed again. "I'm not sure, but I think we have to try. It's our only option."

Rachel nodded.

"Does that side table move?" Galia jumped up to grab it but was met with a solid resistance.

"No. It's bolted into the floor. I've tried about a hundred times to get a piece off of it, but no luck."

Galia sat back down, and images raced through her head. Horrible images which provided a means from this place to their freedom. It made her detest who she was. What she was thinking of doing to another human being. But Jack wasn't a human being. He was a monster. She knew she wasn't above whatever it would take to get them out of there. She owed it to Rachel. She owed it to her dad.

Her dad. A small smile formed on her face despite her present circumstances. It was her hope in the darkness. Her helium balloon.

CHAPTER 19

Jack knew time was his enemy and worked feverishly to pull what he needed from the garage. He set the ladder against the wall and climbed up to the loft, where he grabbed a large tarp and threw it to the ground below. He jumped midway from the ladder onto the ground, moving quickly to gather duct tape and more zip ties. He threw it all into the back of the van and ran to the driver's side door.

Jack opened it, but stood silent for a moment, rubbing his forehead. He drew in a deep breath, smoothed the hair back on his head, and then ran back into the garage. Walking back out with a five-gallon container of gasoline, he added that to the items in the back of the van. After closing the back doors, he jumped in the driver's seat, slammed his door shut, and took off.

* * *

Galia got up off the bed and walked over to the water spicket to rinse her hands. She bent down and tried to turn the faucet handle counterclockwise.

"It's not on," Rachel said. "He turned it off yesterday after I... well, after I said a few choice words that probably should have stayed in my head."

Galia stood back up and looked at her hands again. She tried to rub them gently with the bottom of her shirt, but there was too much mud that had already dried. She winced every time she touched her wrists, and finally gave up and lowered herself into the beanbag chair.

Rachel laid back on the bed. "Do you think he's coming back tonight?"

"I don't know."

"Galia?"

"Yeah?"

"You know... even if we can manage to take him..." Rachel paused.

"What?"

"I mean... this shackle. We're going to need the key. He keeps it on him."

"Yeah, in his shirt pocket, right?" Galia asked.

"Yes. Yes, that's where he pulls it from." Rachel paused again. "If we're going to get the key, that means he has to be out cold, or we have to be able to hold him down. Like, for real."

"I know." Galia responded, now watching a spider move along the floor. She was exhausted, and her body wanted nothing more than to sleep. She wanted to sleep and wake up from this horrible nightmare, but with the injuries to her head, she knew she couldn't allow herself to lose consciousness. Although she couldn't see herself, she knew her injuries were significant. She could feel that much.

Galia straightened up, keeping her eye on the spider, wishing she could move about as easily as he did. She wondered what nefarious intent that spider crept along with. Nefarious. That was a word they used online describing Jack. They just didn't know it was Jack yet.

Galia found herself wishing she had been more upfront about him when she called. Maybe she wouldn't be sitting here. Maybe she would be sitting in a different kind of prison, but at least it wouldn't be a judgement of execution she was now waiting for. The spider crawled into the drain and disappeared. Galia closed her eyes for a moment to rest.

"Hey!" said Rachel, just louder than a whisper.

Galia opened the eye that wasn't swollen shut. "What?"

"Shhh!" Rachel was now sitting up, so Galia propped herself up on one elbow, wincing as the pain radiated up into her shoulder. Both girls strained to listen.

Galia got up off the bean bag chair and limped over to the door. She flattened her back against the wall, opposite the side where it opens, holding one finger up to her lips and motioning for Rachel to come over by her. Rachel moved next to her and Galia whispered in her ear. "When Jack comes in, we're going to wait until he's in the middle of the doorframe, and we're going to slam the door on him."

Rachel shot her a disapproving look.

"What? It's all we have. Do you have any better ideas?" Galia looked at her, waiting for her to respond.

Rachel just nodded and shrugged her shoulders in surrender. Then she whispered back, "Let me go in front. I think I can push harder. I just have to make sure the chain reaches."

Rachel lifted the chain attached to her shackle to prevent the noise of it scraping and walked slowly to the other side of the door. She nodded and assumed her position just ahead of Galia. Sweat beaded on Rachel's forehead as they waited.

Rachel reached down and grabbed Galia's hand, forgetting about her wrists. Galia did her best to ignore the pain so she could provide some comfort to Rachel. The truth was, she needed it just as badly. She knew they were both afraid, but had no better plan.

They stood in eerie silence for some time. Galia looked up at the wall by the bed and read the words quietly to herself. Her body was riddled with pain, but she had to push through it. This was it. This was their shot. She had no idea how this would all play out, but she kept reminding herself it was two against one. The odds were in their favor. She had to do what she had never been willing to do before. Fight. Fight for her life. Fight for the life of this girl she had just met. Fight for the thing she hadn't known for years. Freedom.

She kept saying the word over and over in her head until she was interrupted by that familiar and unsettling click of the door lock. Her heart raced as the door popped open. Rachel looked over her shoulder and gave Galia a determined look. Now was not the time to take the easy way out. This was not a fork in the road. This was their very lives. This was their freedom.

Jack pushed the door open and peered his head around the corner, trying to locate the girls.

"Now!" Galia yelled, and the two girls pushed the door with all their might, slamming it hard into Jack's head. Rachel pulled the door open, and Jack stumbled backwards into the entryway and onto the floor.

"Go! Go! Go!" she yelled at Galia as she held the door open.

Galia hesitated for just a moment, then pressed herself against the opposite wall of the entry way while Jack tried to hoist himself to his feet. They hadn't thought beyond this point. Jack was supposed to be knocked unconscious, but he wasn't.

Rachel could just get her arms past the threshold. She reached in and grabbed Jack's foot, bringing him back to the floor long enough for Galia to get out of his reach. Once outside, Galia spun around and looked frantically in every direction for anything she could use as a weapon. Just a few feet away was a pile of metal scraps.

She could hear Rachel yelling to her but could hardly make out the words over the ringing in her ears. She made her way to the pile and quickly located what looked like a metal bar. She heard Rachel yell again and turned to look over her shoulder. Jack was through the door and coming toward her, fast and furious. This was it. It was do or die, and she had no intention of dying today.

Galia grabbed a metal bar with both hands, using the weight of her body to hoist it into the air. The weight of the bar made her arms burn, and her midsection felt like it was on fire.

By the look on Jack's face, she didn't think he saw it coming until it was too late. The metal bar smashed into the side of his head, stopping him in his tracks. He stood upright for a second, as if he was unfazed. Galia was about to hit him again when his eyes rolled back into his head, and she watched as he dropped straight down to the ground. Galia dropped the bar and fell to the ground beside him, completely spent.

★ ★ ★

"This is Special Agent Grant. We're approaching Price's residence." Agent Grant let his finger off the radio button and waited for dispatch to confirm receipt of their location. The assembly of vehicles pulled quietly onto the property.

"All is quiet." Agent Grant reported. "We're going to circle and assess quick before we send the team in to look around."

"Copy. Standing by," responded dispatch.

"Pretty dark and quiet. You think we're at the right house?" asked Police Chief Reynolds.

Agent Grant stood quietly, looking over the yard. "That's what we're here to find out."

* * *

Galia staggered to her feet. Her vision was blurred, and she tried to shake off the ringing in her ears. Jack lay on the ground, motionless, and Galia looked at him, feeling almost disembodied from the moment. She had to fight to recall what had just taken place.

"Galia!" screamed Rachel.

The sound snapped Galia out of her haze, and she turned and moved toward the door, dragging her leg behind her as she moved slowly forward. She kept looking back over her shoulder at Jack, panicked by the memory of the unexpected tackle when she was trying to leave his house earlier that evening. She was unable to see out of one eye and her head was throbbing. The bruising in her midsection along with the searing pain radiating from her knee severely compromised her movements, and her wrists stung as dirt mixed deeper into her cuts with every motion.

She could hear Rachel crying. Determined, Galia moved as deliberately as her broken body would allow, until she reached the entrance of the room.

"Galia!" yelled Rachel. "You're okay! Where is–"

"We have to get you out of this." Galia grabbed onto the chain of the shackle. "Grab the chain with both hands. We're going to pull. We've got to see if we can free this from the wall."

Rachel looked uncertainly at Galia. "Come on! We don't have much time!"

Rachel jumped in response and followed Galia's lead. The two girls gripped the chain and pulled with as much force as they could, grunting as they tried to rip it free from the wall.

"It's no use! We're not strong enough." Rachel said, throwing the chain in her hands onto the floor.

"Go again," Galia said, motioning for Rachel to grab the chain. "Come on, Rachel. We've got to try."

It took everything for Galia just to be standing up straight, let alone exerting any force. She was hoping the weight of her body pulling backwards would be enough, but desperately needed Rachel's head in the game. "Let's go. One... two... three!"

The girls gave another mighty tug. The chain creaked as they pulled on it, but they could see the chain plate remained unaltered. It made a loud noise as they dropped it back onto the floor.

"Oh my God. Oh my God." Rachel began to unravel. "I'm never going to get out of here." She turned to look at Galia. "You need to go."

"What?"

"You need to go! You need to go and get help! Go!"

Galia stood looking at Rachel and was about to leave, when she heard a groan come from outside. Galia broke out into a sweat and paced, looking at Rachel.

"Just go, Galia! Go!"

"No. There's no way I'm leaving here without you." Galia studied the shackle around her wrist for a moment and then locked eyes with Rachel. Swallowing hard, she asked, "Do you trust me?"

Rachel's eyes widened. "Yes. Yes, why?"

"I'm sorry," Galia said emphatically, as she glanced over her shoulder.

Rachel scrunched up her face. "For what?"

"For this." Galia moved more swiftly toward Rachel than she should have been able to, but adrenaline was her painkiller. She grabbed Rachel's hand with the shackle on it and, before Rachel could make sense of what was happening, pulled back on her thumb with enough force to break it from the socket.

Rachel screamed out in pain. She lay on the floor, moaning and cradling her hand.

"I'm so sorry, Rachel, but listen to me." Galia grabbed the tops of her shoulders. "It's going to hurt, but you're going to be able to bend your thumb into the palm of your hand and pull your hand out of the shackle."

Galia glanced back over her shoulder again but couldn't see or hear any sign of Jack. "Do it! Do it now!"

Rachel, still reeling from the pain, cried out as she used her opposite hand to press her thumb into her palm and slide her hand down, through the shackle. The metal clamp hit the cement floor and Galia let out the kind of laughter that only comes from a marriage of relief and fear.

"Come on." Galia reached down to help her up and could see a look of horror come across Rachel's face, as Rachel looked up and behind her. A sense of dread overwhelmed Galia. She turned unsteadily to see Jack coming through the doorway. Galia was exhausted, and she knew she had zero chance of running from him. Rachel had a much better shot than she did. Galia pushed past her fear, threw herself into Jack, and yelled to Rachel.

"Run! Rachel, Run! Run!" she screamed as commandingly as she could, as she clutched Jack's arms, bringing them both onto the floor.

Rachel stood, holding her hand, but hesitating.

"Run!" Galia screamed again. "Run!"

Rachel paused for one more second, and then bolted out the door.

Galia lay on the floor as Jack loomed over her. It was amazing to her how many thoughts she had in the short time she was staring death in the face. A flood of memories assaulted her, like waves crashing on the shore. They were momentary flashes of precious times tucked away in her subconscious, programed to emerge upon critical failure.

How odd, she thought, how the mind works. She wondered how it decided which memories deserved center stage during the final act. Pictures passed through her mind and stopped abruptly on her dad. The last known image of him in her brain. The one from television. The one of him crying. She too, closed her eyes and cried, not wanting to see the final act of Jack's rage. She only wanted to picture her dad's face.

★ ★ ★

"Jack Price." Agent Grant spoke slowly into the bullhorn. "This is the FBI!" The dark FBI vehicles and backup squad cars were arranged in a circle about thirty feet from the shed door. Squad car doors were open, shielding armed law enforcement.

"There's someone coming through the doorway!" yelled one of the officers. The quiet clicking of the rifles and hand guns being taken off safety echoed across the line like a harmonized symphony, and law enforcement stood waiting in position. Special Agent Grant sent his hand rapidly up in the air.

"Hold your fire!" he called out. Officers relaxed their position, as they watched the shape of a person move through the doorway and take form.

"She's got something in her hand!" yelled someone from behind the squad cars. In response, the officers tensed and resumed their position. Agent Grant put his hand up again.

"I said hold your fire!" he yelled even louder than before, then directed his attention to Galia. "Young lady, put down whatever you're holding and put your hands in the air."

Galia, unable to see through the flood lights, opened her hand and looked down at what she was holding. She extended her fingers and let it slide down and onto the ground and stood, staring at the blood on her hands. "Put your hands in the air. Do it now." Galia turned her face away from the light as she slowly moved her hands up into the air, now realizing where she was. Officers moved in to secure her.

"That's Galia! She saved me! She saved me! Let her go!" Rachel yelled from behind the squad cars. "He's still in there! Jack's still in there! Please! He's still in there!"

As the officers brought Galia behind the line, Agent Grant waved his hands forward and other officers advanced to the door. They moved swiftly, guns up, disappearing inside.

A policewoman was holding a blanket over Rachel's shoulders, trying to tend to her hand, but Rachel threw the blanket off and ran to meet Galia.

"This is Agent Grant. We're going to need an ambulance." Agent Grant walked to meet the girls. "Rachel McGinnis?"

Rachel nodded enthusiastically.

He turned his head to Galia. "Sweetheart, did your friend here say your name was Galia? Are you Galia Gregor?"

Galia nodded her head.

"My God," Agent Grant said out loud. "Dispatch, I'm going to need you to contact Eli Gregor and tell him to meet us at the hospital." There was a pause between his sentences as he fought to maintain his composure. He turned to face the officers assembled there and said loudly enough for all of them to hear him, "We've got Galia Gregor too!"

The officers erupted in cheering, which made Rachel burst into tears. Their celebration was quieted by the voice across the radio.

"Sorry, come again?" Agent Grant asked.

"We've got him." came the voice across the radio to the walkie. "Unsub is deceased. Location is secure."

Agent Grant took in a deep breath, then pressed the button down. "Copy that."

Rachel looked at Galia with shock on her face, but Galia remained silent, looking at her hands. Rachel put her good arm around Galia and cradled her head on her shoulder.

Galia let out a sob. Her knees gave way and she fell to her knees. Rachel lowered herself to the ground and continued cradling her.

* * *

Agent Grant assigned officers to stay with the girls and took two more inside the compound with him. He paused just inside the wooden door and studied the heavy metal door before him. He turned to look at the other officers standing behind him and they exchanged a look of disbelief.

Agent Grant shook his head and continued on into the room where the girls were held. He stood with his hands in his pockets. It was a little trick he conditioned himself to do early on when he worked in the field more often, as not to inadvertently touch something before forensics got there. He scanned the room, his eyes immediately going to the body on the floor by the bed. It was Jack Price. He lay on his back, blood running from a large wound in his neck onto the floor and into the floor drain nearby. He looked over the items in the room and rested his eyes on the carving in the wall beside the bed. "What's that?"

"It's a scripture out of the Christian Bible," answered one of the other agents.

"Hmm." pondered Grant. "What did you pick up outside? What'd she have in her hand?"

"Scissors," answered the agent.

"Really?" Grant bent down by Jack's body, looking over the neck wound. "She did all that with a pair of scissors?"

"Looks like it. Forensics will be here shortly. They'll confirm. She talking?" asked the agent.

"I haven't spoken with her yet. She seemed pretty rattled after she walked out. And in pretty rough shape. Wanted to give her a minute to get checked out by the medics." Agent Grant got close to the body again and took a few notes. "Darndest thing, isn't it? Who would have imagined we'd find two of them in here? Hell, I would have been ecstatic to find one of them alive, let alone both."

"I wonder which one of them did that on the wall?" asked the agent.

"No idea... Maybe neither. Maybe it was someone else entirely." Agent Grant sighed hard and long. "I hate to say this, but I sure am sorry he's dead. He was our only lead to the other girls."

"Maybe one of these two know something," responded the agent.

"Yeah." Agent Grant paused. "Maybe." He stood to his feet and stepped backward, looking at the wall again. "So if the Son sets you free, you will be free indeed. John 8:36. Hmm."

Agent Grant's phone rang, and he walked back outside to answer it. After hanging up, he walked over to the ambulance, where both girls were being loaded in. Galia was on the stretcher, and one of the ambulance techs had just finished helping Rachel into the back and was about to close the door.

"Hold up!" called Agent Grant.

"Only a second, Agent. We've got to get this one in right away." He pointed to Galia. "We're concerned about some of her injuries, specifically her head."

"No problem. I'll be quick." He leaned into the back. "We're really glad to see you two girls are okay." He looked at Galia, now able to see the full extent of her facial injuries under the light of the ambulance, and tried to hide his reaction. "I just wanted you to know we'll be following you to the hospital. I know you've just gone through a lot, and you're not feeling very good, but we really need to get statements from the both of you, to the best of your abilities."

Rachel nodded, and Galia tried to do the same through the oxygen mask attached to her nose and mouth.

"I also wanted to let you know that Rachel, both your parents are on their way and Galia, your dad is too."

* * *

The sound of the ambulance sirens made Galia's head pound. Her mind felt as broken as her body, as she tried to process what Agent Grant just said. She was likely minutes away from seeing her dad for the first time in seven years and found herself haunted by the worries and fears Jack had spent years conditioning her to feel. She was aware of the facts as she heard them on TV, but it was like telling a person trying to quit smoking to just ignore the muscle memory of lifting the cigarette to their mouth. Galia could hear Jack's voice in her head telling her she was dirty and broken. She could hear him saying her dad would never look at her the same way. That he would never love her the same way again.

Galia felt disgusted. Even lying dead in the prison, she was still letting him exert control over her. Fresh tears pooled in her eyes as she lay on the stretcher. Rachel reached down and stroked her hair with her hand. The pain, physically and emotionally, overwhelmed Galia, and she could feel herself fading in and out of consciousness.

Caroline Klug

CHAPTER 20

The last thing Galia remembered was being in the ambulance. The faint sound of beeping and people talking brought her to a state of hazy awareness. She lay there with her eyes closed and her body still, trying to connect with what she was hearing and feeling around her. She was trying to remember how she got to this place with a soft pillow cradling her head and soft sheets holding her so tight. Then she realized the sheets were not tight around her body. What she was feeling was her hand and arm being squeezed. The sound of the beeps got louder as her consciousness returned. She felt the grip on her hand tighten as she stirred awake.

"Galia? Galia, sweetie?"

"Mmm..." Galia let out a low moan as she stirred and fought to open her eyes.

"Nurse! She's waking up!"

Not fully awake yet, Galia raised the hand that wasn't being squeezed and brought it to her head to explore whatever it was she was feeling was wrapped around it. A hand met hers and brought it back down to her side.

"It's okay, Ms. Gregor. You're okay. You have some bandages around your head. You have a few head injuries," said the nurse, as she returned Galia's arm to her side and took her vitals.

A deeper voice spoke. "That's right, sweetie. You're going to be okay."

The voice she heard was like a distant memory. A pleasant one. She smiled, believing she was having a dream.

"Galia, sweetie? Bean? It's Dad."

Those words rang through more clearly and she snapped her eyes open. Her blurred vision cleared to see a face unfamiliar to her. He was tall with olive skin and dressed in a suit. She watched the nurse walked past him and out the door.

"Hey, sweetie!"

There was the voice. She turned her head to the opposite side of the bed. Tears and emotion overtook her in a matter of seconds.

"Daddy?" Galia could hardly get the word out. "Daddy, is that really you?"

Eli tightened his grip around her hand even more, laughing and crying all at once.

"Yes, Bean. It's really me. I was thinking the same thing about you." He let out another laugh which was quickly stifled by the sob that followed. She could see his nose running, but he didn't seem to notice, keeping his hands tight around hers.

Galia tried her best to return the grip of his hand. The pain radiating into her wrist made her wince, but the gesture was enough to say what her words couldn't. She followed his glance back over to the man with olive skin, who was still standing on the other side of her bed.

"Galia, this man is Special Agent Grant. He was one of the people who helped rescue you. He needs to ask you a few questions."

Galia watched Agent Grant's face turn serious as he pulled out a small pad of paper and a pen from the inside of his suit coat. She looked quickly at her dad, then back to Agent Grant. Her face twisted with recollection. She remembered. She remembered all of it. Galia could hardly process the flood of images all coming back to her. She cried and wrestled herself out of the sheets around her, pushing everything away.

* * *

Pictures passed through her mind and stopped abruptly on her dad. The last known image of him in her brain. The one from television. The one of him crying at a podium. She too, closed her eyes and cried, not wanting to see the final act of Jack's rage. She wanted only to picture her dad's face.

Jack kicked her once more in the stomach, and she let out a loud heaving sound and rolled to her side. This is the part where she was programmed to close her eyes and succumb to the fate awaiting her. She could hear her dad's words about taking the path of least resistance – the one that didn't require anything hard or complicated of her. Freedom was literally steps away. She could do what she always did, take the path of least resistance and die here in this prison. Or she could do the harder thing and maybe, just maybe, she would live.

Galia opened her eyes to the reality around her. She reached for the leg of the bed frame to help pull herself up. As she grabbed for it, something unusual caught her eye. Her heart raced, remembering from so many years ago, and her adrenaline gave her the extra energy she needed to pull herself along the floor toward the other leg post.

Jack laughed. "Where do you think you're going?"

Galia ignored him and used her forearms to pull herself around the corner of the bed. She reached under the frame, groping for the bedpost closest to the wall. Once there, she slid her hand across the floor, praying it was still there. Her fingers connected with the thin metal blades and she thrust her hand forward to grab the scissors. Jack grabbed onto her legs and she screamed while he pulled her back out. Galia tucked her hands underneath her while Jack turned her over and straddled her.

He screamed obscenities while he pressed her into the floor. "I should have done this years ago."

Jack grabbed Galia's neck with both hands and squeezed. As she gasped for air, Galia pulled her hand out from under her. She held the scissors in her hand, with the blades exposed.

With every ounce of strength she could muster, Galia thrust the sharp points into Jack's neck. She could feel the warm blood spray across her face and neck. Before he could push himself away from her, Galia twisted the scissors into his wound.

Jack grabbed the scissors out of his neck and threw them to the floor. He staggered off to the side, clutching his hand over his neck, looking at Galia with something like shock. After a few seconds, Jack dropped to the floor.

Galia laid on the cement floor next to him, trying to breathe. She watched him choke and sputter as the thick blood ran down his neck and pooled on the floor beside him. The pool of blood expanded until the force of the declining floor sent a single path of blood breaking free, starting a new path down to the floor drain.

Galia pushed herself backwards, to move out of its way. She picked up the scissors, got to her feet, and scuffled backwards, facing Jack. He was no longer making noise, but she was scared he might still be alive. Gripping the scissors, ready to attack, she leaned down carefully toward him, listening for his breath and trying to watch his chest to see if it was moving.

He was still.

Galia could hardly process what was happening. She raised herself up and took a few more steps backwards, still watching him, fearing an unexpected comeback. After she had inched past the metal door, she turned around to find her way out. It was nighttime, but she was met with an intense light.

Galia gripped the doorframe with one hand, trying to steady herself, her other hand up, shielding her eyes from the spotlight. Maybe this was death. Maybe Jack did succeed, and her body was still lying back in the prison room. Then she heard a voice cut through from the darkness around the light.

"I said hold your fire!" the voice yelled. "Young lady put down whatever you're holding and put your hands in the air."

Galia, still unable to see through the light, opened her hand and looked down at the scissors. She extended her fingers and let them slide down and onto the ground. Then she stood, staring at the blood on her hands.

* * *

"Oh God! Oh God!" she cried.

Galia was now sitting up in bed with her knees pulled up to her chest, rocking back and forth. The blankets she kicked off were hanging over the side of the bed. "I'm sorry. I'm so sorry. I didn't have a choice."

Eli grabbed her shoulders and tried to settle her back into the bed as Agent Grant pulled her blankets back over her. Galia's cries turned to sobs and she grabbed the edge of the blanket and pulled it up to her face like a small child afraid in a dark bedroom.

Eli sat on the bed, took Galia in his arms and rocked her back and forth.

Agent Grant took a few steps back. "I'll give you two a few minutes," he said, and quietly left the room.

"My sweet girl," her dad said gently. "It's going to be okay. You did what you needed to do, and no one is blaming you for that. Everything is going to be all right." Eli sat back down in his chair beside the bed, still holding onto her hand. His eyes were sad as he looked at the bandages around her wrists. "I'm so sorry for all of the horrible things you had to go through. So many years stolen from you." Eli choked up again but continued through the lump in his throat. "I'm sorry."

Galia shook her head and turned her body toward him. "Dad, no! You shouldn't be the one apologizing. Not after..." She paused and looked down, unable to make eye contact. "Not after everything I've done. What I became." Galia cried. "I'm so sorry, Daddy. I know how ashamed you must be of me. I'm... I'm so ashamed. If I could take it back I would. Please don't hate me. I can't bear the thought of losing you again." She buried her face in her hands and the weight of her guilt pressed heavily on her, making her head throb again.

"Bean," he said, trying to get her to look at him.

Galia sat with her hands in her face.

"Galia!" Galia lifted her head slowly, wiping the tears from her face as she looked up at him. She suddenly felt like that small child – the one who got engine grease all over his bright yellow sweatshirt. She was quite certain there was no way to repurpose this one.

Eli stood, leaned in and took her face into his hands, making sure she was looking him in the eyes. "Oh, Galia. I could never hate you. We all make mistakes. We all do things we regret and can't take back. After you went missing, I blamed myself. I was so broken because I felt it was my fault."

Galia tried shaking her head but he used his hands to steady her again.

"Listen to me, Bean. I know now that it doesn't matter who's fault it was. Sometimes bad things just happen. Whether it happens to us or because of us. But someone once helped me understand that it's not about what happens to us, but what we choose to do with it... how we choose to use it to make ourselves or others better. What you did when you were out on the streets..."

Galia tried to look down again but Eli lifted her head to resume eye contact. "Those things you did you thought you had to do to survive, right?"

Galia nodded her head.

"In hindsight, those things may not have been the right choice, but now that you're here... sitting right here with me… you can make different choices. You can use what you've learned to have a different path forward."

"But all those things I did. All those horrible things. Daddy, I did so many bad things. And there were drugs. Painkillers. Different kinds of drugs." Galia was fighting to talk through her sobs. "So many families ruined. I ruined." Galia buried her head in her dad's shoulder and cried.

Eli smoothed the back of her hair. His hand ran past the edge and onto her back the first few times as he adjusted to the shortened length of her hair.

"All those things were unfortunate, but they were just part of the path to get you where you are right now. Now you have a new set of choices. Are you going to use them to live in this place of darkness or are you going to use it to be the best version of yourself and maybe even help someone else?"

For the first time since they'd started talking, Galia stopped crying. She shook off a few involuntary sniffles and sank back into the bed.

"How could I ever help someone after what I did? Who would listen to me?"

Eli smiled so warmly, it almost made Galia forget the pain for a moment.

"My sweet girl. It's because of what you did that people will listen to you. It makes you human. It makes you someone who can understand what someone else is going through. If you're struggling with something, who would you rather listen to – someone who's never walked in your shoes, or the person who has and is in a better place now?"

Galia let his words rest on her, knowing the answer to his question was easy, but she was still having a difficult time applying that same level of mercy to herself.

"So, you don't hate me? You're not... ashamed of me?"

Her words and scared look choked him up again and he sat back on her bed, threw his arms around her and held her tight. "No, Galia. I am not ashamed of you."

Galia could hear him muffle a faint cry.

"On the contrary, I'm proud of you."

Galia could hardly understand his response. "What... why... why are you proud of me? I'm dirty. Unclean."

Eli looked at her, confused. "Who told you that?"

Galia looked down again. "Jack."

Eli held her and stroked the back of her hair again as he spoke softly, but deliberately. "You're not dirty. You're beautiful. You're a fighter. You overcame circumstances most people would never have survived. You did some things you regret along the way, but you regret them. That tells me who you are. Who you're going to be. And for that, I'm so proud of you. You overcame so many difficult odds, and I know..."

Eli pulled himself away and looked into her eyes again. "...that you are going to use all of these things, learn from them, and do something amazing with your life. I have never felt prouder to be your dad. Galia Gregor, I love you, I've always loved you, and I always will. You're home now. You're home."

His words washed over her like a healing balm. They were better than the drip of whatever was in her IV, dulling the pain.

"I don't even know what to say, Dad. I was so worried you wouldn't want me back."

Eli laughed. "That's because you're not a parent yet." He grinned at her. "Someday, I hope that you find out just what I'm talking about. Someday, I hope you realize the power of a parent's love, and how nothing you do can change that love."

"Dad." She said quietly. "I just want you to know it was you."

Eli looked at her confused. "What was me?"

"It was your face I saw when I thought I was going to die. It was the thought of you that made me want to fight and survive. The thought of seeing you again and making all of this right. You gave me that strength."

Eli's eyes teared up and he gave her another hug. Galia sat with her chin on the top of his shoulder, tears of gratitude spilling from her eyes.

There was a quiet knock at the door, and Galia released the grip on her dad and looked up. She blinked to clear her eyes but could hardly believe what she was seeing. Galia wiped the tears from her face again, suddenly aware of how she must look. She took a deep breath to stop from crying.

"Hey." His voice was deeper than she remembered, but that charming grin had the same effect on her as it did seven years ago.

"Teddy?"

Teddy smiled even wider, and there were tears in his eyes too. "May I come in?"

Galia cried again. She couldn't help it. She couldn't believe how lucky she was to be sitting in that room and looking at the two people she most had wished to see over the last few years.

"Of course! Oh, Teddy, I can't believe you're here. You look so... so grown up."

For a moment, she let herself forget about all the bad things, and felt the possibility of being okay. Eli smiled at the two of them and got up from the bed.

"I'm going to grab a coffee quick. Can I get you anything?" he asked Teddy.

"No, thanks, Eli. I'm good."

"Galia, are you okay if I step out for a few minutes?"

Galia grabbed his hand, fearful of being separated again.

"It's okay, Bean. I'm not going anywhere far. I promise. I just want to give you two a minute to catch up."

Galia looked at Teddy, who was still smiling, and then nodded.

Eli left the room and Teddy made his way around her bed and sat slowly into the chair beside her.

The two of them talked and it was as if seven years turned into seven seconds. It was as comfortable as it was when they were in high school, catching up like best friends do.

Teddy lifted his hand from his lap and, not wanting to scare her, moved it slowly toward her face, watching her for any sign of hesitation. Galia's heart raced. A part of her felt scared – the conditioned part of her. But the deeper part knew he was good. She let him run his fingers over her cheek and chin. He was tender with her, keeping eye contact the entire time. Galia flushed at having him so close to her. He broke his gaze, looked at her hair and took a lock of the platinum hair into his hand.

"Oh, that. Jack did that. He said it was good to disguise my real look, so it was harder for the police to find me."

Teddy furrowed his brow, clearly confused.

"He said because of being a part of…" Galia paused, reliving again the shame of her past with someone else.

Teddy reached down and put a hand on hers. "It's okay, Galia. I know. I know about everything. It doesn't matter. The only thing that matters is that you're here now."

Galia tried to continue but couldn't. She lowered her head and cried as she let Teddy hold her hand.

"Galia, I can only imagine what you must feel and what you must be going through right now. In a way, I kind of do. You saw me after I killed my dad. I was a mess and never thought things would be okay. But then, one day, they just were. They still are. Look at me."

Galia raised her head.

"Your past doesn't have to define your future. Only if you let it."

Galia nodded, overwhelmed by mercy. She took a deep breath and continued. "Jack told me because of belonging to that prostitution ring, the police had issued a warrant for my arrest, and hiding was the only way to keep me from going to jail."

At this point, Eli and Agent Grant re-entered the room. They stood by the window as Galia proceeded to tell Teddy, and them, everything. Teddy, outwardly angry, let go of her hand and paced the floor beside her.

"I am so angry with all of the lies he told you. You don't believe him, right? You can't believe him. That man is Satan incarnate, and God will deal with him."

Galia searched his face. "So, you're still tight with God?"

Teddy got control of his emotions and sat in the chair beside her, grabbing her hand once more.

"He sure is!" said Eli. "He's an assistant pastor now at that church he belongs to."

Galia looked over at him with surprise. "Really?"

Teddy nodded.

Galia, suddenly aware of his hand on hers, slid it slowly away.

Teddy's confused look turned to humor and he put her hand back into his. "I'm a pastor not a monk. I can hold your hand." He grinned at her again.

Old feelings rushed her, and her face flushed, which made her dad chuckle.

Agent Grant stood and walked closer to the bed. "There was one thing Jack said which was true."

Everyone looked up at Agent Grant.

"Police did break up the prostitution ring, but there's no warrant for your arrest, Galia."

Galia let out the breath she was holding, but quickly stifled the feelings of relief. "But..." she stuttered. "What about... Jack."

"Self-defense. A clear case of self-defense. Galia, I'm not sure you quite understand. You're not in any trouble. On the contrary, you're being hailed as a hero. You saved Rachel McGinnis."

Galia's eyes widened. "Rachel! Oh my gosh... is she okay?"

"Yes, she's fine. Thanks to you."

Galia moved as if she were going to get out of bed. "Can I see her?"

Agent Grant put his hand on her shoulder. "In a little while. She's with her parents right now."

Galia looked down at her lap, and then back up at Agent Grant. "Wait. You said before that prostitution ring was broken up. What exactly does that mean?"

Agent Grant sat down next to her. "There was a young lady who called 9-1-1 the night of your abduction. She saw it happen."

Galia's mind spiraled to imagine who that might have been.

"Unfortunately, we weren't able to connect it to you right away, as she said she didn't know your real name."

Galia's eyes grew wide again.

"That call is what led to further investigation, and having an informant in the ring, and what ultimately broke that up."

"What happened to Ronny?" Galia asked, concerned.

"He was arrested, along with several others."

Galia's eyes searched something unknown in the room. "The girl who called 9-1-1... was her name Lacey?"

Agent Grant nodded.

"Yes, that was the young lady who made the call."

Galia felt another lump in her throat.

"She was very brave and gave us a lot of information to stop the ring, as well as information that helped us with you later, once we were able to make the connection."

Galia teared up again. "Is she... is she okay?"

Teddy nodded, squeezing her hand. "Yes! She's okay."

Now Galia was really confused. She looked inquisitively at Teddy. "How do you know Lacey?"

"This is the craziest thing." Teddy almost looked excited. "I met her at a homeless shelter when we were there serving dinner one night. I invited her and some of her friends to church for a service. They show up now and then. When they recently reopened the investigation…" Teddy looked at Eli. "I offered to give Eli a ride to the station when they wanted to re-interview those connected. We got to the police department, and there she was."

Galia gasped. "So, she's okay? Lacey's okay?"

"When we got word of you here…" Teddy smiled. "I put word in with the homeless shelter."

Galia's face dropped. "She lives at a homeless shelter?"

Teddy smiled again. "No, she helps at one. She's really changed her life a lot, Galia."

The hope that had so eluded her suddenly poured down on her like a rain shower. It ran down her head, into her hair, over her face and down every part of her body. Galia sat, unable to speak.

"I still can't believe you were the roommate she talked about. It's so crazy, isn't it? So crazy. She was crying on the phone when I told her you were here and safe."

Galia smiled, once again overwhelmed with what she felt was so grossly undeserved. She had dreamed of a second chance, those nights she spent lying on her bed in that tiny prison. She thought she got that gift years ago from Jack. In reality, she was only just receiving it now. She had no idea she would be trading rehabilitation for redemption.

Agent Grant and a few other offices spent time with Galia over the next few hours, gathering information from her. Galia shared what Jack had said about his parents, about the box of personal items and articles, and about the woods behind Jack's house.

★ ★ ★

In the weeks that followed, a team recovered the bodies of seven more girls, including that of Cami Roberts – the girl from the warming well with the silver necklace. It made Galia sick to think of the grief of those poor families, but Agent Grant comforted her by saying it was important to bring them closure. Galia understood that, but grief remained by her side for some time.

CHAPTER 21

Five Years Later

Galia sat quietly in her chair, drinking in the atmosphere and twirling the long, black strands of hair around her fingers into ringlets, letting go and feeling them bounce straight again. The worship team was up on stage setting up, and ushers were separating the service programs into neat stacks for each entryway. A countdown clock was projected on the screens, with only a few minutes left until service started.

People poured in from the lobby to take their seats. Blue and purple lights filled the stage and illuminated the paper lanterns hanging from the ceiling. The lanterns were all different sizes, hanging in various heights from the ceiling. It was mesmerizing to look at, and Galia felt as though she could sit there all day. She closed her eyes. A peaceful smile came across her face as thoughts of gratitude filled her heart. Her eyes were startled open as she felt a gentle hand on her shoulder.

"You ready for this?" Teddy asked.

"Yes. I am," Galia said confidently. "I've been ready for this for a long time now."

Teddy squeezed her shoulder and walked toward the stage. Looking back over his shoulder, he gave her one of the boyish grins she liked so much, which made her smile back at him.

She watched as Teddy gave the worship team some final instructions before sitting down in the front row.

When the clock on the screen ran down to zero, the worship leader welcomed everyone to stand and join in as they sang together. They were playing "Who You Say I Am" by Hillsong, and the only thing lovelier to Galia than the music were the words she was singing.

"Free at last, He has ransomed me. His grace runs deep. While I was a slave to sin, Jesus died for me." Galia raised one hand in praise as she sang. "Who the Son sets free, oh is free indeed. I'm a child of God, yes I am."

As worship was winding down, Teddy got up and walked onto the stage. No one was singing anymore, but the worship team continued to play music softly as Teddy read a scripture. "1 Peter 2:9 tells us, 'But you are a chosen people, a royal priesthood, a holy nation, God's special possession, that you may declare the praises of him who called you out of darkness into his wonderful light."

He closed his Bible and looked at the congregation. "A chosen people. A royal priesthood. A holy nation. God's. Special. Possession." Teddy was silent for a moment. "Wow. Those are some powerful ways God sees us. How does it make you feel when I tell you God is speaking these things about each of you? Some of you probably feel gratitude. You know where you came from and you know where you are now, so your heart can connect with God's ridiculous grace. Some of you might feel convicted. You know where you've been because, the truth is, you're still there. Some of you may feel skeptical – I'll talk to you after service."

The congregation laughed, and Teddy fell silent until the church was quiet again. "I'm guessing some of you feel sad." His statement was spoken more like a question, which Teddy let hang in the air for several seconds. "Maybe you're struggling with something that causes guilt or shame in your heart and prevents you from accepting labels like chosen or royal or holy or special. Maybe you don't *feel* special. Maybe no one on this earth has ever taken the care enough to make you feel special."

A few sniffles echoed through the church.

"One of the biggest lies Satan tells people is that they are unlovable because of who they are or the things they've done." Teddy paused again. "You all know my story. You know what I did when I was just in high school. And for those of you visiting with us today, without going into a lot of detail, I'll tell you I killed my own father."

There were a few gasps in the crowd.

"Yes, that's right. I did that. Now, I did it while protecting my mother, but I did it. And I was angry and had hatred in my heart when I did it. I consider that sin. Yet, here I stand. Do you know why that is? Because God sent his Son, Jesus to die on a cross so I didn't have to. He loved me even when the world told me I was unlovable. He forgave me even when I had trouble forgiving myself. He led me to this amazing church and these amazing people who taught me that my past didn't have to define my future."

Teddy looked at Galia, who was smiling, remembering those words spoken to her when she was in the hospital, and now knowing they were truth. "There's a lot more I could say on this, but I want to allow some time to do something a little different today."

Galia straightened her posture, knowing this was her cue. She thought she would be more nervous for this, but she wasn't. She felt strong and calm.

"We have someone special to me here today, who's agreed to tell us her story. She's someone who's faced a lot of adversities. She's struggled with the kind of sin most people won't admit to, let alone talk about, and she's fought for her very life against the hands of evil. You all know her, but you may not know these things *about* her. Not only is she one of the bravest people I've ever known, one of the most kind and loving, one with an amazing heart for Jesus..." Teddy stopped and looked lovingly at Galia. "She's also my wife. Galia, would you please come up here and join me?"

A quiet murmur went through the congregation as Galia stood and walked to the stage.

Teddy offered her a hand up the stairs, gave her a hug, and left her on center stage.

Galia stood, looking out across the audience. She smiled warmly at her dad sitting in the front row. Next to him was Lacey. Since Galia had been home, she and Lacey picked up and strengthened their sisterhood. They continued going to the streets, but for a very different reason. They wanted to help other girls better their lives. Lacey had brought several of those girls to church with her today.

Galia suddenly felt pressure, hoping her words would be enough to speak hope into the lives of those girls. She took in a deep breath and let it out slowly. Just before she began to speak, she looked out a few rows and was surprised to see Rachel McGinnis and her parents. All three of them had brilliant smiles, and Rachel's mom was holding one hand over her heart, as if she were giving Galia a silent and heartfelt thank you. Galia smiled back, tears forming in her eyes. That was all she needed to take another deep breath and tell her story.

By the end, tissues were a wanted commodity, as there wasn't a dry eye in the house. Galia concluded, "You don't have to be a prostitute on the streets to be living in darkness. I mean, that's one way to do it, but..."

The audience laughed nervously with her.

"No matter what your circumstances are. No matter how bad you think they are, there's always a way out if you're brave enough to have a little faith. My dad, Eli Gregor..." Galia pointed to her dad sitting in the front row, and he smiled. "...used to tell me when I was younger that I always took the path of least resistance. Which was true."

A chuckle ran through the audience.

"He tried to encourage me to be better. To be stronger. He taught me that hard things were not easy, but they were worth it. He was right. Those words are what saved my life and the life of another that night in that tiny prison."

Galia could hear Rachel's mom audibly choke up and watched as Mr. McGinnis smiled and took his wife's hand. Galia looked across the audience, about to thank them and step down, when she found herself gripping the sides of the podium in hesitation.

She drew in a long breath. "I'm no pastor, and maybe I should step down now, but I feel something burning in my heart to say to all of you."

Galia looked at Teddy for permission, and he gave her a nod to continue.

"I talked about the prison I was in. That tiny prison with the heavy metal door. It was bad in there. It was mostly dark, cold and musty, and it smelled terrible."

Galia could see Rachel McGinnis leaning forward with her elbows on her knees and her hands over her mouth, tears streaming down her cheek. "There was a bucket in there. I'm sure you are all smart enough to imagine what that was for, and why it smelled bad in there."

Galia's cheeks flushed, and nervous laughter filled the air, along with a quiet murmuring. "Between the metal shackle I talked about, and the heavy metal door, it was a true prison. I wasn't able to physically get beyond those things. But I endured a worse prison that I didn't talk much about today, and I would be remiss to leave here if I didn't."

Nobody made a sound. The audience was quiet with anticipation.

"It was the prison I chose to live in. You could call it Jack's house. Or you can call it what it really was. A choice. My choice. He may have played a part in lying and manipulating me, but I was the one who let fear dictate what I did. I took the path of least resistance. I lived in that house for five years."

Galia choked up and looked at the floor while she tried to compose herself. "I allowed five years of my life to be stolen, all because I was afraid to do the right thing. That decision caused years of pain to those who loved me and were looking for me. Sometimes, that's how Satan works. He convinces us that the right thing will cause us more pain when, in reality, it's the right thing... the truth... that ultimately sets us free. My mind was my own worst prison."

Galia paused again. "Are any of *you* in a prison? Maybe one of your own making?" She scanned the faces in the room and watched while some avoided eye contact. "Are any of you believing lies that just aren't true? My situation is dramatic, I know. But we all have situations that are dramatic in their own way and keep us locked away from the truth. Maybe you had an affair, and you're too scared to come clean. You think telling the truth will break your marriage, so you live with that dark secret, eating away at you like acid. Maybe you're overweight and you've told yourself you aren't pretty or worth someone's attention. Maybe you've had difficulty learning and you've told yourself you're dumb and you'll never be smart."

Galia paused again. "Maybe someone is hurting you, and you've believed the lie that you don't deserve anything better."

By this point, there were several tear-stained faces in the crowd. Galia looked over at Teddy, and with tears now spilling from her own eyes, she looked back at the crowd, lifted her head, smiled and spoke proudly.

"Chosen. Royal. Holy. I am God's special possession. Some of you can and might judge me. But I know the truth now. I'm not perfect, and I still make mistakes. Just ask my husband."

The crowd laughed between their tears.

"But I know the truth, and it's set me free. It can set you free too."

★ ★ ★

The service ended, and Galia saw her dad walking toward her with a smile that said everything his words were about to say.

"I'm so proud of you, Bean. I mean, I'm really, really proud of you. You have grown into a woman of grace, and I am so thankful to have the privilege of being your dad."

Once again, tears formed in Galia's eyes as she wrapped her arms around him. "Thank you, Daddy. It means so much to me to hear you say that. More than you know." Galia watched as her dad pulled something out of the front pocket of his pants. It was a folded piece of paper, and he handed it to her. Galia could see it was old and a little tattered. She grabbed the note and opened it. Tears welled in her eyes and she looked up at her dad in disbelief.

"Go ahead," he said, motioning with his hand. "Read it."

Galia looked back down at the note and had to wait a minute for the tears in her eyes to clear. Then, she read slowly and softly. "Dear Dad, if you're reading this, it means I've left. Since mom died, I've had such a darkness inside of me. Everything around here just reminds me of her. Of that darkness. You're in pain too, and I know I'm only making things worse for you. I think I need to go my own way for a while. I need to figure out how to be me again so I'm not a burden to you any longer. I love you. Love, Galia (Bean)."

Galia could hardly make it through the note. Tears spilled from her eyes again as she looked up at her dad, who also had tears in his eyes. "Dad... I'm so sorry..."

Eli shook his head at her as he smiled. "No, no need to be sorry. We've covered all of that ground already."

"But... this note... why–"

"In the years after you left, it was the last connection I had to you, and I used to read that over and over. After you were found, I almost threw it away. I decided to save it... to save it for the right time to give it back to you. Well, Bean, I think now is the right time."

Galia moved her head to the side a little, uncertain of his meaning.

"Your story this morning was beautiful. What you said at the end... I want you to hang on to it, because I think it's a part of your story."

Galia stood quiet, trying to understand.

"You talked about the prison you were in... the one at Jack's house."

Galia nodded silently.

"The lies didn't start there. They started here," he said, pointing to the note.

Galia let out one quick and involuntary sob, lowered her head to look at the note, and then returned her eyes to his. "Wow. You're right."

The two of them stood silently for a few seconds.

"Why are you always right?" She let out a small chuckle through her tears as she tucked the note gently into her pocket.

"Gal!" Lacey yelled. "There's some people here to see you!"

Eli gave Galia a nod. They hugged again, and Galia turned and gave Lacey a hug, too. She worked her way through the girls Lacey had brought with her, giving each one the kind of hug you get from someone who's known you for a billion years.

Teddy waited patiently for her to finish with the other women. When they had gone, he walked up to her and gave her a big hug. "Wow. That was beautiful. You did a really amazing job up there."

"Thanks." Galia smiled and touched the side of his cheek. "I couldn't have done it without you."

"Oh, I think you could have." Teddy laughed. "But I appreciate the ego boost."

They both laughed.

"If there's one thing you are, Mrs. Fenton, it's strong. Strong. Beautiful. Smart..."

"Stop! Okay, maybe a few more." Galia teased, and Teddy continued.

"Funny. Right a lot of the times, but kind of irritating sometimes when you're not right but you think you are. Cute when you make that clicking noise when you..."

Okay, okay!" Galia chuckled. She smiled, cocking her head to the side and looking at Teddy as if he could do no wrong. "You are one fantastic husband. I have so much to be thankful for, but you are the best of all those things." Galia teared up again.

Teddy wiped a tear off her cheek with his finger and kissed her on the forehead. "Does that mean I'm the best husband on the whole east side of West Allis?" he asked with a grin.

"I don't know about the whole east side, but you're certainly at *least* the best in the whole north east quadrant." Galia's tears turned to laughter. She wiped away the last tear and gave Teddy a satisfied look. "Come on, Dad!" she called across the church lobby. "Let's go get lunch. I'm starving!"

They got their things and headed out the door. On the way out, Galia saw one of the girls who was at the service with Lacey leaning against the side of the building. Galia stopped and looked in her direction. The girl had an expectant look on her face but stayed where she was.

"Give me a second," Galia said to Teddy and her dad and walked over to the girl. "Amy, right?"

"Yeah. That's right," the girl said smiling, seeming surprised that Galia had remembered.

"I'm really glad you were able to make it to service today. I hope you liked it."

Amy nodded her head. "I..." she stopped and let her eyes fall back to the ground.

"What is it? It's okay. You can talk to me."

Amy looked up, summoning her courage. "You know that prison you talked about? Like, not the one with the door, but the other one?"

"Yes."

"Well..." Amy continued. "I guess I live in one too. At least I think I do."

"Do you want to talk about it?" Galia asked softly.

Amy nodded her head.

Galia put a hand on her shoulder and nodded back, then turned toward the men. "Hey!" she called out to Teddy and her dad. "You guys go ahead. I'm going to have lunch with my friend, Amy."

"Are you sure?" Teddy asked.

"Yeah. I'm sure." Galia turned back to Amy and gave her a smile. "What are you hungry for?"

The two girls walked to a nearby café for burgers and fries. Over the next few hours, Galia listened to Amy's story and shared more of her own. The two girls laughed and cried together. For Amy, there was a third and unexpected companion at the table. That companion's name was *Hope.*

Galia no longer felt stolen. Maybe borrowed for a time, but now she was home. Where she belonged. Where she always belonged.

Her dad had been right. The lies started way before she ran to the streets. They always start before. After all, they are the catalyst for what makes a person run in the first place. She could get lost in regret for ever running, but that felt like another prison, and Galia wouldn't be going back to that prison again. She had traded those shackles in a long time ago.

Galia looked down at the faint scars on her ankle and smiled as she returned her eyes to Amy. There had been many tears shed that morning, but none so beautiful as the tears shed in gratitude of a life redeemed.

Caroline Klug is an author of inspirational fiction, using thrillers and short story collections as a way to bring insights to people all over the world.

In addition to fiction, Caroline writes Christian Living books that teach, inspire and encourage.

To see other books by this author visit:
www.CarolineKlug.com

Caroline Klug

www.ingramcontent.com/pod-product-compliance
Lightning Source LLC
Chambersburg PA
CBHW031621100726
47898CB00006B/1894